FINDING BILLIE

JEAN GRAINGER

To Diarmuid

CHAPTER 1

*B*illie Romano gazed out the tiny window as the 737 touched down at Logan. Raindrops were sucked along the glass by the velocity, and she gripped the armrests as the landing bump jolted her. There. She was down.

She stood but decided to wait until almost everyone had disembarked.

'No point in rushing is there?' said a short man a few years older than her, with thinning hair, a straggly effort at a beard and glasses.

'No, I guess not,' she agreed, and chose to ignore the look in his eye that suggested he'd like the conversation to continue.

He reached up to take her carry-on from the bin overhead though she was perfectly capable. She sighed. *No need to get ratty. He's just trying to help.*

'So home for Thanksgiving?' he asked.

'Yes, just for a few days,' she replied. Her voice sounded flat even to her own ears.

'You get back much?' he persisted.

'I come back to visit my grandfather a few times a year, but I haven't lived on the East Coast for a while.' Every fibre of her being wanted to tell him to back off, but it wasn't the guy's fault – he was just being nice. And they were stuck in this aisle with people pulling on coats and dragging bags out of the overhead bins, so to say anything to stop the conversation would just make it more awkward.

But she did not need this now, not on top of everything else. Even if she didn't have 500 other things on her mind, he was not her type. She guessed he thought the heavy-framed glasses made him look hipster, when in fact they just made him look geeky. And not in the cool way like the new guy at work. Rob managed to pull off geeky-cute; this guy just looked like he was trying too hard. His accent was pure Boston, Southie probably.

'Where you based now?'

He was determined, she'd give him that.

'California.' She hoped by giving one-word answers he'd get the hint.

'Nice. I was there once. My sister married a guy from Santa Barbara. They got divorced though, so...' He shrugged and gave an apologetic shrug as if the failed marriage of the sister of a guy she'd just met would be sad news for her.

'Santa Barbara's nice – lovely beaches,' she said as she took her bag.

'You been out there long?'

They shuffled slowly along the aisle.

'Three years.' She could see the air stewards bidding everyone goodbye.

'And what do you do out there?'

'I'm an animator. I work for Visionboard.' Although she did not feel like being hit on, she was proud to tell him who her employer was.

'Visionboard, huh? Wow, you must be good. I took my nephews to see that new one, the martial arts one, a few weeks ago. They loved it.'

She smiled. 'Ninja Dragon?'

'Yeah, that's the one.' He beamed, delighted to have found a point of connection.

'I worked on that. It was a lot of fun.'

'Well, my sister's boys spent the rest of the night trying to put each other in the ER after it, doing the moves, you know? So she wasn't happy, but they loved it. It was funny too.'

'Yeah, it was,' she agreed.

Finally, they reached the door, and she nodded in response to the cheery 'Happy holidays' from the steward who'd spilt water on her as he served the mysterious substance they called lunch.

As she strode through the air bridge towards the glass doors of the terminal, the bearded guy kept up with her.

'I'm going home too. Well, actually, I live here, in Boston, but I was in Pittsburgh on business, a corporate thing, and I just went there for a few days. How come you came through Pittsburgh?'

'The flight was routed through Pittsburgh, I don't know why.' As she approached the terminal, she felt the lump of anxiety she'd been supressing all day. 'So...er...nice talking to you.'

Mercifully, there was a ladies' room coming up. She peeled away from the surging crowd and joined the line for the bathroom.

'OK...bye...and happy Thanksgiving.' He sounded defeated.

For a brief second, she felt bad. He was just a nice guy making conversation, but she wasn't in the mood.

Eventually, her turn came and she went into a stall and locked the door. Tears stung her eyes.

'Stop,' she reprimanded herself, taking a steadying breath. *Getting all upset isn't going to solve anything.* It was four days. She could do four days. Pops would be there; she could even handle her mother.

She emerged from the stall, examining her face in the mirror as she washed her hands. She looked like she felt: tired, worried, sad.

Logan did that to her. It held so many memories. Going off to college, her parents so proud of her, even if they had no idea what she was actually studying. Her mom was a real estate agent, and her dad worked construction all his life. The arts and movies were way outside their experience, but that didn't matter. Since she was a child, she'd loved cartoons. Creating them was all she wanted to do, so she'd moved to Providence immediately after high school to study animation at the Rhode Island School of Design. Her final-year project had earned her an internship at Visionboard, the winner of the Oscar for Best Animated Feature Film that year. Visionboard was the dream for anyone in the animation business. She'd been selected – one of only two people from her graduating year – and the opportunity to go to California and work for the company that had dominated animated movies at the box office for the last ten years or so was a dream come true. She remembered her dad's face when she told him. A sharp stab of pain almost winded her. *Don't go there*, she admonished herself. *It won't do any good.*

But still the memories came flooding like a movie through her mind. When she got the email, she was so excited she could hardly speak, and she remembered her dad's voice on the phone as she told him. He knew then he had cancer, but he wouldn't rain on her parade, so he cheered her victory like he always did and held his pain inside. The internship turned into a contract, and now after three years, she was a permanent member of the staff.

She tried to wipe the image of her dad coming to the airport to collect her out of her mind. Big Matt Romano would never be there to meet her again. Never again would she rush into his arms and have him lift her off the ground in a bear hug. He was dead. And her mother didn't even have the decency to wait a year to remarry. Billie suspected Marko might have been waiting in the wings. Donna surely didn't meet and marry him within four months of her father's death. The thought of her mother flirting with another man while her dad battled the cancer ravaging him made Billie furious and so sad. She hoped her dad never knew.

At least the Boston guy was gone when she found the carousel with the luggage from her flight. She took her small case from the belt, slung her carry-on over her shoulder and headed for the exit.

She saw them through the glass. What was going on? She thought Pops was collecting her. She'd agreed to do Thanksgiving dinner with her mother, but Donna picking her up was not part of the plan. *That oaf beside her must be Marko.* She'd managed to avoid meeting him up to this point, but it seemed now an introduction was going to happen. There in Logan, where she'd always met her dad.

Tears stung her eyes. She could not do this. She didn't go to their wedding. It was a small affair, and she was sure she wasn't missed. She'd made an excuse about work. She always stayed with Pops when she came back, and she only met her mother once each time. A short meeting over a quick cup of coffee, enough to placate Pops but not enough for anything but the most superficial of conversation. She knew her mother tried – she tended to gush a bit – but Billie always remained implacable. It was torture for her, and she suspected her mother didn't enjoy it either. For Billie, it was a box-ticking exercise, just like the occasional text, the cards on birthdays... Nothing you could pinpoint as totally dysfunctional in a mother-daughter relation-ship, but dysfunctional was exactly what their relationship was.

What were Donna and Marko doing there? Had something happened to Pops? Cold dread started in her throat and worked its way through her shoulders, settling in her stomach. She thought she might vomit. Was Pops dead? Someone bumped into her as they enthusiastically walked through the glass doors to a joyful reunion. She watched it all unfold – people embracing each other, tears, screams of delight. And yet she was rooted; she could not make herself walk.

Don't be ridiculous, she told herself. He had texted as she boarded to say have a safe flight. Pops was fine. She was just panicking.

Her gaze rested on her mother, who looked tense in a navy trouser suit. Donna hadn't seen her yet. Billie shook her head incredulously. Her mother looked so polished and poised these days.

The woman who waited outside bore very little resemblance to the woman who raised her. She remembered her mom – before their lives imploded – in their small untidy house, baking cookies and watching *Dynasty*, the TV show from 100 years ago that she loved. It was constantly on repeat, and her mother could not get enough of Alexis Carrington and the rest of them with their diamantes and shoulder pads. It was like that woman disappeared and had been replaced by this totally different person.

Marko. She recognised him from the photo in Pops's living room. Apparently, he was Ukrainian, and he'd emigrated to the US a decade or so ago.

She recalled the horror she'd felt when her mother called to say she was getting married. Daddy had been barely in the ground. She couldn't believe her mother was so callous.

Someone else bumped into her. She began walking again; they were getting closer now.

Donna and Marko were the oddest match, and Billie could not understand the attraction. He looked nothing like her father, but then she realised bitterly that was probably exactly why her mother married him.

Billie forced her small suitcase out ahead of her through the doors, and then there she was, her mother.

'Billie! You came!' Her mother hugged her awkwardly, and Billie tried to stifle a tart response. She had texted Pops from the airport to say she was boarding, so of course she was there – where else would she be?

Marko nodded and, without a word, took her case. She caught his dark eyes and held his gaze for a moment. He was tall and stocky, and she noticed he wore a gold bracelet that glinted on his hairy wrist. He had on a charcoal-grey suit with a cream shirt and an emerald-green tie. Who on earth went to pick someone up from the airport in a suit? He had slicked-back, suspiciously dark hair and was sort of menacing or something. He was smooth-skinned, not one wrinkle despite being almost sixty years old. He might have had work done.

Billie knew she and her dad would have shared that look, the one that said 'Can you believe this guy?' if they'd met him. He reminded Billie of a reptile. His eyes were cold, and he seemed to be weighing every situation.

Her mother's highlighted blonde hair was cut in a glossy bob, and her large brown eyes were made up perfectly. Not a wrinkle showed on her face, but Billie guessed that was more to do with regular Botox injections than anything else. Her lips were filled as well. As they walked out, Billie caught a whiff of her mother's signature scent these days – Joy by Jean Patou. She'd asked her mother the last time they met what it was, more for something to say rather than any real interest, and afterwards, Billie looked it up on the internet. It was hideously expensive, and it took twenty-eight dozen roses and 11,000 jasmine flowers to make one bottle apparently.

Donna chatted nervously as they walked to the car.

'Is Pops OK?' was the first question Billie asked.

Donna had sold their family home in South Dorchester, Marko sold his apartment near Boston Common, and they bought a place out by the Head Island Causeway really close to Pops's place. Billie had been dismayed when Pops told her, as it suited her much better to have Donna on the other side of town, but her grandfather said he was happy to have Donna nearer. He was sixty-nine years old and very fit apart from needing knee surgery, but he liked the idea that his favourite daughter lived close by now. Billie's aunt, her mother's sister Diana, was married to a military guy, and they moved around a lot.

'Yes, he's so excited to see you. He wanted to come to the airport, but he's been having trouble with his knee again, so he went to see the doctor this morning.'

'On his own? But I thought he couldn't drive until he had the surgery?' Billie knew her voice sounded accusing, but she didn't care.

'Not on his own.' Donna kept her voice light. 'He's got a lady friend, would you believe? He met her at an active retirement meeting. Her name's Marilyn, and she's such a nice lady. They go dancing!' Donna beamed.

Billie wondered why Pops never told her anything about this Marilyn. She considered asking her mother about her, but she didn't want to admit how little she knew about Pops's life. Her grandfather called every week, and they talked for an hour or so. Billie would have gone crazy with grief in these past years if it were not for Pops. The fact that he was seeing someone was such a huge thing, and it hurt her that he'd never mentioned it. She recalled all of their conversations, but then remembered guiltily they were usually all about her – her job, her friends, her grief. Had she ever actually asked Pops how things were with him?

He was Donna's father, but he'd loved Matt, and the feeling had been mutual. For Pops, Matt was the son he never had. Donna's mother died when she was a girl, so Pops raised her and Dianne on his own. As far as Billie knew, he'd never had another woman in his life, so this really was big news.

Her mother was talking about their new house, and how excited she was for Billie to see it when she came for Thanksgiving dinner. At least it was something that she didn't have to go back to her old home, the house in South Dorchester. It would have been too hard to see Marko where her father should be.

As they emerged from the oversized elevator in the parking garage, Marko took a fob out of his pocket, and a large sleek silver Mercedes beeped in response. Billie tried not to show her surprise.

The trunk door popped automatically, and Marko lifted Billie's luggage in, then held the back door open for her, still without saying a word.

She slid into the sumptuous interior and tried not to gasp. This was not a normal back seat; instead, there were two cream leather reclining seats with a console between them for drinks, snacks and entertainment. The windows were tinted, ensuring privacy, and the aroma of leather pervaded her nostrils. She'd never been in a car like it.

It was as far from her dad's van, filled with tools and sandwich wrappers, as it was possible to be, and she hated it.

Her mother sat in front beside Marko, and the car purred as he manoeuvred it out of the high-rise parking lot.

'So Marko and I boxed up all your stuff. It's in the garage, so you can go through it and decide what you want to keep, or take back with you, or leave with us – whatever you like. I didn't throw anything away when we packed up the house, just in case.' Donna caught her eye in the rear-view mirror.

Billie hated how her mother was fawning over her, trying to get back in her good books. It was going to take more than a few boxes of old high school yearbooks and teddy bears to make Billie overlook such a betrayal. It had been three and a half years, but she was still so angry and hurt. Had her mother cared for her dad at all? Clearly not. And he'd loved her so much. It wasn't fair.

'OK,' Billie said. She knew she sounded like a sullen teenager, but her mother infuriated her. And it wasn't just the marriage to the reptilian Marko; they'd not had a good relationship for seven years. Her father had been her person, the parent she loved and trusted.

Her therapist tried to get her to focus on flashes of memory of good times. She and Gio and Mom and Dad. But those days were long gone. It was hard to remember who her mother was before Gio. After that...well, nothing was ever the same again.

Gio would have been so psyched by this car. She'd had so much therapy to try to come to terms with the fact that her only sibling died when he was twelve years old, but none of it helped. She knew the psychobabble behind it: Gio drowned as Donna lay on the beach reading a book, Donna felt guilty, she couldn't get past it, all the rest of it. But Donna was absent from her family from that day on. Billie had worked through the sadness at the loss of Gio, then the loss of her mother to an impenetrable fog of grief and the feelings that her mother must have loved Gio more. Billie even wondered if it had been her that had drowned, would Donna have cut her brother off the way she excluded her? Gio, or Giovanni, named after her dad's beloved Italian grandfather, was a fun-loving boy. It was just an accident. He had been fooling around with his friends, when one of them paddled out too far and panicked, so he went to help. The friend managed to cling to his boogie board, but Gio got tangled up in something – that's what the coroner said – and drowned. Right there, on a sunny day at the beach on Castle Island, where they'd gone a hundred times.

Her dad was devastated too, but his grief included Billie. He cried with her, they took long walks, they sponsored a bench on the headland near where Gio died, which now had a little plaque with his name on it. He comforted her and held her as she sobbed for her brother. He tried to do the same for his wife, but it was impossible. Billie remembered her dad telling Donna over and over again it

9

wasn't her fault, nobody blamed her, but it was like she couldn't process it. She rejected her daughter and husband and shut herself away. She didn't go to the little ceremony for the plaque, and she sat bolt upright, like a marble statue, at the funeral.

Billie was only half listening as Donna went on and on and Marko drove. Her mother was talkative again now. Billie wasn't sure when that had happened. Maybe when Marko showed up? Who knew. But the damage was done.

She gazed out at the familiar sights of the city. Boston meant opening old wounds. First Gio, then her dad.

As her mother's husband expertly manoeuvred the Mercedes through the traffic on Massport Haul Road, navigating effortlessly towards the causeway, he murmured something she couldn't hear to Donna and Donna reached over and put her hand on his leg. He turned his face to her and smiled.

Billie fixed her gaze out the window; she could not watch that. Every time her dad tried to touch her mother in the years after Gio's death – put a hand on her shoulder, help her out of a car – it was like she'd been given an electric shock. Billie knew that they had separate bedrooms, though they pretended it was because of her dad's snoring, and it just made her so sad. Her dad deserved better.

He had been just a regular working guy; he didn't earn tons of money like Marko clearly did. Her dad would have called him a *giamoke*, an Italian word for an idiot. But her father was decent and honest and told her the truth about everything.

She'd trusted him completely, and his family was his world. He spoke about his grandpa, who'd come over to the States from Italy before the war; he'd died when Matt was a teenager. And her dad's parents were nice; Billie remembered them vaguely. They'd lived in New York so they didn't see them much, and they both died over twenty years ago in a house fire. There was an aunt, but she married some Italian guy and went to live in Sorrento. Her dad always said he'd like to visit them, but that never happened. His family was Donna, Billie and Gio, and that was all he'd cared about.

She glanced at the back of Marko's head, wondering what his story was. Pops tried to talk about him sometimes, but Billie always changed the subject. Donna never mentioned him in their brief exchanges; she knew better than that. He must be very successful to have a car like this, but maybe he was a drug dealer or something. He certainly looked the part. Billie wondered how he'd got so far ahead in business considering he hardly spoke.

CHAPTER 2

*C*onor O'Shea tried his best to find something to ask the young woman in front of him that would not embarrass her. The interview was going from bad to worse – she had no experience and had never worked in the hospitality industry. She had a first-class honours degree in business and Japanese, which is what made the agency think she might be suitable, but they were wrong.

This was the second attempt at finding someone to be a deputy manager to fill in for Carlos Manner. Conor's South African assistant manager had broken his ankle, wrist and tibia in a hillwalking fall.

He'd interviewed a month ago as well, but nobody suitable applied. The agency assured them that in the new year, the prospects would be better. But the busy Christmas period was coming up, and he needed someone now, though where these miraculous candidates were going to suddenly spring from was a mystery. Another case of the agency overselling and underdelivering by the looks of things.

He'd hardly seen Ana and the boys for weeks, as he was so busy and rarely got home before midnight. It was exhausting and he missed them, but since Katherine O'Brien, the head receptionist, was on her honeymoon and Carlos was out sick, he was left managing everything himself.

He glanced at the clock. The interview was less than ten minutes in; he would have to stretch it out another bit.

'So what do you like to do in your spare time?' he asked, not giving a flying fadoodle what she did to entertain herself.

'I do taekwondo,' was the short response. This young woman clearly had no interview skills either.

'Oh, I see. My sons do that too. They love it.' He said, hoping she might elaborate a little to run down the clock.

No response. That obviously wasn't a statement worth answering.

'And are you good with computers?' he asked helplessly.

'Well, all people of my generation are better than the old folks, so I suppose I am. I think it's because we were born with them, whereas your generation had to learn?' She shrugged sympathetically, and Conor tried not to wince.

Her eyebrows looked unnaturally dark and a weird shape, and her teeth were ridiculously white. He suspected there was a lot of cosmetic investment in that face, but it had the effect of making her look odd. She also had that annoying upward inflection at the end of every sentence, popular among young people in America and increasingly with young Irish people too.

Right, he thought. He'd had enough. He was too busy for this rubbish.

He stood, offering his hand. 'Thanks very much for coming today. We'll be in touch.' He smiled, and she stood and took his hand in a vice-like grip.

'When?' she asked.

'When what?' Conor gave her a quizzical look .

'WHEN WILL YOU CONTACT ME?' She fixed him with a confident stare.

'Um… Well, we have some more people to see, so once we've made a decision…' He needed this full-of-herself young one out of his office.

'And when will that be?' she asked again as he opened the door, pointedly glancing at the empty row of three seats outside his office.

'In due course. Now, I'm sure you can see yourself out?' He turned back towards his office where his phone was ringing. Relieved, he shut the door, leaning for a moment against it. Some days, he wished he was still driving tours; life was much simpler then. Being a forty percent owner of the amazing Castle Dysert resort on Ireland's west coast looked impressive, he knew, but it was such hard work. He thought of letting the phone ring out, but guilt got the better of him. He strode over to his desk.

'Conor speaking.'

It was Sheila Dillon, head of housekeeping. 'Conor? I know you're interviewing, but we have a situation here.'

'Go on,' he said wearily.

'One of the young lads we hired last week to do the laundry has been staying in the castle with his girlfriend, along with several more young people, in the bedrooms in the annex that we closed off for the winter. Artur went to check that the heating was coming on intermittently and found the place like a squat.'

Conor closed his eyes and rested his head on the back of his high leather office chair.

'What should I do?' Sheila, like everyone, was harassed and short-staffed.

'Have you him there now?'

'Yes.'

Conor sighed. 'For the boy's own safety, tell him I am not coming down now. Tell him I said if he wants to avoid a criminal prosecution for theft and malicious damage, he and his mates better get that annex in the way they found it and before tonight. When that's done, tell him I want to see him.'

'Right, will do.' Sheila hung up.

The rest of the interviews were a disaster. Not one of the candidates could be left minding a cat let alone a beautiful old castle and five-star resort.

'Conor.' Deirdre, the new receptionist, stuck her head around the door. 'Sorry now, but the printer is jammed again, and I can't print a guest's receipt, and he needs it...'

He took a deep breath. He needed Katherine and Carlos so badly, but this girl was doing her best, so he'd better help her.

'No problem.' He passed her and went over to the printer, used the implement his father-in-law and maintenance manager, Artur, had made specifically for the purpose, and extracted the concertina of paper that had got jammed.

'Can you phone the company and get someone out to sort this properly, please? They were here last week, but obviously the problem is ongoing,' he said as he returned to his office.

'Of course, and who are they?' Deirdre asked.

He had no idea – Katherine dealt with all of that. She probably had a note in her diary.

'They're in Katherine's… Never mind, I'll do it myself.' He sighed and closed the office door. He was at a snapping point, but it wasn't poor Deirdre's fault.

Corlene was on the missing list – again. She wasn't much use when she was there anyway, as she just annoyed everyone. When she'd convinced him to invest his legacy from an old American friend in the project of renovating the dilapidated castle and its tangled grounds into Ireland's premier resort, she'd made out like they would be partners. And at the start they were, but Corlene had her own business in Dublin, and anyway, she was all about the scene in the capital. He only saw her on the society pages of the Sunday papers these days.

Katherine was not due back from her round-the-world cruise with her new husband for another five weeks, and Carlos was totally incapacitated.

There was no way that stupid kid would have moved himself and all his mates into the hotel if Carlos Manner had been prowling around. Carlos kept a very close eye on everyone and everything, and while he was not loved – or even liked – by the staff, and he had to be kept away from guests as much as possible, he ran a very tight ship and was as loyal as a dog. He was a stickler for detail and noticed every single thing. He and Katherine combined were a force to be reckoned with.

Conor was about to call the agency again and tell them that none of the people they had sent were suitable. The trouble was it was winter, and many of the seasonal workers only came for the summer. Not everyone wanted to relocate to the Irish wild Atlantic coast in November.

He pulled up the reservation screen for the coming month. Christmas was set to be mad – he'd be working day and night at this rate. They were full to capacity every night. Because of lack of staff, they'd closed the new annex they had added for extra rooms. It was a real problem.

Their remuneration package was excellent. They paid all of their staff above the going rate and offered extra holidays and membership to the state-of-the-art gym and pool complex in the castle. They would even accommodate them if needs be, there were staff apartments on the grounds, but the people of the calibre he required were just not there.

As he scrolled for the agency's number, an incoming call caused the phone to buzz. Carlos.

'Hi, Carlos. How are you feeling?'

'Bad, but one mustn't complain. How did the interviews go?'

As usual with Carlos, there was no small talk, just straight into business.

'A disaster. Not one I could even consider,' Conor replied. 'I was just about to call the agency again when you rang.'

'They won't have anyone today they didn't have yesterday,' Carlos said unhelpfully.

'I know, but I have to try. I can't just advertise on the newspaper or whatever. Remember what happened when we tried that? Swamped with applications from every clown in the country, thinking they could run this place when they couldn't run a tap...'

'That's it. I'm coming back to work. I've one good arm, and while I'm in a wheelchair, at least if I am there, I can direct the existing staff. Because, with respect, Conor, you do not know the day-to-day running and you need me, at least until Ms O'Brien gets back.'

'Mrs Burns, you mean.' Conor grinned, still getting used to the idea of Katherine as a married woman himself. Katherine was a lady of a certain age, as the phrase went, and she was prickly at best, but she had a heart of gold and was one of Conor's dearest friends. She'd given up on the idea of ever meeting anyone, when an American came to stay at the hotel and they just hit it off. He made her laugh – no mean feat with the dour Katherine – and they were perfectly suited. It cheered Conor up to no end to see his old friend happy at last.

'Indeed. So I will return to my duties, inasmuch as I am capable, in the morning.'

'But, Carlos, don't be mad. You've a broken leg and a broken arm and wrist. You can't come back to work, especially as Christmas is around the corner.' Conor could think of nothing he wanted more than for Carlos to appear, but he would have to be some kind of a slave driver to get the man out of his sickbed.

'I can and I shall. Tomorrow at eight.'

'Well…if you're sure…and nothing except supervising…' Conor felt awful for not protesting more, but Carlos seemed determined.

'I am. Goodbye.'

Carlos hung up, and Conor knew by now not to be offended. It was just his way. When he first met the small, neat South African, Conor was assistant manager at the Dunshane – the hotel he spent most time in when he was a tour driver and where he'd met his wife Ana – and Carlos was tormenting the staff there, Ana in particular, so the two men had locked horns. Conor remembered the horror he felt when Corlene hired Carlos for Castle Dysert without consulting him, but in hindsight, it was a stroke of genius. Carlos was a tremendous asset to the hotel.

True, he wasn't a warm person, and to many – well, in truth, to everyone – he was snippy, but he was determined that Castle Dysert be seen as Ireland's best hotel. Guests never found a leaky tap or a cobweb in their rooms, and the suppliers all went through Carlos, so he ensured top quality at best prices. He oversaw staffing in every department and made it his business to know every single one of the employees, and in his own way, he was a decent man of principle.

A thought struck Conor, and he picked up the phone – he could solve one problem immediately. The internal phone down in housekeeping rang several times before Sheila got to it. She was flat out as well. The laundry of sheets, tablecloths and towels took up the entire day.

'Housekeeping. Sheila speaking.'

'Sheila, it's Conor. On second thought, send that young fella up to me now, will you, please?'

'Right. He's on the way.' He heard her sigh. 'Any luck getting us more people down here? We're way behind.'

'I'm working on it, I swear. Can we send more out?'

Though Carlos claimed the standard was not maintained when they outsourced anything, it might have to do for now.

Moments later, a very sheepish-looking lad whom Conor recognised as one of the people he'd interviewed the previous week appeared at the door of his office.

'Er...Mr O'Shea...I'm really sorry...' He was beetroot red, which clashed with his auburn hair.

'Are your friends still here in the hotel?' Conor asked coldly. He felt sorry for the kid, but he would never let on.

'Yes, they're tidying up now and –'

'Good. Mr Manner is back to work tomorrow.' Conor watched the colour drain from the boy's face. However worried he might have been facing Conor, the prospect of Carlos was a whole other story.

'He will want to press charges – I'm just giving you fair warning – and this is his area, not mine, so I'll let him handle it. I thought it only fair to let you know.'

Conor knew the lad was only working the Christmas and New Year season to make enough money to go to Florida to his brother's wedding next April, so a criminal conviction would put paid to any visa application for the United States. He had no intention of doing anything of the kind, but it would do the kid no harm to rattle him a bit, teach him a lesson.

'I swear, Mr O'Shea, we'll have the place perfect, seriously, if we have to stay up all night! We've stripped all the beds and are washing everything, and they are hoovering and dusting and the whole lot.

You'll be able to eat your dinner off the floor in there by the time we're finished, I swear.'

Conor knew he could not crack too soon. 'Well, whether or not it is up to our standards, that will be for Mrs Dillon to decide. She'll inspect the rooms when you've finished, but as I said, it's not up to me.' He started writing in his diary. 'So I think you'd better get on with it, don't you?'

'Yes, Mr O'Shea, and I'm sorry again...'

'Shut the door on your way out,' Conor responded.

He checked his watch; it was half past seven. If he left now, he'd see Joe and Artie, his nine-year-old twins, before they went to bed. He grabbed his jacket and made for the door. As he was about to pop out the back, he overheard Deirdre trying to reason with someone.

A guest was being difficult, complaining that the Wi-Fi signal was too weak in the gym for him to watch Netflix on his tablet. Conor thought he should probably step in, explain that the guest needed to connect to the gym Wi-Fi rather than the main building's, but he just wanted to get home so guiltily he snuck out the back door.

His sons were watching *The Simpsons* in their pyjamas when he got in, and Ana was loading the dishwasher, dinner over.

'Oh, Conor!' she exclaimed. 'I thought you will be late! We would have waited for you to eat dinner if I did know you were coming home...'

He wrapped his arms around her and kissed her. 'I ate in the bar earlier so I'm fine. I wanted to get home to put the lads to bed for a change.'

'Dad!' Joe flung himself at Conor, almost toppling him. He was constantly astounded at the speed at which his boys were growing up. They seemed to stretch over the course of even a day. They were tall and long-limbed, with shocks of white-blonde hair. Both Artie and Joe were athletic, though undoubtedly Joe was the better sportsman and Artie found schoolwork easier than his twin. They were identical, but their personalities were very different. Joe was rough and tumble, couldn't give two hoots about maths or Irish and was always up to some mischief, but Artie was quieter, more contemplative. He was a studious boy and hated to get anything less than full marks in a test. They both loved hurling, the Irish national sport, and they both easily made the team, but Joe edged ahead of Artie ever so slightly. It was because Joe was fearless; he'd launch into any tackle with total disregard for his own safety, sometimes making his parents wince on the sidelines.

'Hi, Joe!' Conor ruffled his son's hair and, despite his weight, managed to lift him up in one arm. Joe hugged him. 'How did the game go?'

'Two points down at half-time, but Fiachra scored a goal and I got two points, so we won easy.'

'Good man,' Conor said, then asked more cautiously, 'And did you play, Artie?' He sat on the sofa between the boys.

'No, I came home,' Artie said, not taking his eyes off Smithers and Mr Burns.

Conor and Ana shared a glance. Artie was like this these days, distracted, answering only what he was asked.

'How come?' Conor nudged him gently. 'You love hurling, and you're a brilliant corner back. Billy Cantillon was only saying it a few weeks ago, how you and Joe are an impenetrable backline.'

Conor never let on that he knew Joe was the better hurler, just as he never made Joe feel that he was less able than Artie academically.

'I just didn't feel like it.' He never took his eyes off the screen. Conor was tempted to switch it off and demand that his son talk to him, but he knew that wouldn't help the situation at all. Artie was sensitive. When they met with the teacher, Mr Bredin, and explained they were two very different personalities despite being identical, the instructor didn't seem to take much notice. Conor wondered if Mr Bredin was the problem. They'd always had female teachers up to this point, and they'd loved them, but this guy was very old school. He was close to retirement, and every one of the local children dreaded his class. He could have said something to Artie to upset him, but there was no way of knowing until the boy opened up, which he flat out refused to do.

Artur and Danika, Ana's parents who had moved from the Ukraine and were very close to the boys, tried to reach him, but no luck.

He'd even asked his own father, Jamsie, who'd only turned up last year after an absence of almost five decades, to try, but he drew a blank as well. Conor was disappointed, as he thought Jamsie might be able to get Artie to open up. Though he was a new arrival in the boys' lives, they loved him and really looked forward to his visits from Dublin.

'So will we read Harry Potter? We are just about to discover who Scabbers the rat really is.' Conor chose to ignore his son's recalcitrance.

'Great! Here or upstairs?' Joe asked.

Conor felt so sorry for poor Joe. He was bereft without Artie as his shadow. Conor wished he could be home more. They really needed him, but so did the hotel.

'Upstairs. Now, teeth first, and I'll see you up there in five minutes. Three, two, one – go!'

Joe scrambled up the stairs. His competitive streak meant he loved to beat Artie in a race, but his twin gazed at the TV.

'Earth to Artie… Teeth, mister.' Conor spoke gently, but he did flick off the TV. Artie didn't object but slowly dragged himself from the couch and made for the stairs.

Conor waited until he heard them both in the bathroom. 'Ana, what are we going to do? He looks miserable.'

'I know. It is the same in school. He don't play with the other boys, he don't play with Joe, and we all try to talk to him but nothing, just like what you see there.' Ana blinked back tears. Her Ukrainian accent became more pronounced when she was upset. Her darling boys had been through so much already. Last year, her breast cancer diagnosis had thrown their lives into a spin, and though she was in remission, she knew they both worried it would come back.

'Do you think it's the teacher? Because if it is, I'm going to go down there and have it out with him.' Conor let out an exasperated sigh. He was a problem-solver, and yet here was his own child clearly unhappy and he had no ideas. Bredin had irritated Conor the only time he'd met him; the man had a terrible attitude and seemed to make no allowance for the fact that the kids in front of him were only nine years old.

'I don't know. I ask Joe if he say anything to Artie, but he just says Mr Bredin is very cross and very strict but he is not more worse for Artie than the other boys and girls. Maybe we can talk to him again? Not like blaming him, but just talk, say we are worried?'

'We tried that before, and it was a disaster. That man should not be around children in this day and age. He's like one of the auld fellas that taught me, all sticks and terror. Those days are gone, or they should be at least. No, I think we need to go to the principal, and failing that, maybe we need to get him some counselling or something... I don't know. We've all tried, but he's so closed off, and it's getting worse.'

'Dad! Come on... We did our teeth!' Joe yelled down the stairs.

'Right, I'll read to them for a bit... See you soon.' He kissed Ana and went upstairs with a heavy heart.

CHAPTER 3

*B*illie lay in bed, gazing at the ceiling. It was Thanksgiving morning. She wished she were back in her little studio apartment in Glendale with the sun streaming through the windows. The Boston winters took some getting used to, and she was out of practice.

Outside, snow was piled high, though Pops had paid someone to clear his driveway for the first time ever. He'd always done it himself, but his knee wouldn't allow it any more. She knew Pops hated admitting he was slowing down, and it was only a little, but she could see it. His house was familiar and homely, and all around were family photos and books. If she could just stay with him, and keep her mother and Marko out of it, she could manage. Boston was hard for her – so many memories. She usually just holed up in her grandfather's house, caught up with him, maybe met up with a few old friends for drinks, and then left for LA again. This time, though, he was insistent that they go to her mother's for Thanksgiving dinner. She'd avoided Thanksgiving and Christmas for three years and had planned to do the same this year, but Pops had been unusually adamant. Billie knew he really wanted a reconciliation. She'd tried to explain. It wasn't that they weren't speaking as such, but there was no relationship to repair. Her mother had stopped being anyone's mother the day Gio died, and those years were gone. Billie genuinely saw no future for the relationship, and she wished Pops wouldn't try to force something that wasn't there. But she loved him, and if it was what he wanted, then she could do it. At least he was bringing his girlfriend, Marilyn, to dinner too. Having someone else there always diffused the tension, and Billie was intrigued at the idea of meeting her.

They sounded ideal for each other. After Marko and Donna had dropped her off the previous night, she and Pops talked over hot chocolates and buttered toast, her favourite treat since childhood. She was touched to see Pops's face light up when he spoke about Marilyn. He didn't have a picture, but Billie imagined a sweet old lady with white hair and a nice dress and cardigan. Pops explained how they met at a book club in the senior centre. He said he had been reluctant to go there at first but now really enjoyed it, and he seemed to have made a lot of new friends. They both loved to read, but Marilyn's eyesight had deteriorated and she found it hard to make out the small print in the novels she enjoyed, so Pops had taken to reading to her every night over the phone. She lived downtown, and neither of them liked driving in the city at night. They were ploughing through all the Agatha Christies they could get their hands on, interspersed with some P.D. James and Inspector Morse, both being big British whodunnit fans. She liked to cook and had what he called weird tastes, but she was gradually widening his palate as well. Pops confided that he was thinking of asking her to go on a vacation with him. The Boston winter was long, and he said he needed some sun on his bones. She had smiled, as she was so happy for Pops that he'd found someone.

She wished someone would talk about her like that, but apart from a few casual flings in college, she'd never had a proper boyfriend. She knew it was probably because she was prickly and hard to get to know, but she just couldn't talk about everything that had happened with her family and so didn't want to let anyone get too close. It wasn't a conscious decision; it just happened. When she went out, guys hit on her, but she'd never met anyone she could consider opening up to. Except maybe Rob, and well, that was unlikely to ever happen.

She wondered what he was doing right now. Was he gone home for Thanksgiving? She realised she didn't even know where home was for him. West Coast for sure – he had that relaxed way of being that didn't exist back east – but she didn't know anything about him. She wanted to text, but on Thanksgiving, a text was not like a normal 'Hey, how are you doing?' text. Nobody texted a casual thing on Thanksgiving, unless of course you were a total loser.

Emily was probably right that Rob was not the guy for her. He was nice to everyone, and though she'd tried to be a bit flirty – not her strong point – he was oblivious. It was pathetic. She was twenty-five years old, for God's sake, and she was behaving like a middle schooler with their first crush.

Emily had heard he was seen with a woman at Le Pichet, the fanciest French restaurant in Glendale, so for all they knew, he could be married or in a relationship. He was one of the senior animators and worked upstairs in the Concepts department. They came up with the ideas and storylines and worked with script writers and directors, and once that was done, it was all handed down to her floor. She and the rest of the team did the actual drawings. She loved her job, but her dream was to be upstairs. She had so many ideas but needed to cut her teeth at the coal face for a few years first. The studio boss, Noah Coulson, was a big believer in everybody doing everything, and she knew he watched each person's work closely. Noah was as likely to do the sandwich run when they were flat out on a project as anyone else, and he checked in with everyone all the time. He was nice, and approachable as a boss, but he expected the highest standards. If you were not delivering, then you had no place at Visionboard. She knew how lucky she was – there were animators all over the world who would kill to have her job.

Rob had been headhunted, according to the rumours that went around. He'd been at another studio and had worked on their huge smash hit, the remaking of the *Pied Piper of Hamelin*, and suddenly he was at Visionboard. It was quite a coup for the company. He was exactly her type, lean with longish hair and a beard. He was a yogi and a vegan, and Emily had found out from stalking his Facebook page that he was really involved in the organic food and fair trade movement. Billie had tried to be a vegan – it was the done thing in Glendale these days – but she loved meat, though she would never order it if she were out; people judged you for that.

Just last week, Rob had asked about her weekend. It was nothing more than office chit-chat, and she should see that, but she'd blushed to the roots of her red hair and mumbled in embarrassment. He must have thought she was a total imbecile.

Then, on the day before she left to come home for Thanksgiving, she had been caught gazing at him while he worked. Tina, the most annoying woman on earth with a laugh like a braying donkey, nudged her and whispered, 'Careful, he'll notice your lovesick puppy act.'

She managed to avoid being teased by spluttering that she was watching and learning his technique, but Tina gave her one of her annoying knowing glances. No doubt she'd told everyone over the water cooler that Billie liked Rob.

'Billie! Happy Thanksgiving! Breakfast in fifteen!' Pops called up the stairs.

She threw back the covers and got up. 'I'm just going to grab a quick shower, Pops,' she replied, trying to inject some cheer into her voice.

She stood under the jets and allowed the water to drum on the top of her head. She breathed deeply as so many therapists had shown her.

Maybe if she'd stayed in Boston, she would have got over it all much quicker – facing the memories every day might have desensitised her to it – but coming back four times a year was so gruelling. It was as hard now as the first time. She missed her father with such a deep longing. She didn't just love him, she needed him – still.

She remembered those days after Gio's funeral. She'd only just started at Rhode Island when he drowned. She came home for the funeral and went back to college in a trance, then failed her first year. Drinking, drugs, partying, sleeping with random guys – it was like she was on full-on self-destruct. She woke up one morning, when she should have been sitting an exam, in some frat house, no idea why she was there, and just collapsed. It was her dad who came to collect her. He rented an apartment near campus, looked after her and let her cry for her brother. He made her eat properly, and she stopped all the drinking and drugs. He was her rock, and after she begged him not to, and against his better judgement, he never told her mother. They talked and cried and walked for miles. Her dad never once said a bad word about Donna, just that he was worried about her, that he wished he could reach her, that he knew how much she was hurting. He talked about Gio all the time, laughing at the funny memories of a boy who should not have died. She fell asleep in his arms, the first proper sleep she'd had since Gio, and when she was ready, he went with her to the dean while she explained the situation as best she could. The dean had said she could do summer school and sit the repeats in the fall. From then on, she'd begun to pull herself together, at least on the surface.

Her had dad texted or called every single day, just checking in with her, and her first thought every morning – even now – was to hope for a text. Stupid, she knew, but it had never gone away.

She wrapped herself in a towel and sat at the dressing table. This was her room. Pops still called it her room, and it was full of her stuff: the Harry Potter duvet cover from the time she was obsessed with all things Harry, her old college things, clothes she'd not worn in years. Everything was as she left it.

She tied her auburn hair up in a ponytail. She usually wore it down and straightened and normally had a few blonde highlights to take the real red look off it, but she'd had no time in the weeks leading up to Thanksgiving. Getting away from the studio at this time of year was a nightmare, so she'd worked late into the night to get the current project off her desk.

She examined her face. Did it betray how utterly allergic she was to the upcoming events of the day? She hoped not, for Pops's sake. Donna was his daughter, and he loved her. He just wanted his family, or what remained of it, to be close, but Billie knew in her heart it wasn't possible. She applied a little make-up, using concealer on the dark circles under her eyes. The passport-sized photo of her and her dad clowning around in a photo booth at the mall when she was twelve was stuck to the corner of the mirror. She'd always thought that she had her father's grey eyes, though she admitted hers did look blue on occasion, and despite the Californian sun for the past three years, her skin was as white as a sheet. Her friends teased her, tagging her all the time in that Facebook meme of the girl sunbathing who blended perfectly into the white sand beach.

The only colour Billie had on her skin was her sleeve, a riot of hues from her wrist to her bicep, cartoon characters from the last 100 years. She had no other tattoos, nor did she plan any. She liked the effect the sleeve created – it sort of shocked people because it was at odds with the rest of her.

She looked very girl-next-door, she knew, five foot five, normal build, and she liked to wear long-sleeved tops and jackets, only revealing her full arm of colour when she felt inclined. She'd worked all summer at Burger King when she was sixteen to save up the money to do it. She'd researched meticulously until she found the right artist and got it done without telling anyone.

She'd never forget her dad's face when he saw it. She had no idea how he'd react, but he'd loved it, thought it was very cool. Her mother had been less enthusiastic, worrying that people would judge her. But Billie didn't care about that – she adored it.

She was ready, and took a deep breath. Today was going to be hard, but she was just going to do it, nail a smile on her face and just get it over with.

Billie was surprised Donna and Marko were making such a big deal about Thanksgiving considering he apparently had never celebrated it before. Her mother had explained how he'd been driving all over the place to get all the things for dinner...as if she cared. Allegedly, Donna even sent Marko out for some of the Dutch Edam cheese Billie liked; the grocery store they normally went to didn't stock it, so he went across the city to a deli especially. But she'd be just as happy to have a quick glass of wine and a potato chip and get the hell out of there. She knew her mother wanted her to feel grateful that Marko was going to such trouble, but she wasn't.

She'd said as much to Pops the previous night.

'They are doing it for you,' he'd said. 'They know you loved Thanksgiving as a kid, so even though he's not American, he and Donna are getting into the spirit of it for you. So maybe cut them a bit of slack, eh?'

Billie was taken aback. It was the first time Pops had ever reprimanded her – even gently – and it was a shock.

'Well, I didn't ask them to. I can't stand them, and he creeps me out,' she said, knowing she sounded like a bratty teenager.

'Billie,' he said, 'I love you, you know I do. And it was a hard blow to lose your father. He was a great man and we all miss him. But your mother has been through a lot – maybe you could show a bit of kindness when she tries to make something nice for you?'

He'd sat down opposite her as he spoke. 'I know you don't want to hear it, but it's true. She is trying, and I know she switched off from us all, but she blamed herself for Gio and couldn't get past it. She's my daughter – sometimes I think you forget – and she's a good person who has suffered a lot. She deserves to be happy. Surely even you can see that? Her refusing Marko wouldn't bring either Gio or your father back, so why do you want her to be miserable? Are you denying your own mother a bit of joy after all she's been through?' Pops's brown eyes had bored into hers, his own pain there for her to see.

Tears had sprung unbidden, and Billie disintegrated under a wet blanket of grief. She missed her brother and father, and now Pops was being hard on her. Maybe with good reason, but it hurt.

'I just can't bear...' she began.

Pops had leaned back, making no effort to comfort her as he normally would. 'Can't bear what? Seeing her happy? Because she is, Billie, she really is, and it does me good to see my girl smiling for the first time in years. Sure, Marko's nothing like your father. He's hard to read sometimes – he's deep, that one – but y'know what, kid? He's OK. He's been very kind to me, and not every guy is willing to move to be near his wife's old man, but he insisted. And anyway, it doesn't matter what we think of him. Your mother loves him, and he makes her happy, and that should be enough for us – it's enough for me anyway. Can it be enough for you?'

She had looked up and caught the reflection of her tear-stained face in the glass door between the kitchen and the living room. She looked a wreck.

'Can you do it for me?' he asked, reaching across the table and holding her hands.

'I'll try,' she said.

'That's all I'm asking.' Pops nodded and patted her hand. 'I know it's hard and that you miss your father, but hating Marko or your mom won't bring him back, OK?'

She nodded slowly. 'OK,' she'd whispered.

She would have to make more of an effort today. She could not bear for Pops to look at her with sad disappointment in his eyes again.

She wore what her mother would call a nice dress – black, long-sleeved so her sleeve of tattoos was covered, fitted to the waist with a tulip skirt with dark-red lining in the pleats. She teamed it with the red shoes that Emily called her Dorothy shoes. She wished she could click her heels now and say, 'There's no place like home,' but the truth was she had no home. Pops's place was as close as it came. She rented a nice little studio apartment in Glendale, but it wasn't hers, and her family home was sold.

Two more days. Just two more days. Do this for Pops. You can do this.

She went downstairs with an artificial smile on her face. As she approached the living room, she could hear voices, and upon opening the door, she was greeted by a woman with a Southern drawl.

'Well, look at this beautiful young lady!' a woman she assumed was Marilyn exclaimed as she crossed the room. Marilyn had a head of grey curls that tumbled luxuriantly down her back and twinkling green eyes, and she crossed the room in a second, lithe in her movements. She wore a long magenta kind of tunic and wide-legged black satin pants. She had several silver bangles on her wrist, under which was a large tattoo of what looked like pagan symbols. A big chunk of some kind of blue stone hung from a cord around her neck. She was a million miles away from the sweet old lady Billie had envisaged. She looked like a glamorous old hippie.

'Sol has told me all about you, and he's been so excited that you are visiting!'

Billie found herself enveloped in a hug of sandalwood and citrus.

'Hello, Marilyn, it's lovely to finally meet you.' She said, amused and delighted by Pops's new girlfriend.

'Can I get you a drink?' Marilyn asked.

'Um...I might just make a coffee...' Billie began.

'Nonsense! It's Thanksgiving, so let's be thankful for all the wonderful things in our lives. Sol, knock her up a cocktail.' She gestured to Pops with a wave of her jewelled hand. 'His strawberry daiquiris are amazing.'

She was tiny, no more than four foot ten or eleven and seemed to have Pops wrapped around her finger.

Billie caught Pops's eye and grinned as Marilyn led her to the sofa and he dutifully did as he was told.

'Now, tell me everything. Sol tells me you make movies! How wonderful. I love the movies. I took Sol to see *Fifty Shades of Grey* a few weeks back. He was horrified, of course, but I thought it was interesting. I love that we can be who we are these days, not tied up with all that "what will the neighbours say" rubbish.' She stopped and hooted. 'Tied up! Ha! *Fifty Shades* must be subliminally working my brain. You'd better watch out, Sol.' She nudged Billie conspiratorially as Pops handed them each a festive-looking red drink.

'It's called a Rose Kennedy. Marilyn and I took a cocktail class at a bar downtown last month, so we've been making all kinds of concoctions,' Pops said, and Billie suppressed a smile. She never would have had Pops down as a cocktail guy. 'Of course, she didn't tell me it was a gay bar until afterwards.' He chuckled.

'The guy who owns it, Gino, has a huge crush on Sol. He's begged me to bring him over again, but after Gino pinched his butt, your grandpa said he's had enough visits to the Closet to last a lifetime.'

Billie giggled.

'She's not joking. The guy is pretty relentless, so I'm staying out of the Closet for the foreseeable future,' Pops said, sipping his Coke.

'Oh, are you not having one, sweetie?' Marilyn asked.

'Someone's got to drive, remember?'

'Oh, let's take a cab. It's only five minutes away. Or we could walk... A guy I know from my drumming circle just last week walked barefoot through Grand Forks, North Dakota, all the way across the city.' She explained, as if that were a normal thing to do.

'Why?' Billie asked.

'I think he wanted to atone for a past life transgression, and he also had corns, which have gone, so killed two birds...' Marilyn explained, as if this suddenly made it all clear.

'I don't mind driving,' Billie offered. She'd only sipped the cocktail, so she was fine.

'No, come on, guys,' Marilyn pleaded. 'It's Thanksgiving. I'll call Kaffir – he's my postman, but he drives with Uber to meet people and speak English. He'll take us to Donna and Marko's and come back for us afterwards.' She left the room to make her call.

Billie whispered to Pops, 'She's so funny! I love her.'

Pops smiled and nodded. 'I do too,' was all he said.

'She has something tattooed on her arm...' Billie began.

'It's her spiritual name, Achara. It's Sanskrit apparently.'

Billie paused. 'OK, so is she Hindu or something?' she asked, fascinated.

'Nope, she doesn't belong to any one religion, but she subscribes to lots of ideas, bits of Christianity, bits of Judaism, bits of Islam and a whole mishmash of Asian stuff. I can't keep up with her, but she sure is interesting.'

Marilyn reappeared, chatting animatedly in some strange language. Then she hung up.

'What language were you speaking?' Billie asked in amazement.

'Pashto.' She grinned. 'Kaffir is from Afghanistan. He's sweet and drives me a lot. Especially since the cocktail course! Most days I end up totally unable to drive home from here, so I get to have a sleepover with your lovely Pops. I've even left a toothbrush here now.' She nudged Billie conspiratorially as she sat beside her again, and Pops blushed slightly.

Billie sipped her drink gratefully. Marilyn was right – it was delicious. She was going to need it to get through the day.

All too soon, they were on the way to her mother's new house. They rode in the back of a beat-up old sedan that smelled odd and had all sorts of things dangling from the rear-view mirror. The seats were covered in some kind of embroidered fabric with little mirrors sewn inside.

All the way there, Marilyn and Kaffir chatted, Marilyn often emitting gales of laughter. At one point, Kaffir had to pull the car over, he was laughing so much. Neither Pops nor Billie had the faintest idea what was so hilarious, but they were happy to be part of it.

'She knows everyone,' Pops said quietly to Billie in the back. 'I swear, we walk down the streets where she lives, and it's like Sesame Street. At the beginning, I honestly thought she was in a circus or something because she knows so many, shall we say, off-beat people. What she's doing with someone as straight-laced as me, I'll never know.'

'You're lovely, that's why.' Billie squeezed his arm. 'How amazing she can speak that language though, right?'

'Oh, she can speak loads of languages. I thought I was showing off one night with my Yiddish, but she can speak Spanish, French, Arabic... The list goes on and on.'

'How come? Like, where is she from?' Billie was intrigued.

Kaffir was explaining something to Marilyn in a most animated way, using his fingers to count something he was most anxious she understand. Billie would have preferred he kept his hands on the wheel, but somehow they were staying on course, so she just hoped for the best.

'She's from the South, but she's lived all over the world: ashrams, kibbutzim, refugee camps... She lived on a canal boat in Amsterdam! She's lived a lot of lives, that lady.'

Billie could hear the admiration in his voice, and perhaps a trace of wistfulness too. 'She's incredible,' she said.

As Billie spoke, they drove through a large pair of electric gates and up a winding driveway flanked either side by manicured lawns. There were marble statues and fountains and a large turning circle in front of a very elegant mini-mansion.

Billie was dumbstruck. Nobody had mentioned to her that Marko was wealthy, though the fact that he and her mother went on a private yacht for their honeymoon was a clue – one of her friends' parents had shared the photo on Facebook. And there had been the Mercedes yesterday. But nothing had prepared her for this. It was, she had to admit, just beautiful.

The house itself was white and had marble pillars, but off to one side was a beautiful sunroom, finished in oak and glass. Marko was inside, polishing glasses beside an exquisitely laid table. Pops hadn't been joking – they'd pulled out all the stops.

It could not be more different from the 1,000-square-foot house of her childhood – three beds, one bath and a large communal living room on Talbot Street in South Dorchester. Their home had been warm and welcoming, and packed to the brim with stuff, but it was modest by anyone's standards. It had been full of magazines and mementos, letters stuffed behind books and the detritus of family life all over the place. Her parents had bought it when they got married and stayed there until...well, until he died. At least her dad had died in his own house – that gave her some comfort – rather than in a hospital or a nursing home. He would have hated that. She could not imagine what he'd think of this place. She felt like she was betraying him by even being there.

Billie braced herself as the huge moss-green door opened and her mother emerged. She was dressed in a fitted white dress and jacket, pearls at her throat and in her ears. She looked absolutely filthy rich, Billie thought as she walked towards the house with Pops and Marilyn.

Kaffir left Marilyn off reluctantly; he was clearly only getting started with the saga that needed so much counting, but Marilyn managed to extricate herself somehow. They walked into the huge lobby, and Donna kissed Billie's cheek.

'Welcome, Billie. I'm so glad you could come.'

Everything in her mother's house was white, cream or peacock blue. It was slick and modern, and her mother's heels clicked on the terrazzo tiles as she led them to a large lounge room. Cream leather furniture, an enormous fireplace inset with a blazing fake gas fire, deep-pile white carpet and a few tables dotted about here and there made the room look like a place where the occupants could just walk out and no trace of them would give an indication of who they might be. Except for the photos. One big picture in a crystal frame stood on a table. Billie remembered the day it was taken. Gio's little league team had won the cup, her dad was the coach, and the picture was of her little brother, still in his uniform, raising the cup triumphantly. Pure joy shone from his face. He had such a cheeky grin. She felt like she'd been winded. The other picture was of her, aged twenty-two, the day she graduated. Dad and Pops had come to the ceremony, but her mother wasn't there. Her father said something about her being sick, but they both knew the truth. Gio had been dead for four years at that stage, but her mother was in a dark place.

Luckily, Marilyn chatted on, exclaiming over this and that, complimenting Donna on how lovely the house was, though she'd been there before, Billie knew. She and Pops had helped Donna and Marko with the move.

Marko offered her a drink, and she took it. It was some kind of warm punch, and though she hated to admit it, it was delicious.

Marilyn sipped and exclaimed, 'Oh my, Marko! What is this stuff?'

'You don't like it?' he asked, his dark eyes revealing nothing.

'No, I love it!' Marilyn said. 'It's delicious. What's in it?'

Billie watched him, realising it was the first time she'd heard him speak. She thought he would sound foreign, but he didn't. He had a cultured generic East Coast accent, like a newsreader or something.

'In Kiev, we make this in the winter – it is so much colder there. Sweet red wine, cherry liqueur, half a lemon, cinnamon and cloves. You warm it slowly, and this is the result.' He gave a ghost of a smile.

'It's really warming,' Pops said. 'My folks used to make something like this, *glühwein* we called it, but it was slightly different.'

'Yes, *glühwein* is the German version – I think lots of European countries have a variation of it – but this is ours.'

'Bet you're glad Kaffir is collecting us now, eh, Sol?' Marilyn chuckled.

The conversation went from the weather to the traffic out that way compared to South Dorchester to the film club Sol and Marilyn were members of, and Billie sat back and observed. Though they were all trying their best to seem like any regular family, she felt she was the elephant in the room. She knew Pops and Donna saw a lot of each other, and Marko and Marilyn would have made up the foursome, so Billie was the odd one out.

She excused herself to go to the bathroom. She wandered into the long cream corridor, then stopped. There, facing her on one expanse of white wall, was a large painting. She'd never seen it before, but it was instantly recognisable. It was of her and Gio and their parents, taken at a picnic organised by the construction company her father used to work for. She had loved the annual picnic, when all bets were off as regards to pop and candy and chips, and they ate hotdogs and played dodgeball till the sun went down. As she got older, she still enjoyed it – lots of cute boys were there and she was proud to be Matt Romano's daughter. Everybody respected her dad. He had worked his way up, and by the time he was diagnosed, he was the supervising foreman on a huge project. But he never forgot his roots. He spoke to everyone with regard, and he was loved. The big tough guys with tears in their eyes at his funeral were a testament to that.

The photo from which the artist must have done the painting was taken just a week or two before Gio died. Her parents were lying on their stomachs on the grass, Gio kneeling beside his mother, Billie leaning on her dad's right side, her face turned up to the evening sun, and Donna's head was on Matt's left shoulder. The relaxed joy on their faces had transcended the film and been captured by the artist. She could not stop staring at it. Her dad was wearing a green polo shirt and khaki shorts, her mother a pink summer dress; she was in a bikini top and denim cutoffs, and Gio wore a Red Sox t-shirt. She didn't know who took it, one of her dad's co-workers probably, but it was the last time she remembered them being happy.

She forced herself to walk on and went into the bathroom. It had a claw-footed marble jacuzzi bathtub in the centre of the room, and as she washed her hands, she caught a glimpse of herself in the huge gold-framed mirror. She looked like she felt – heartbroken.

Dinner was delicious, she had to admit. Donna might be a crap mother, but she was a great cook. Afterwards, she ushered everyone into a room they called the study. It was smaller than the other rooms they'd seen and seemed cosier. In there, the colours were muted greens and blues, and while the space was less intimidating than the rest of the house, Billie knew it had come straight from the pages of *Architectural Digest*. On a table were several inexpertly wrapped gifts. They were the only things in the room that weren't perfect.

It was Thanksgiving, not Christmas. What was going on, she wondered. Maybe they were early Christmas presents? Pops was Jewish, so he celebrated Chanukah as well as Christmas. She'd post his gift, which she'd already ordered online. His was the only gift she ever put any thought into these days. She'd bought him a book called *Sephardic Genealogy* because he was really interested in tracing his roots. It had been on sale in an Israeli bookshop and had been expensive to buy and then have shipped, but it was old and she knew he'd love it. His parents had survived the Holocaust by getting to China. He'd lived in Shanghai, a city that did not require Jewish refugees to have a visa. He'd lived there until he was eight years old, before moving to the United States. So many of his aunts, uncles and cousins – and all four grandparents – perished in the Nazi death camps.

Once everyone was settled with a digestif – some very fine cognac – Pops stood beside the stack of boxes. He looked excited.

Billie felt a surge of love for him. He looked like he always did, tall and thin, with thinning grey hair. He wore a navy sweater she'd bought him for his birthday and chinos. She guessed he looked kind of 'generic old guy', but he meant the world to her.

'So I know Christmas is the time for gifts, and this is Thanksgiving. But soon it will be Chanukah, and actually there are lots of parallels to be drawn between the flight of the Maccabees and the Pilgrims' quest for religious freedom. But anyway, I digress.' He went on. 'This year, I wanted to do something for us as a family, so I got these for everyone – I think they're neat. They're from a company called 23andMe, which makes a DNA test that can tell you your ancestry going back thousands of years. Marilyn got one for me a few months ago, and I was fascinated with the results. All you do is open the kit, register online with the number on the box, fill the little tube with saliva and send it off. They analyse it, and then you can log on the site and get your results. Turns out I'm mostly German, which I knew, but with Italian, Scandinavian and – I can't believe this – I'm six percent Irish. An old German-Jewish guy has a bit of Irish in him, can you believe it? And you know how I feel about them,' he said darkly.

Marilyn caught Billie's eye and gave a little eye-roll. Pops had always had a thing about the Irish for some reason. He wouldn't be drawn on why, but he had never liked them.

'So since we are an international family now – Marilyn is sure she's part Romanian, and I think she looks like a wild gypsy too, doesn't she?' – she slapped him playfully – 'I thought it might be fun to see where we all come from. Let's do it today, and then we can plan a family dinner in a few weeks to reveal our results. I think there might be a significant birthday coming up for someone,' he said with a rueful expression.

'Oh, don't worry. We hadn't forgotten.' Donna smiled at her dad.

He handed around the boxes, and soon everyone was logging into the site on their phones.

'This is a fun idea, huh?' Marilyn asked as Billie opened hers.

'I guess.' She managed in return. She had no interest and couldn't care less about any of it – what did it matter where your ancestors came from – but Pops loved all that stuff, so she mustered up some enthusiasm for him.

Marko seemed quite animated for once, helping Donna download the app on her phone and put in the serial number.

'Do you have any ideas about your DNA, Marko?' Pops asked.

'No. It was just my sister and I growing up. She looked after me as my parents were not there, and we didn't have any relatives – that we knew about at least – so it will be a complete revelation to me.'

Billie noticed a shadow pass over his face. She found herself wondering where his parents were.

'So, Billie, have you registered? You need to use the code on the box. That's how they match up the samples. You send back the box with the barcode on it.' Pops was so excited to be helping everyone. He'd embraced technology in a way that eluded many of his generation, but he loved the possibilities it brought.

'Yup, just doing it now, Pops.' She grinned at his childlike enthusiasm.

'So I thought we could all get together again, maybe in February. Everyone will have their results by then, but no peeking, OK? Keep your results till the night we get together.'

Soon the whole group had spit into tubes, and Pops gathered all the boxes. He planned to post them all together.

In the comradery that the DNA kits had created – Marko's was all bubbles and not enough saliva and Marilyn was cursing her new iPhone as she tried to log in – nobody noticed the worry cross Donna's face.

CHAPTER 4

*C*onor and Ana were dumbfounded. They'd been planning to visit the school, but before they could, the school secretary called and asked them to come in. When they got there, not only was Mrs O'Donovan, the principal, waiting but also the school's psychologist as well as the head of the Special Needs Department, Mr McCarthy.

'Conor, Ana, you're very welcome.' Imelda O'Donovan greeted them warmly and led them into her office. 'You know Gerard, and this is Julianne Moore, the school psychologist and counsellor.'

Conor and Ana nodded hello and took the seats offered around a round table.

'So I asked you both here today to talk about Joe.' Imelda held their gaze. She was a woman Conor had admired since the boys started at Star of the Sea National School five years earlier.

'What about him?' Conor asked, confused. Artie was the one they were all concerned about – what was wrong with Joe? He tried not to sound defensive.

'Well, as you know, we have been worried, as Artie has been withdrawn in recent weeks. He doesn't play with his friends anymore, he's dropped out of sports, which he loved, and he doesn't even seem to be connecting with Joe the way he used to. Now I know you've spoken to Mr Bredin about this, but there hasn't been an improvement in the situation. In fact,' – she glanced at the psychologist – 'there has been an incident.'

'What kind of incident?' Conor asked as Ana sat rigidly beside him. She never got along well with teachers, mainly because she was a teacher herself and felt like teachers in Ireland often spoke down to her because she was foreign. Conor had no idea if that were true or not, but it was how she felt.

'Joe was in a fight,' Imelda explained. 'He won't tell me what caused the fight, but he punched another student and hurt her quite badly.'

'Her?' Conor said incredulously. He couldn't believe one of his sons would hit a girl.

'Yes, it was a female student, and her parents are understandably very upset. They've taken her home, and she may need to see a doctor – he punched her in the stomach.'

Conor looked at Ana.

'I can't believe Joe would hit anyone, but especially a girl.' Ana was as appalled as he was. 'Our boy is not like this,' she said decisively.

'And what did he say when you asked him why he did it?' Conor asked.

'He wouldn't tell me. Though to be honest with you, I think it may have something to do with Artie. He was crying this morning at break time. One of the teachers went to him and took him inside to try to figure out what had happened, but then two other teachers had to run and break up the fight between Joe and this other child. Joe won't say, but I think the two incidents are connected.'

'Artie, he is gentle. Something is upsetting him. He is not so like this in usual times. I think it is his teacher – he don't like him and he don't understand Artie. He is sensitive…and if someone would say something to upset Artie, then Joe would defend him.'

'Ana, I understand and I agree, but what caused it or whether Artie likes his teacher or not is beside the point.' Imelda was not having this. She'd heard it a million times before from parents, the 'not my

Johnny' syndrome in which parents blamed everyone but their own child.

'I think we're just very upset to hear this, Imelda,' Conor interjected to try to defuse the situation. Ana was on edge, and she was like a lioness when it came to the boys. 'Of course we don't condone what Joe did. Please offer our sincere apologies to the little girl and her family, and of course any costs, doctor's visits or whatever, we'll cover. But we are really concerned about our sons now. You know them – they're not like this. Something is up, and we've tried, especially with Artie. I agree with Ana – Joe would have been defending his brother. If we can get to the root of Artie's problem, Joe's will be solved too. We've tried countless times, his grandparents have tried, but we can't get through to him.'

Imelda looked at them both sympathetically. 'So that's why I've invited Julianne to join us today. I think perhaps it might be time to come at this from a different angle. Artie is troubled, there's no doubt about that, and we must try to figure out what's going on with him. On the other hand, I cannot have a student physically assault another student without consequences – I'm sure you understand that? So we'll deal separately with both boys.'

'Of course,' Conor replied, before Ana could erupt again. His wife was calm and rational around most people, but when it came to school, she could be very fiery.

'Well, Conor and Ana,' Julianne said, and Conor could almost feel Ana wince at her tone. The psychologist didn't mean it, he was sure, but she came across as a bit patronising.

'I'm really hopeful that I can help Artie. You mentioned that you both and members of your extended family have tried to get him to open up, but to be honest, we often find children are more willing to speak to strangers. It's no reflection on his relationship with you, but when kids are in emotional turmoil, as Artie clearly is, they are often worried about the effect their words might have on their parents, so saying whatever is bothering him to someone with no emotional investment can work.'

Ana spoke. 'And what is this? You talk to him with us or on his own?'

'On his own, but you or your husband could be outside the door. It's important for Artie to feel like the therapy room is a safe space where he can say whatever he wants without fear of upsetting anyone he loves.'

'I don't know... We will have to talk, Conor and I...' Ana got up to leave. Conor knew she was moments from tears.

'One other thing before you go.' Imelda stood up. 'I will have to suspend Joe from school, just for three days. I don't do this lightly, but I'm afraid it has to be done. Children need to learn consequences, and restorative practice is part of our ethos here, so Joe will be excluded for a few days. Then he will need to reflect on his actions and apologise to the child in question. I hope you understand?'

Conor stood. 'Fine. Can we take him now?'

'Of course. Artie will be going home at the normal time, but I think it's best for everyone if Joe leaves now. He's in the time-out room. I'll go and get him.' She walked out with Conor and Ana.

'I'm going to the car. I don't want him to see me upset,' Ana said in a strangled whisper. 'I just need a minute...'

Conor nodded and gave her a one-armed squeeze. 'It's going to be fine. We'll sort this,' he whispered gently in her ear.

Ana went to the car, and Conor waited for Imelda, who had been waylaid by a teacher with an unrelated query. She solved it in her usual efficient manner and, before going down the brightly decorated corridor to fetch Joe, turned to Conor. She spoke conspiratorially. 'Look, Conor, strictly between us, the child he hit was Emma Doyle, Kieran Doyle's daughter, and he's not happy. There's something going on there. I don't know what yet, but I'm working on it. Julianne is very good. Honestly, if anyone can get it out of Artie, she can. I know it feels like the end of the world today, but it's all a part of growing up, just a bump in the road.'

He nodded and gave her a small smile. She was a good person and an excellent principal. But he sighed inwardly. Of all the kids to attack, Joe had to pick Kieran Doyle's. Kieran and Conor had had words the previous year when Kieran was roaring abuse at the kids during a hurling game. He was the selector for the team the twins played on. Conor had approached him at that time, saying, 'Kieran, they're just young lads and shouting at them isn't going to help. Maybe just tone it down a bit?'

But Doyle was not going to be reprimanded. He'd made a big deal of it on the day, and when the kids won the cup, he made a speech about how some parents were raising namby-pamby boys when everyone knew that kids nowadays needed toughening up. The speech was clearly aimed at Conor.

Whatever was wrong, Kieran Doyle was not going to let this go.

Conor waited patiently until Imelda came back with a very upset Joe. He'd been crying, and he dragged his school bag and coat behind him. Conor's heart melted to see his little boy in such distress. Joe was a fixer – he was the one in the family who noticed if Conor or Ana or Artie was a little down and tried to cheer them up.

Whatever else he needed, he did not need to be reprimanded, no matter what he'd done. Joe was behaving totally out of character.

'Come on, Son.' He put his hand on Joe's thin shoulder and took his bag and coat. 'We'll be in touch, Imelda, thanks.' Conor nodded and led his son outside, neither of them speaking.

Once he got out of sight of the front of the school, Conor led Joe over to a small wall and sat him down. He crouched down to be eye level with the boy.

'You're not in trouble, OK? Me and Mammy aren't cross with you. What we are is worried about you because this isn't like you and we don't know why you hit that girl. But we are going to help you, not give out to you, do you understand that?' He spoke gently and tipped Joe's head up by lifting his chin with his forefinger.

Joe's blue eyes met his fathers and filled with fat tears.

'It's OK, Joe. It's all going to be OK. Mammy and I can fix everything, every single thing. We just want our happy little boys back.'

Joe wasn't going to talk, that much was clear, so Conor took his hand and led him to the car. Ana was sitting in the back, and immediately, she extended her arms and her son collapsed into them, resting his head on her chest as she cuddled and kissed him while Conor drove. She held him all the way home.

Dinner that night was sombre. Joe looked totally dejected, and Artie barely touched his dinner though it was his favourite, shepherd's pie.

As Conor and the boys cleared the table – it was the house rule that the boys cleared away, loaded the dishwasher and wiped down the table – they went through the motions without speaking. Usually they were messing, putting suds on each other and generally joking around.

Artie went upstairs unbidden to do his homework. Joe went to get his school bag too, though he was going to be excluded from school for the next three days. As his son dragged the bag to the kitchen table, Conor sat down beside him.

'Joe, I know this is all really upsetting and you hate being suspended, and I'm guessing it has something to do with Artie, but can you tell me what's been going on?' he asked quietly.

Ana was in the bath and Artie was upstairs. Conor hoped that getting Joe on his own might get him to open up.

The more easy-going of the twins looked guarded.

'I know you and Artie are really loyal and you don't rat each other out, which is a great trait in brothers, but we are really worried about both of you now, and me and Mammy can't help if we don't know what's going on, you know?'

He looked into Joe's eyes and saw the tears threatening there once more.

His phone beeped. He glanced at it. It was Carlos. *Call me.*

Conor threw his phone on the sofa. Carlos could wait; Joe and Artie were much more important.

'Can you tell me, Joe?' He pressed for an answer.

He could see the conflict on his son's face. Loyalty to his twin wrestled with wanting to help him.

Eventually he blurted, 'Just that Emma Doyle is horrible. She's mean to everyone, but she picks on Artie all the time saying Mammy is a refugee and that she came on a boat illegally and that you...' He stopped.

'That I what?'

'That you like really young girls 'cause Mammy is way younger than you and that she was only a child when you got together with her and that you are a weirdo for that.'

Conor fought the urge to react. *So that's what Kieran and Tracey Doyle are saying over their dinner table?* No child could make that up. 'And what else?' he asked.

'That Babusya and Didus are refugees as well, and that we'll probably all get deported out of Ireland because we're only half Irish. And that we should all be in some kind of place they put illegal people who come into the country with no passports or something, I don't really know. And she's always saying that Artie is a weirdo because he's so smart, and that he's got special needs but nobody will tell him.'

Conor could see the relief on his son's face at finally unburdening himself.

'And sure I'm the one who goes out to Mr McCarthy for help with maths and Irish and stuff, not Artie, so if anyone has special needs, it's me, but she kind of ignores me. It's Artie she picks on the most – she never leaves him alone.'

'And what does Mr Bredin say?' Conor asked, wanting to throttle that little madam Emma Doyle.

'He doesn't care. And anyway, she never says anything when any adults are around. It's at lunchtime in the yard or before school starts. She's always got Chloe Brennan and Aoife Molloy beside her too, and that Aoife Molloy would flatten you. She once clattered Tommy Clancy, and his mam had to get him stitches.' Joe was warming to his theme. 'And Chloe's mam is the school secretary, so nobody says anything to her 'cause they're afraid of Kathleen.'

Conor supressed a smile. Kathleen Brennan, who worked in the school office, was nicknamed 'the Rottweiler' by the parents because she was so vicious. It came as no surprise that her daughter was following in her footsteps.

'And what do you do when they start on Artie?' he asked.

'I try to lead him away, just to get away from them. It's not fair, Daddy. If she were a boy, we could hit him a clatter or give him a kick or something, but we're not allowed to hit girls, and they are so mean.'

'Well, you seem to have abandoned the "Don't hit girls" rule,' Conor said ruefully.

'Yeah, I know, and I probably shouldn't have hit her. But in the yard today, she was on at him again, saying we came out of an orphanage and that we'd have to go back to Russia, even though we're not even Russian, and that we are really way older than we are because kids that come out of Russian orphanages, nobody knows how old they are. And I just got sick of her. She was mocking Babusya's cake she gave us for lunch, you know the lovely one she makes with all the coloured layers? But Emma was doing a stupid accent, mocking her and Didus too.' Joe looked so sad.

Conor fought the urge to say something and instead continued with his questioning. 'And how come Artie doesn't play sports with you anymore?'

'Those girls stand on the sideline laughing at him and pointing and all that kind of thing. So he stopped. And he doesn't want to play hurling with the club because Emma's dad is one of the selectors now, and he wouldn't pick Artie. He picks me but only 'cause I'm one of the best on the team and everyone knows we'd lose if I wasn't playing.'

Conor made a disapproving face at his son's arrogance.

'Ah, Daddy, I wouldn't say that to anyone else, but it's true.' Joe looked so innocent, and he was right. He was one of the best – possibly *the* best – players the team had.

'Right.' Conor pulled his son in for a hug. 'Thanks for telling me, Joe. You did the right thing. And I know you are out of school for three days, and you shouldn't have hit her, but you were sticking up for your brother and she did provoke you. So while I don't want you to ever do that again, we'll just let it go. We'll sort this out now. Go and play with your brother – pull out the Lego or the Dinky cars or something.'

Joe scampered off, and Conor was relieved a few moments later to hear them emptying the box of toy cars out onto the carpet upstairs. He had kept his old Dinky cars from when he and Gerry were kids – one of the few things he took from his mother's house when he sold it – and he loved that his boys got such a kick out of racing them and lining them up on the track Santa brought them when they were five. They especially loved an old Aston Martin that Jamsie had bought for Conor's sixth birthday before he took off. It made Jamsie tear up when Joe showed it to him one day, all these years later. Most of those small die-cast cars were as old as Conor, but the lads got a great kick out of them.

He sighed and made himself a cup of coffee. He wondered, not for the first time, why people had to be so mean. He had no gripe with the Doyles, apart from telling Kieran to cool the language and the aggression at the match, but did that warrant this onslaught of racist abuse Artie was now dealing with? How could it be that someone was handed a lovely little baby and, in a few short years, manage to allow her to become so horrible?

Ana would be so upset. And while she was in remission, she wasn't a 100 percent herself yet, so he wished he didn't have to tell her the reason Artie was being bullied. But he had no choice.

He let them play for a while and then took over bedtime. He brought Ana up a cup of fennel tea and her book when she decided she was getting an early night. She got tired easily, and he was anxious to keep her life as stress-free as he could. His working all the hours wasn't helping, but when he suggested getting someone in to help her last week, she nearly bit his head off. Her mother did all the laundry and most of the cooking, her father took care of the garden and bins and all of that if Conor wasn't around, and she'd demanded to know what exactly she'd need help with.

She apologised afterwards for snapping, and she'd cried. It was taking time to get back to her old self, and her body and her emotions were frustrating her. She was bored, but if she tried to do anything like gardening, which she loved, it wore her out too much.

The twins showered and got in their pyjamas, and they clambered into Conor and Ana's huge bed with their mother. He was about to call them out, but he saw that they needed her...and maybe she needed them as well. He gathered the boys' dirty clothes and watched them from the doorway. Ana was propped up on pillows, Joe on one side and Artie on the other, as she told them a *kazka* called *The Story of the Forty-First Brother*. They loved their Ukrainian heritage, and Ana and her parents kept it alive for them through folk tales, history and songs. The twins could converse fluently in the language and had even taught Conor the rudiments of it, so while he couldn't write in it or discuss anything complex, he could understand and participate in everyday conversations.

Artur told them bits of the history of the country, and Danika taught them old songs. They loved to hear about the tsars who hunted in the Ukrainian forests long ago, and the Cossacks with their long military traditions and excellent horsemanship. Conor had seen his boys mesmerised as their grandfather explained in his own language how they'd fought against the Bolsheviks, who had destroyed the tsars. His boys were proud that they were part Ukrainian. They even got football shirts that had the Ukrainian strip on one side and the Ireland strip on the other, both cultures equal in their eyes. It never occurred to them that people would be racist, or look down on them because of their background. It was their first brush with xenophobia, and Conor hated that they had to see it. To have their Ukrainian heritage ridiculed and made little of was heartbreaking.

He couldn't care less what the Doyles or anyone else thought of his family, or the fact that he was older than Ana, but he cared very much when those people upset his kids with their racist bigotry. He wanted to go around there and have it out with them, but he knew that wouldn't be wise. Joe did hit their daughter after all, no matter how much the little witch deserved it.

He had got Joe to confide in him, and that meant he had to make good on the promise that he would solve the problem. That teacher was as useful as a chocolate teapot, so it would be no good trying to reason with him. Should he tell Imelda what he knew? Would that make it better or worse for Artie? Would the girls guess Joe had told on them and include him in the bullying? It was so hard to know.

He loaded the washing machine and considered how best to handle this situation and ensure the best outcome for the boys.

Ana, once she heard, would have to be restrained from going over there and ripping their heads off. She loved her adopted country, but sometimes the attitudes towards her, just because she didn't have an Irish accent, frustrated her. Some people assumed she had no education or that she was from a very backwards place when they heard her speak, and they tended to speak slowly and loudly. He'd seen it himself and was appalled. Ana said it was a daily occurrence.

One of the mothers down at the school had asked her if she'd be interested in cleaning her house. Ana replied coldly that she would not, and ranted at Conor for an hour that evening about the audacity of the woman. There was nothing wrong with cleaning – of course not – but this woman assumed she was a cleaner because she was from the Ukraine. She wouldn't have asked any of the Irish mothers that.

Artur and Danika berated their daughter when she spoke like that. They were grateful to their adopted country and insisted they were only met with kindness and hospitality, but Conor knew little things went on that other people could have considered a slight.

For example, the new curate at mass asked people to volunteer as readers for the liturgy, and Artur volunteered. His English was accented but quite good, and he and Danika were daily churchgoers, getting up each morning to make 7 a.m. mass before work. But he was never taken up on the offer. Things like that irked Ana, but Artur and Danika had seen a lot in their long lives, much spent under a Communist regime, and were more likely to let things go. Conor could have had a word with his friend Eddie, the parish priest, but Artur would know and it would hurt his pride, so Conor left it be.

He went outside to lock up the cars and close the gate, and while out there, on impulse rang his father. Jamsie and he had had a very rocky start – not seeing your father for forty-something years would do that – but Conor had forgiven him and was glad to have him back in his life. Jamsie was a terrible father, he knew, but he was sorry and what was the point of holding grudges?

'Conor. How are you, Son?' Jamsie sounded thrilled to hear from him as he always did, and Conor felt a pang of guilt. He'd been so busy lately, he hadn't stayed in touch like he should.

'Fine, Jamsie, fine.' Though the men had reconciled their differences, Conor called him by his first name. It was too late to call him Dad.

'You don't sound fine if you don't mind me saying so?' Jamsie's voice was tinged with concern.

Conor sighed as he locked the gates and took the boys' toys that were scattered around the lawn into the garage.

'Ah, we're just really worried about the lads. I finally dragged it out of Joe. Artie's being bullied in school by a girl – well, a few girls, but one in particular. I had a run in with the father, and the child's been saying all sorts of nasty racist things about the boys and Ana and even Danika and Artur. And to put the tin hat on it, she's decided that apparently I'm some kind of a child molester because Ana is younger than me. It's really winding Artie up and upsetting him. Today, Joe hit her a box, and apparently she needed medical attention and the whole lot. When I tell Ana what's going on – and I have to tell her – she'll lose the plot completely, and I don't know what she'll do. She's like a dervish once she gets going, no stopping her.'

'And why would you stop her?' Jamsie asked. 'The most powerful instinct on earth, humans, birds, animals, you name it, is for a mother to protect her young, and that's what Ana is doing. What's so wrong with that?'

'What is wrong with that is if I let her go over to the Doyles' house, she could leave that child for dead. You haven't seen her when she's riled up, but I'll tell you, it's not pretty.' Conor chuckled.

'Well, it sounds to me like that little madam, whoever she is, needs to learn a lesson.'

'Not if it ends my missus up in jail though,' Conor said with a sigh.

'True.' Jamsie thought for a moment. 'I know I shouldn't say it, but good on Joe for giving her a dig anyway. And Artie hates that teacher, doesn't he?'

'Well, he doesn't hate him, but he's very old school and angry, so they are a bit afraid of him, to be honest. He's like the brothers that taught me, but kids aren't used to that anymore. Nearly all the teachers nowadays are nice.'

'Well, maybe scary or not, that man needs a bit of a talking to about what's going on under his nose. But I know what you mean. If you go in there all guns blazing, you could make things worse for the poor lad, and for Joe for being the one who told.' Jamsie exhaled in thought. 'I've not much parenting experience, as you know well, but I'd talk to the principal and the teacher, swear him to secrecy, and if there's no improvement, then you'll have to think again.'

'Yeah, that's what we'll probably do. Thanks. Listen, I better go in and face the music. If you feel earth tremors in Dublin in the next hour, that'll be my wife, losing her reason down here,' Conor said, only half joking.

'T'would be worse if she didn't care. She's a grand girl. You're a lucky man.'

'I know.' Conor agreed. Ana was always fiery, and he loved it about her. She was not a docile little wife at home; she had her own opinions, and when it came to the boys, she was fiercely protective. The idea that Artie was being harassed because he was half Ukrainian would really make her mad.

A thought struck Conor before he hung up. 'Jamsie, are you around next weekend? It's Ana's birthday, and I've been neglecting her. I want to take her away for a night – not too far, but treat her like she deserves. Would you come down and look after the lads? Artur and Danika would be around as well, but they are so good to us during the week helping out, I hate asking them on the weekend. Normally I'd ask Laoise and Dylan, but they're in Australia on a tour. What do you think?'

Conor had often invited his father for an overnight stay, and he'd come for Christmas, but Jamsie always waited to be asked as he never wanted to impose. But Conor had never asked him to babysit before.

He took a second to answer, and Conor was about to ask if he was all right when he replied.

'I would absolutely love to mind my grandsons. Thanks, Conor, for asking me. I...' Jamsie was unusually choked with emotion. Conor realised his request meant a lot to his father.

'All right, don't go getting all emotional on me now. I've enough tears and all of that to be dealing with today. I'll see you Friday, so?'

Jamsie chuckled. 'See you Friday.'

Just as Conor was about to go in, his phone rang. It was the Head-land Heights in Ardmore.

He'd rung yesterday, from work, before any of this blew up, and gave his name. The receptionist had taken the booking for Conor and Ana for Saturday night.

Conor answered, and it was the manager, Antoine Barry, a fellow Corkman. The two men had both attended several tourism confer-ences, and Conor liked him.

'I hear you're coming to spy on the competition, are you?' Antoine laughed.

'You caught me,' Conor replied with a chuckle. 'Antoine, how are you?'

'Yerra, tipping away. I just saw on the reservations that you were coming. Well, we better put on our best show. I hear you got a Michelin star last month? Congratulations.'

'We did. Our new head chef is something else. We poached him from a place in London, but yeah, he's definitely the real deal. Swing by someday if you are up around West Clare and see for yourself.'

'I'll take you up on that. Maria and I are off to Sardinia for the weekend. She says she needs to get away in the off-season because once it starts…well, you know.'

'I do indeed. I'm at the same thing myself. It's my wife's birthday actually, and she loves the Headland Heights. My lads, though, prefer the mobile homes below on the beach, I'm afraid.'

Conor and Ana had taken the boys to a caravan park in Ardmore a few times, where there was a playground and amusements and a chip shop and a huge expanse of beach. They were in heaven when they were there. The campsite was located just below the magnificent hotel.

'I don't blame them!' Antoine chuckled. 'I look over at them myself some days and think, wouldn't it be nice? A simple life in your little self-contained unit on the beach. And sure for kids, it's pure heaven.'

'They love it. Sea, sand, chips, ice cream, fishing, no school. We have a place out in Spain, but to be honest, I'll probably sell it. We don't get there often enough, and the lads prefer Ardmore anyway.'

'Delighted to hear it. And by the way, your money's no good here. You really gave me a dig out with that corporate group that we double-booked back in June. I'd have been rightly goosed if you hadn't been able to take them, so I owe you one.'

'Not at all, 'twas no bother, and us Cork lads have to stick together.' Conor chuckled.

'No, I insist. This one's on us. See you Saturday.'

'Thanks, Antoine, I appreciate that, if you're sure. See you then.'

He went in and supervised getting the boys out of his and Ana's bed and into their own and then went down and made Ana another cup of tea. He brought it up and closed the door of their bedroom behind him. She looked up, as their room was always open.

'What's wrong now?' she asked, a note of panic in her voice.

'Nothing. I just need to talk to you without little ears tuning in,' he said, handing her the cup.

'OK,' she said, relieved, and sipped her tea. 'Ah, tea…so strange. When I come here in the first years, I don't drink this stuff. I think it nasty. But Ireland has wore me down with this, and now I love it.' She sipped again gratefully. 'Thanks, Conor.' She smiled and leaned up to kiss him. He responded and gave her a squeeze.

'OK, Ana, I am going to tell you something, but I need you to listen and not go mad, OK?' He said.

'This does not sound good,' she replied, placing the cup on the bedside locker, her eyes wary.

'It isn't.' He sighed. 'I spoke to Joe earlier, and I finally got out of him what's been happening...' He told her the whole sorry tale of Emma Doyle and her needling Artie constantly. He held nothing back – the mocking of Ana's parents, the allegation about Conor's sexuality, everything. She sat and listened, not saying a word. When he finished, she held his gaze for the longest time.

'I want to kill her. With my bare hands, go there and kill her,' Ana said in a low voice as her green eyes glinted with fury.

Conor understood. 'I know you do. And with that accent, it would scare the living daylights out of her, but she's a kid. A nasty little brat, no doubt about it, but a kid nonetheless, so we can't approach her.'

'But we can't do nothing.' Ana was furious.

'Of course not. We'll go down to Imelda in the morning, explain what we know, and see if she can do something.'

'And if she can't or won't? Then what we will do?' Ana's eyes blazed with the injustice of it all.

Conor drew her onto his shoulder and kissed the top of her head. 'Then I go round there and batter every single one of the Doyles.' He chuckled.

'I wish you were not joking. In Ukraine, if this happen...' she said ominously.

'I can only imagine.' Conor had heard enough stories from Artur and Ana about the type of rough justice that was meted out in their home country.

'So we've a plan now. Let's take it one step at a time, all right? We'll solve this.'

He was going to leave his treat at the weekend a surprise but decided to tell her. 'Now, you know how you love the Headland Heights hotel in Ardmore?'

They'd gone there for coffee one day, and the hotel rivalled, but not quite trumped, Castle Dysert in terms of luxury. Ana had said at the time that she'd love to stay there.

The Headland Heights was a five-star hotel built into the cliff face in the seaside town in County Waterford. It had an outdoor hot tub, and the views of the Atlantic as the headlands stretched out on either side of the bay were spectacular. Both headlands were popular with walkers, and the hotel was the jewel in Ardmore's crown. The lads loved the walk up the cliff. There was an old monastic well, a World War II lookout and a lifeboat station, not to mention a few old wrecks to examine far below amid the crashing surf. In the summertime, they jumped off the pier into the icy crystal-clear waters below.

Conor looked at Ana and held her gaze.

'Yes, it is lovely, but what...'

'Well, I'm taking you there on Saturday, just the two of us. Jamsie is coming down from Dublin to mind the lads – he actually choked up when I asked him, and he'll be grand with them – and your parents are around as well, so...'

'Conor!' Ana looked upset. 'Thank you, and I know it for my birthday and it is kind, but I can't leave Joe and Artie like this, I just can't.'

'We can.' Conor held her hand. 'Look, Jamsie adores the boys, and the feeling is mutual. They're upset, sure, but now we know what's causing it, and you know they'll be spoiled rotten. I think it'll be good for them just to have their granda for the weekend – it takes the pressure off. He knows what's going on as I spoke to him earlier, but the lads don't know he knows, so they can just be normal.'

He tilted his head to the side and made a funny face. 'Come on, please. We need some adult time. They need a bit of spoiling, and it's only for one night...'

'But I –'

'I booked you one of those seaweed treatments, where they wrap you up in warm muddy seaweed and cover you in fluffy blankets...'

She smiled. She had been introduced to the idea of a spa by

Corlene when they opened Castle Dysert. Corlene had insisted that Ana test drive the treatments offered, and ever since, she was hooked.

'And what about you? You going to have some treatment?'

'Nah, sure I'm a big tough guy, you know that!' Conor grinned, delighted she'd given in.

'A big tough guy who loves foot massages,' she teased.

'Shh! Don't tell anyone – it'll ruin my image.'

'OK, our secret. What about the way you love Downton Abbey, should I not say that?'

He started tickling her and she screamed.

'Definitely not,' he said as she wriggled away from him.

He caught her and the tickling turned into kissing.

CHAPTER 5

*B*illie could not bear to face the world, not after the debacle of the previous night. She blushed to the roots of her hair when she recalled the way the events unfolded. It was mortifying.

The wrap party for their latest feature film had turned into an all-nighter, going from the really swish venue with the free bar where all the big-shot executives hung out to a club she'd never heard of before and would never go to again.

She tried to piece together the horrible moment when, emboldened by a bottle of wine and several Mojitos, she decided to come clean to Rob about her attraction to him. She had made a complete spectacle of herself, she just knew it. She had no idea who overheard it, and the fact that Rob was so nice about it made it a hundred times worse. The whole thing was a blur of humiliation, but she did recall him saying that he was engaged and was getting married next month. Then he'd kindly called her a cab. *Oh God, he must have paid for it too.* She remembered she had no more cash in her purse. How could she ever go into work again?

She'd call Emily – at least her friend would know what she was facing.

She looked at her phone. Seven missed calls, one from Rob. *Oh no.*

Another from Pops, but she definitely couldn't take that in this condition. She was due to go back to Boston the day after tomorrow, for Pops's seventieth. He was probably calling to get her flight details.

She opened Siri. 'Call Emily,' she croaked. Her mouth felt like the bottom of a birdcage.

'Calling Emily,' the automated voice responded.

'Hey,' Billie said.

'Hey yourself. I've been trying you all morning.'

'I know, just woke up.'

'Well, were you thinking of coming to work today?'

'No…I was thinking of jumping off a large bridge. How bad is it?'

'On a scale of one to ten?'

'Yeah.'

'Six thousand?' Emily giggled.

'Oh, um…what am I going to do?' She could feel her face flaming in shame.

'Look, come in and face the music, get it over with. Nobody died. You're going to get a hard time – Tina is crowing like a witch that she knew for ages you fancied him. Rob got really ratty this morning and told everyone to shut up about it, if that's any consolation?'

'It's not. Is Noah there?'

The thought of her boss hearing about what went on was another point of mortification. At least he went home early, sober, like a sane person, so he didn't witness her humiliation, though no doubt by now someone would have told him.

'He is, and he came by your desk twice looking for you, so I'd get myself in here pronto if I were you. Gotta go – he's coming.' Emily hissed the last bit and hung up.

The moment the call ended, the screen flashed again. Incoming. Pops. She groaned.

'Hi, Pops.' She tried to inject some brightness into her voice.

'What happened?' he asked.

How does he know anything happened?

'What do you mean?'

'All over your Facebook feed, you're tagged in about five memes about the most embarrassing thing ever, and lots of LMAO and emojis, so what happened?' He was persistent if nothing else.

'I…um…' From nowhere, the tears came. She hardly drank at all, but since coming back after Thanksgiving, with the trip having dragged up all the stuff about Gio and her dad and then Mom being married to Marko, she found herself reaching for the bottle much more.

'Ah, Billie, I'm worried now. What's going on there, honey?' The kindness in his voice just made it all harder.

'I got drunk at a party and told a guy at work I liked him in front of everyone. He's engaged, and now everyone is laughing at me, which is totally understandable, but I just can't face going in there today…' Her words turned to a sob.

'OK, OK, is that all? So you did a dumb thing – it's not the end of the world.' His soothing voice was so familiar. No matter what happened, Pops was right there by her side.

'I can't face them, I just can't, and now my boss is looking for me,' she blurted tearfully.

'Look, here's what I would do.' She heard him suck on the contraband cigarette he was supposed to have quit on doctor's orders. If Marilyn or Donna found out, they'd murder him.

'Call your boss, tell him the truth, that you feel like you made a total schmuck of yourself, you are embarrassed, you're gonna take a few days to visit your family in Boston, and you'll be back to work on Monday, yadda yadda. You were coming on Friday, anyway, so just come today instead.'

Billie smiled. He still used old Jewish expressions. 'But I can't just…'

'You can. You totally can. Get on a plane. You've got the voucher, so just use that to pay for the change. I'll pick you up at Logan tonight. Hey, did you check your 23andMe account?'

She'd completely forgotten about it. 'No… Didn't you say we were all to do it together on your birthday?'

'Good girl. Your mother peeked at hers, I know she did. OK. Text me with your flight. I gotta go...' He hung up. Obviously, someone was coming and he needed to get rid of his cigarette.

She lay back on the pillow, her head pounding – it felt like her brain was about to explode. Maybe Pops was right, and she should just go to Boston earlier than planned. Noah was OK – a bit serious but generally a nice guy. If she asked him and promised to make the time up, he'd probably OK her early departure.

She cringed at the thought all the same. He'd feel sorry for her – stupid Billie, making a total fool of herself with the hottest guy in the building. Her boss might be OK, but he wouldn't understand. He'd never do something that embarrassing.

She'd noticed of late he was giving her more and more challenging assignments, and she thought it might be in preparation for moving her upstairs. She hoped her work was impressing him; she put in lots of extra hours and really wanted to be promoted to Concepts. Surely now she'd undone all her progress in one stupid moment.

She tried to visualise him in his office. She could picture the smirk that would be on Tina's face as she put the call through. Billie didn't have his cell – she had to call the office. She swallowed the lump in her throat. He wasn't a monster. He was very professional and would be fine.

Noah didn't look like most people in the industry, very styled and conscious of themselves. Emily joked that he looked more like an accountant than a film-maker.

He'd been really sweet when she had to go back east when her father was dying, and she'd only been at Visionboard a few weeks then. He was in his thirties, so really young to be an executive producer with such a huge company. Some of the girls tried to flirt with him to get the best projects, but he was oblivious. They speculated that he was gay, but Billie didn't know. It seemed to her he was just very professional.

Reluctantly, she scrolled for the office number, praying anyone but Tina would answer.

'Hello, Visionboard, how may I direct your call?' Tina's sing-song voice.

'Tina, it's Billie. Can you put me through to Noah, please?' she asked, infusing her voice with as much confidence as she could.

'Billie, how are you?' Tina's mock concern made her want to scream. She was such a gossip.

'Oh, fine, thanks. Can you put me through to Noah, please?' she repeated, forcing her voice to stay neutral.

'Sure, Billie. Take care of yourself.'

Billie was sure she heard a derisive sneer in the other woman's voice.

A few clicks and then she heard Noah.

'Hello?' he answered.

'Hi, Noah, it's Billie.'

'The Billie that should be at her desk?'

'Yes, look, I'm really sorry. I screwed up, I'm sure you heard, and I made a total idiot of myself last night. I just can't face coming in. I'll make the time up, I swear. I'll work all next weekend, Saturday and Sunday, but I think if it's OK with you, I might go and see my family back east today. I was planning on going on Friday anyway. I just need...' She held back the tears.

She heard him exhale. 'OK. Go. But I will hold you to next weekend.'

'Thanks, Noah. You're the best.'

'Hmm. I was young once too, you know. Hard to believe, but I was,' he joked.

'I'd believe it.' She said with a chuckle.

'OK, give my regards to snowy Boston. I graduated from Boston College, did you know that?' he asked.

'No, I didn't. My folks would have liked me to go there, but I went to Rhode Island instead.'

She heard Noah chuckle. 'My dad wanted me to stay in Pensacola and work at his lumber yard, so there you go...'

She waited, wondering if he was going to say anything else. The pause went on, so she spoke. 'OK, Noah, I'm gonna get a flight today. Thanks again. I really appreciate it.'

'Take care, Billie.' He hung up.

She dragged herself into the shower, and when she returned to the bedroom, there were two more texts.

Emily: *Hey, hon, you OK? You coming in or what?*

And one from Rob: *Hi, Billie. I hope you're OK? I'm so sorry about last night. I didn't mean to embarrass you. I think you're great, and if I wasn't committed elsewhere, I'd be flattered and delighted. Take care. Rob.*

'Aargh!' She threw the phone on the bed. He felt sorry for her. Of course he did. Oh, God, why was she such a moron?

Robotically, she changed her flight to Boston to that afternoon. She needed to get away from California.

CHAPTER 6

*A*na and Conor lay in the huge bed, watching the sun setting over the Atlantic through the floor-to-ceiling windows of their suite. The Headland Heights had not only given them a complimentary stay but had upgraded them to a premium suite, which enjoyed uninterrupted views of the bay. The sky blazed in streaks of vermillion and ochre as the sun sank slowly behind the horizon. Conor had opened a bottle of champagne, which was in an ice bucket beside the bed. He poured Ana a glass and handed it to her.

He kissed her bare shoulder. 'You taste seaweedy,' he murmured.

She'd spent the afternoon in the spa while he did 100 lengths in the pool then relaxed in the bar with a beer and a book his father had bought him for his birthday.

They had dinner reservations, but not until eight, so they'd decided to avail of a bedroom with no possibility of a small boy interrupting them.

He traced his fingers along her abdomen, touching the silvery lines there, stretchmarks that had faded after her pregnancy with the twins. They had tried for years to have another child, but it never happened, and then the cancer came last year so their priorities shifted.

'Do you ever regret that we didn't try IVF?' he asked quietly.

'Sometimes,' she answered. 'You know Caroline Leavy, from the school? She and her husband was trying to have a baby for lots of years, and she go to have this IVF, and now she has twins.' She smiled. 'I don't know if more twins would maybe kill us, though?'

'I think we are so lucky. Joe and Artie are so perfect, and it would be nice if it happen some years ago, but God decide we have enough. If it was meant to be, it would happen.'

Conor marvelled again at Ana's simple but unwavering faith. He didn't share it, but he respected it. 'True. We're so lucky. The boys, our parents and, most importantly, your treatment. One full year clear of cancer, one more year to go before the risk of return is significantly diminished. I don't know what I'd have done...' he whispered.

'You would have managed, but now you don't have to.' She kissed him tenderly. 'I think it is gone, Conor. I feel like it is over, all the doctors and hospitals and all of it, you know? Like I am ready to get my life back, to do everything I did before.'

'I'm so relieved. Every day, I am just so grateful for everything. But let's make sure you take it easy all the same though, right?'

'I'm tired of taking things easy. I get so frustrated sometimes, so bored, just waiting for the boys to come home. I want to do some-thing, you know...something useful.'

'You are so useful! You're an amazing mother and the best wife any man could want, and you're funny and clever and brave. You can do whatever you want, sweetheart.' He kissed her deeply.

'We must do this more often. I'm sorry I've been so caught up with the hotel. I don't mean to neglect you and the lads, but sometimes it feels like I'm pulled in fifty different directions. In lots of ways, even though I was away, driving tours was easier.'

'Yes, but then you sleep in hotels, not in your home with your family. So even if it is bad now with the castle, you sleep with me every night.' She never berated him about how hard he worked, though she missed him. Her father was a hard-working man too, and Ana knew everything Conor did was for their family.

'Well, I'm determined to find someone good as assistant manager, even though the last two rounds of interviews were an unmitigated disaster. Carlos is great at his job when he's fit and well, but he's like a cut cat these days. Being stuck in that wheelchair is torture for him, I know, but he's making everyone else's life hell as well. He's eating the head off anyone who looks sideways at him. Katherine's the only one he won't rear up on – she'd leave him for dead if he tried – but she's not back for ages yet. Even when she's back properly, I need someone anyway. We are just too busy these days, and while they both have lots of skills, people management isn't really one of them.'

'And now Katherine is married, she will want to use her time off,' Ana said, then sipped her champagne as she rested against Conor's chest.

'Exactly. Sure I'm trying to get that woman to take her holidays since she started, but she wouldn't all along. She's entitled to have a bit of fun, God knows she deserves it, but her being all loved up does nothing to solve my problem.'

'And Corlene is no use…' Ana sighed.

Conor knew that while Ana and Corlene had reached a kind of entente cordiale, it wasn't a friendship. Corlene flirted constantly with all men, but she laid it on thick with Conor – she couldn't help it – and it drove Ana mad. He didn't respond, but she was incorrigible.

'None whatsoever,' he agreed.

'And you do all of the work and she does none, and yet she gets more of the profits. It's not fair.'

'Fair or not, it's how it is. She cut me in at forty percent when my investment was nothing like that figure, so she's been good to me.'

'Yes, but you have run the place so well, brought it from nothing to the best hotel in Ireland, even pulled it out of the ashes after the fire. She had nothing to do with that success. All of that was you and your hard work.'

Conor shrugged and sipped his champagne.

'Could you buy her out?' Ana asked, the idea just occurring to her.

'Of the castle? But we're in sixty-forty now – I'd have to come up with sixty percent of the value of a five-star resort. You'd be talking fifty million, I'd say, so no, not a chance.'

'Hmm…I suppose not. It would be nice, though, not to have to consult her or anyone.'

'Well, to be fair, she lets me do whatever I like. She's too busy cavorting around Dublin with Colm MacEntire TD,' Conor reasoned.

'What is this TD they say after some names?'

'It's Irish. It stands for Teachta Dála. It means literally "messenger to the assembly", but it's the name we have for elected representatives. You know the way the parliament is called the Dáil? And the leader is called the Taoiseach and the second in command is the Tánaiste? Those are old Irish words first used in the time of mythology, describing the leader of a clan, the gathering of the leaders, his right hand man.'

'Or woman.' She smiled.

'Well, actually yes. Under the old system here, the Brehon Law applied before the Anglo-Normans invaded in 1169, and women were highly respected. They could divorce their husbands very easily, they kept their own land when they got married –'

'So in the old way, I can get rid of you easy?' She chuckled while running her hand over his chest.

'Yep! If I got too fat to perform my marital duties, for example, or if I was a priest and never told you, or if I told my mates down the pub things about our relationship… Anything like that and you could give me the high road.'

'Really, it is true?' she asked.

'Absolutely. Women had all the power before, so I suppose us fellas have to thank the Brits for something…'

She slapped him playfully. 'Now, I must get dressed. I have a hot date tonight…' She moved to get up.

'Ah, it's only ten to six,' he murmured into her neck, and as always, she turned to him.

CHAPTER 7

*B*illie and Pops sat at the table in the Lebanese restaurant. They were all going out for Pops's birthday on Friday night, but there would be lots of friends at that, so he had suggested revealing their DNA results that night when it was just family. They'd come directly from the airport, and he'd booked the table for seven. It was five past, but there was no sign of Marilyn, Marko or Donna. Pops was so excited. He had asked everyone to email their 23andMe results to him. He was full of interesting facts about genetics these days, and he spent hours doing research.

'I know you're only doing this to keep me happy. Maybe it's an old man's thing.' He chuckled.

'Aw, Pops.' Billie placed her hand on his. 'It's actually really interesting. Like I know Mom's side because of you, but I've no idea about Dad's. His folks, well, they were Italian, but apart from that, they never said where in Italy the family came from, and I don't think Dad knew either. I guess the name Romano could be from anywhere over there, right? It's kind of a common Italian-American name, so I'm interested. I'm guessing fifty percent Italian and fifty percent whatever you and Mom are.' She sipped her sparkling water; the thought of ever drinking alcohol again made her nauseous.

'When death is around the corner, you kinda get interested in your place in the great scheme of things, you know? Like you're just a link in a chain, people behind you, people in front of you. Maybe more so for Jews after everything that happened. Who knows?' He raised his bottle of beer to her in salute.

She was so grateful to him that he hadn't brought up the debacle with Rob. She couldn't bear to talk about it. Pops just knew when she needed to talk and when she definitely didn't.

Billie knew her grandfather was scarred by what had happened to his family. He didn't remember life in Germany, obviously, but the toll moving to China and then the US had on his parents, the loss of their families in the Nazi death camps, was a hurt that would never heal. Maybe if she'd been brought up Jewish it would mean more to her. It was awful, of course, and she remembered sitting in history class as the teacher taught them about the Holocaust. But to her teenage self, it was just another example of how adults were determined to screw the world up. She didn't feel any more outraged at the Holocaust than she did at the slaughter of Native Americans, or those killed in Vietnam. She learned the details and handed in her papers and it was horrible, incredible, what people could do to each other, but it just didn't hurt her the way it hurt Pops.

They looked up towards the door, and there, in a mustard muslin kaftan, covered in what looked like one of those colourful Mexican blankets, stood Marilyn, talking animatedly with Haasim, the owner. She was clearly a regular.

'She's certainly colourful, Pops, in every way.' Billie smiled.

'She sure brightens up my days, kiddo,' he said, then took another sip of his beer. 'After your grandma died, well, I was so busy with work and the girls. She was from Brazil, as you know, so we didn't have a big extended family around to fall back on for support. I never had much time for dating, and then, well, I thought that ship had sailed. But Marilyn convinced me to give it a whirl, and I got to tell you, she's one of a kind. You like her, right?'

Billie was surprised at the note of vulnerability in her grandfather's tone.

'Of course I do, though I could live without the image of you two in some S&M setup,' she teased, referring to Marilyn's interest in *Fifty Shades of Grey*.

Pops coloured with embarrassment. 'That's just talk. She's trying to shock you... She does that...' he muttered.

'I'm just kidding, Pops. I know at your age...' She giggled, and he swiped playfully at her head.

'You'll be my age someday, and see how it feels.'

Marilyn joined them and gave Pops a big hug and planted a firm kiss on his lips before wrapping Billie in a cloud of sandalwood perfume.

'Billie, it's so good to see you. He's been like a hen with an egg all week, waiting for this. He's convinced I opened mine already, but I didn't. I think I'd like to be Indian, you know? I feel very Indian some days, and I knew an Indian guy once, from Goa. I met him in an ashram in Arizona. Wow...we had some fun times. Pity about that snake though. How many snake charmers get bitten by their own snake? What are the chances?' She seemed to be asking a genuine question.

'Quite high I would have thought?' Billie offered.

'I guess, though he never seemed the type to get bitten. He changed from charming an Indian cobra to a Russell's viper. He got the viper from a guy in Indianapolis, not his usual supplier in Madras, so that might have been the problem.' She shrugged sadly. 'Well, we'll never know now, I guess.'

'Er...OK. I'm sorry about your friend,' Billie said, unsure of how to respond.

'Thanks, but he's fine. I met him recently actually...' Marilyn stopped to peruse the menu.

Billie was confused. Hadn't Marilyn said he died? 'I thought he passed away...' she began.

'Oh, he did in that life, but I know him in his next incarnation, or maybe his second one after the snake. Who knows? He works in Starbucks now – his name's Luis.'

Pops and Billie exchanged a glance, and Pops gave his attention to the menu so Marilyn wouldn't see him smiling.

Moments later, Donna arrived, clutching Marko's hand.

'Donna, Marko, we were getting worried. Was the traffic bad?' asked Marilyn.

They chatted idly about the weather and the traffic for a few moments, and the waiter came to take their order. They gave it, and then Pops addressed them.

'OK, folks, the moment you've been waiting for. These results are kind of complex with lots of different markers and so on, but I haven't looked at these. I printed off the emails you sent, and the nice lady at the retirement centre put them in the envelope for me.' He had four sealed envelopes in his jacket pocket and handed one to each of them.

'Let's start with Marko. Open your email, Marko,' Pops said with a grin.

Marko tore his open and scanned the page. There was a coloured map of the world.

'Oh, look, I am mostly Cossack. This is very good. I loved those stories as a boy – my sister would get me books filled with tales of the brave Cossacks who fought the terrible Bolsheviks. And some Russian, some Mongolian, and a bit of Japanese. Amazing.'

Donna opened hers next. 'As expected, lots of German, lots of Brazilian from my mother's side. Some Portuguese, a bit of Spanish, and some Israeli.' She smiled but something about her expression made Billie wonder, as it didn't reach her eyes.

'You next, Billie,' Pops said.

Billie tore open her envelope and gazed at the map. Her brow furrowed, and she looked around the table. 'This can't be right,' she said, confused.

She'd emailed the results to Pops without opening them, as he instructed.

'How much Irish was in yours, Pops?' she asked.

'Six percent, why?' he asked, standing up to walk behind her and look over her shoulder.

'So how on earth can I be forty-eight percent Irish then?' She turned to look up at him.

Pops shrugged and took the page from her. Billie's eyes found her mother's. Donna was as white as a sheet. She opened her mouth as if to say something, but closed it again. Marko reached over and held his wife's hand.

'What's going on?' Billie asked, totally confused. She had assumed it was a mix-up with the test, but her mother's face said differently.

'Billie, I...' Donna paused.

'What?' Billie demanded. 'How am I forty-eight percent Irish? Dad was Italian... You are Jewish and Brazilian... I don't understand.'

'Billie, please...' Donna said helplessly. 'I can explain...'

Suddenly, Billie needed to get away. Whatever her mother was going to say, she didn't want to hear it. Without another word, she got up and walked to the restrooms. She needed to think. She locked herself in a stall and stared again at the single page. There it was in black and white. Some German, some Brazilian, some Portuguese as she'd expect, and forty-eight percent Irish and no Italian whatsoever. Her last name was Romano, her father and all of his family were Italian. This made no sense. Pops had six percent Irish only, so how could she be half?

She heard the bathroom door open and then her mother knocked gently on the stall door.

'Billie, please come out. I can explain.'

Her heart thumped in her chest. There was no escape. Something told her the life she knew was about to be turned on its head again. She was frightened, but she needed to know.

She rose and opened the door. Her mother stood there like a rabbit in the headlights.

'I know you've had a shock. To be honest, I was hoping... Look, I didn't know Dad was going to produce the DNA tests, and I was shocked when he did, but I guess I needed to tell you the truth anyway. I should have told you years ago.'

'The truth about what?' Billie asked, her throat dry.

'Billie, I hope this won't change anything. It shouldn't. Your life,

your memories are real, but I have to tell you that Matt, your dad...
Well, he's...' She sighed. 'He wasn't your biological father.'

All Billie could hear was the thunder in her ears. What on earth
was her mother going on about? That her dad wasn't her dad? Of
course he was! Donna was just saying it because she knew Billie loved
him more than her and she hated that. She was jealous.

'I don't believe you.' Billie pushed past her.

'Hang on a second, sweetheart, let me explain. There was a chance
that you weren't his. He knew that – we both did – but he said it
didn't matter...'

'I don't want to hear this. You're jealous of my relationship with
Dad. I loved him more than you – it's always been that way – and this
is just some kind of twisted –'

'Billie, stop it.' Her mother was firmer now. 'This is a shock, of
course it is, but let's try to be grown-ups. I'm not trying to hurt you –
I'm trying to be honest, so let me speak.'

Billie leaned against the sink, her fingers clutching the marble
plinth. This could not be happening. Her mother's voice crashed over
her, and she didn't want to hear it, but she knew that every word was
true.

'I'm not trying to hurt you, and I would never make this up. I...
The summer of 1993, your dad and I had been going out for about a
year. We were not getting along too well, and we decided to take a
break...'

'You dumped him.' Billie knew she sounded childish, but she
wanted to lash out.

'No.' Donna was adamant. 'Matt was the one who wanted a
break actually.' She coloured at the memory. 'So we didn't see each
other all summer. And I was at the Green River festival out at
Greenfield with some girlfriends, and I met this Irish guy. He was in
a band, and he was nice. His band was traditional, you know, like
Riverdance stuff. He played guitar and violin and a whole heap of
other things, but he and his buddies were working construction.
Anyway, we liked each other, and we spent the whole summer
together. We had plans. Things with me and Matt were over as far

as I was concerned, but I never introduced this new boyfriend to my dad because I thought Pops would think I was hopping from one guy to another, and because he was Irish and, well, we know Pops's feelings on them. So we hung out, and we... Well, we fell in love.'

Billie felt like she was going to throw up. However much she might wish it, she now knew her mother wasn't lying.

'One day, he was at work as normal. I was a student, and I had a summer job mentoring a girls' camp. I was to meet him after work, like we always did, but this time instead of B –' She stopped and took a deep breath. 'Instead of Billy being there to meet me, his friend, a guy from the Midwest someplace – I forget his name – came to tell me that the police had been called to the building site. Something had happened, nothing to do with Billy, but he was asked to show his papers. Anyway, it turned out he was illegal, and he was deported and forbidden from ever entering the US again.'

Billie struggled to absorb what she was being told. Her father's name was Billy – that's why she was called Billie, not after some old tennis player. That was another lie her mother had told her.

'And Dad was fine with you naming me after your old boyfriend?' Her voice dripped with bitterness.

'He never knew his name. Matt said he didn't want to know anything about him. We were a family – me, him, you and Gio. Nobody else mattered.'

'Go on.' It sounded like an order. She couldn't bear to hear her mother use her dad's name. The betrayal was too much.

'I was crushed. I had no address for him in Ireland, and there was no social media or any way of finding him. I just had his name, nothing else. All of the guys in the band were illegal too and worked at the same site, so they were all picked up. Nobody left who knew him had any more details than I had.

'Then I bumped into Matt again, a few days after Billy was deported. He said he'd made a terrible mistake, that he still loved me. And I don't know... I felt vulnerable, lonely, and we slept together. I woke up the next morning and it all felt wrong. I told Matt I didn't want to get back together and asked him not to contact me. He was sad, but I was just so confused and heartbroken, it didn't seem fair.

'Three weeks later, I discovered I was pregnant. I didn't know who the father was. It could have been either of them. I was in my junior year. I didn't think I would ever hear from Billy again. I figured he could have written or something – he would have been back in Ireland by then and he knew where I lived – but I heard nothing.' She looked at Billie, her eyes pleading for understanding.

'Dad worked so hard for me and Diana after my mom died, and putting us through college and everything. I couldn't disappoint him by dropping out. But as a single mother with no support, that was what I would have had to do. I toyed with the idea of a termination, but I just couldn't do it.

'Then Matt came over. He said he just needed to talk. I don't know what made him come back one last time, but he did, and I told him the whole story and I cried. And he just said, straight out, "Let's get married." Just like that. He knew there was a fifty-fifty chance that you were not his biological child, but he didn't care.' She smiled sadly. 'He was a wonderful man, Billie, and he felt like he was one hundred percent your father.'

'Dad knew?' Billie was incredulous. 'He knew I wasn't his?'

Donna nodded. 'Not at first, but you were born with that beautiful hair colour, and your pale complexion. With every month that passed, it was obvious you were Billy's child. But Matt never acknowledged it. You were his daughter, and that was it as far as he was concerned. You have to know that, Billie. It mattered so much to him.'

Waves of despair threatened to engulf her. It felt like the foundations of her life were crumbling.

'But... How could he... Why did nobody tell me...' She could hardly get the words out.

'He convinced me it was all going to be OK. He was working and had a good job and a nice apartment, and he loved us. Maybe I should have left him, but I felt so abandoned, so lost and scared, so fearful for the future. Matt seemed to have all the answers. We both adored you from the moment you were born. Then we had Gio five long years later after we'd given up all hope of having a child of our own. Life seemed perfect...'

Billie winced as her mother mentioned her brother's name. Even now, it was too raw.

'Did he ever contact you, my father?' Billie's voice was hoarse with emotion.

'I didn't think he had, but he did. A few letters. The only address he had was an apartment I shared with a girlfriend for the summer. She and I both moved out at the same time, but the super kept the letters. I was sure we left a forwarding address, but he must have lost it or something. Who knows? One day, almost a year after you were born, a new super was taking over the building. She found the letters and called out of the blue to say she had some mail for me.'

'And what did he say?' Billie asked. 'In the letters?'

'I don't know. I burned them without opening them. Matt and you were my life then, and nothing Billy Joyce had to say at that stage would change anything. You were *our* daughter. He never knew you existed – it was better that way. And the least I could do for Matt was let him be your dad without having to share you, and without Billy hanging over our family.'

'So he doesn't know I was even born?' Billie demanded.

'No,' Donna said, looking exhausted by the whole experience.

'And you would have never said a word, only Pops got that stupid DNA test and your whole sordid little secret is out in the open.' Billie's tone was accusing, but she felt such rage at her mother. How could she lie so blatantly for twenty-five years? She thought about all the conversations she'd had with her dad about how proud he was of her as his daughter, how much he loved her... All of it was a lie.

A thought struck her. She knew her mother loved Gio more than her – the way she behaved after he died was proof – and now she knew why. It led to an even more painful realisation – her father loved Gio more too. Of course he did; he was his son. Billie was... Well, she was nothing to him.

'I'm going now.' She walked past her mother. She needed to get away, to be alone, to think.

'Billie!' Donna tried to stop her, following her into the restaurant. 'It's dark out there and freezing. You can't just wander off on your own.'

Sol and Marilyn tried to talk to her, but she barrelled past them. She needed to get away.

'How about I take you to my place, huh?' Marilyn said, keeping pace with her as she made for the door. Billie noticed her glance back at Pops with a look of 'let me handle this'.

'OK,' Billie agreed, and followed Marilyn out of the restaurant, leaving her mother, Marko and Pops alone.

She slept fitfully, not helped by the huge cocktail Marilyn insisted she drink before bed. Her host had offered her a joint as well, which she'd declined.

Marilyn really was the most unlikely soulmate for the very traditional Pops, but she was sweet and kind and Billie felt safe with her. All night, Billie lay in the strange room, her eyes wide open, going over and over it all in her mind. Huge paintings hung on three walls of the room. They were abstract, the paint almost three-dimensional, lots of reds and blacks and midnight blue. Billie didn't like them; they seemed at odds with Marilyn's sunny disposition.

She lay there and tried to picture her father's face. Her dad, the man she had adored her whole life, was no relation of hers. Some other man, a total stranger in another country far away, was her father. His blood ran in her veins, and yet she'd never even heard of him until the previous day. Eventually, dawn broke, and the pale light shone through the linen curtains. She must have dozed off because the next thing she heard was Marilyn.

'Morning!' the woman trilled, opening the curtains.

Billie groaned and tried to stay asleep.

'I brought you some breakfast.'

Billie struggled to sit up, her eyes bleary.

'Look, kid,' Marilyn said as she stood over her with a tray. 'Last night was tough, but really, what does it change?' She lowered herself to the bed beside Billie and helped her sit up.

'Everything,' Billie said glumly.

'Wrong.' Marilyn poured a cup of coffee from a French press and handed it to her. 'Nothing at all. Your mom is still your mom, Pops is still your pops, and your dad is Matt Romano and always will be. Sure, you got some other guy's blood, but that is nothing. It means nothing. A parent is the one who raises a child, who helps them take their first steps, who pays the dentist bills, who sits through PTA meetings, all of that. Trust me, I know.'

Billie sipped the delicious coffee and took a bite of the hot buttered toast on the plate beside it. 'I didn't realise you had kids,' she said.

'I don't. Well, I had a baby, a boy. I gave birth to him, but he's not my child. Someone else raised him, did all of the things for him that your mom and dad did for you, and so I'm not his mom, not in any sense that matters.'

'Did you ever see him?' Billie asked, and immediately regretted it – it was none of her business.

'Only right after he was born. There was a time when I hoped he'd come looking for me, but he didn't, so that was where it ended. On a cold March twelfth, in a hospital in Tennessee, I gave birth to a little boy. I held him, they offered to take a photo – which was nice, and I have that – and they took him away. I was assured the people were nice folks who would give him the kind of life I never could.'

'Because you were young?' Billie asked.

'Young...and in prison.'

Billie nearly choked on the piece of toast.

'Don't worry, I don't believe in secrets, and Sol knows all about my past. I served fifteen years in Tennessee Prison for Women in Nashville. I was pregnant when I was convicted and sentenced. I could have had him fostered, but it would have been too long, and I had no family, so I gave him up for adoption.' She said sadly. She paused and then said, 'Go on, you can ask...'

Billie couldn't help herself. 'What did you do?'

'Nothing. I was seeing this guy, and boy, did his mama hate me. I was everything she didn't want in a daughter-in-law – poor white trash. I wanted to be a singer, but then so did everyone, and I was not what she had in mind for her precious firstborn son. They lived in a fancy house outside of Nashville, and one night it was burgled. She was assaulted and her husband knocked unconscious – he died later in the hospital, a brain bleed. She testified that there was a woman at the scene, and that it was me. She told that old judge that I was only seeing her son to get access to the house. I only found out later that her best friend was having an affair with that very judge. I was arrested. I had nobody to stick up for me – I was squatting in an old trailer, my parents were both dead – and while I was awaiting trial, they found someone to say I confessed to it in a cell one night. Of course I didn't, but the woman who said she heard me confess got a lighter sentence for framing me. I had served fifteen years when a young student from the Innocence Project took up my case and got it re-examined. I was released, and, well, that was it.'

Billie put her toast down. 'Marilyn, how horrible. I'm so sorry that happened to you. Did you sue the state?'

'I didn't have to. They paid me compensation, or at least they gave me a lot of money. Nothing compensates for taking away fifteen years of a person's life though.' She shrugged. 'But I'm here, I'm breathing in and out, and I'm loving life. I've done more in my life than most. I've travelled, I've had so many experiences, and now I've got Sol. And I love him so much, I really do, and we're happy, you know? I think I have more happiness now than a lot of folks get in a lifetime, so I'm doing OK.'

'Would you ever try to find your son, to explain to him?'

Marilyn shook her head sadly. 'No. If he wants to find me, he can. I can't just show up, disrupting his life. That wouldn't be fair.'

'How old is he now?' Billie asked. Suddenly, her own drama seemed diminished.

'He'll be forty-four next week.'

'You might be a grandma.' Billie smiled.

'No. Grandmas are like moms and dads – they are present. I'm just a connection, someone linking him to his tribe, but nothing more. It's OK.' She patted Billie's hand. 'I reconciled to it a long time ago.'

'It makes my story seem kind of...I don't know...less sad or something,' Billie said.

'It is less sad. The sad part for you is that you lost your father. Whether his blood flowed in your veins or not, he was your daddy and you miss him. I know you're mad at your mom – you were mad at her before any of this started – but she's entitled to a life too, you know?'

'I guess.' Billie shrugged. 'Do you wish he would contact you? Your son, I mean?'

'Of course. Every single day,' the older woman confirmed with a sad smile. Then she changed the subject. 'So what are you going to do?' Marilyn had a direct way of questioning, and her emerald-green eyes were innocent but determined.

An idea popped into Billie's mind. Suddenly, she knew exactly what it was that she wanted to do. Maybe it was crazy. In fact, it was totally crazy, but she wanted to do it anyway.

'I feel like I want to go to Ireland,' she said.

'To find your father?'

'I don't know if I want to find him, or anything about that yet, but I want to go. I...' She paused. Did she dare say the words out loud, the ones that had haunted her since she discovered the truth? Her eyes brimmed with tears. 'I think my parents loved Gio more than me. I know my mother did, but I always thought my dad... Well, he and I were closer, and I thought he loved me the same as Gio. But now I realise I don't belong in that family. I... The man I called my dad was no relation of mine. He was just duped or something by Donna, and I don't belong. Maybe if I go to Ireland, I'll feel like I belong there? I don't know...' She wiped her tears with the sleeve of the pyjamas Marilyn had lent her.

'Can I tell you what I think?' Marilyn said quietly.

Billie looked at the older woman and said nothing.

'I think all the songs and novels and movies are about men and women and their relationships, and they make out like they are so complicated, but that's not true. Men and women are easy – you either love the guy or you don't, he's attracted to you or he isn't.

Simple. The most complicated relationship on earth is between a mother and daughter. That bond is filled with so much love, but also pressure and expectation and doubt and awkwardness. Your mother loves you very much, Billie, and I'm not saying that to make you feel better, I'm saying it because it's true. She knows she wasn't there for you when she should have been – she beats herself up about that all the time – but she wasn't well. Mentally, she just checked out because the pain of losing your brother combined with the guilt that it was somehow her fault just became too much. She didn't reject you. It felt like that, I know it did, but she just switched off.'

Marilyn reached for Billie's hand. 'Sometimes, when I was in prison and I thought I would die in there, I just disconnected. It didn't matter what happened to my body, my spirit, because I wasn't there. I painted those' – she waved at the canvases on the walls – 'when I got out to try to release some of the darkness. It helped actually, and I keep them in here to remind me that I must never allow myself to be dragged back there. Not to prison, but to the prison of the mind. Prison is a scary place, Billie, and when it got too much for me, I was someplace else. The mind is amazing. It can transport you out of yourself when the situation you're in becomes intolerable. That's what your mom did – she left herself. The pain was too hard. It wasn't personal to you – she left the world.'

'Why didn't he tell me?' Billie asked in a small voice.

'I never met him, but from what Sol has told me and the conversations I've had with your mom, your father would never say the words "You are not my daughter" because in his mind, and in his heart, you were.' Marilyn wiped Billie's fresh tears with a tissue from the box beside the bed.

'Do you think going to Ireland is a dumb idea?' Billie asked. 'I mean, he doesn't even know I exist, and he probably doesn't want that bombshell dropped on him. And anyway, he might be awful. You know what Pops thinks about the Irish... Maybe he's right...'

Marilyn tucked a strand of Billie's hair behind her ear. Her dad had always done that exact same thing.

'I think you should take some time, process what just happened.

And if you want to go to Ireland, then you should go. I think we don't regret much of what we do, unless it's to hurt someone, but we often regret what we don't do.'

Billie smiled through her tears. 'Thanks, Marilyn.'

'No problem, kid.' The older woman stood and gazed out the window onto the quiet suburban street.

'Adversity is what grows our character, not ease, Billie. I'm a complicated person, but I like who I am. And all of it – my personality, my beliefs, my values – was born out of hardship. People whose lives are too easy become vacuous – the world is full of them. People who care what the neighbours think, or who let petty jealousies rule their lives, they've had no real struggles. Surround yourself with people who haven't had it easy – they are much more interesting.'

'You're really wise. I can see why Pops loves you,' Billie said.

'He's easy to love too. Lots of adversity in his life, and he's an interesting man because of it.' She paused and turned. She was thinking – Billie could see it on her face.

'I'm going to move in with him.' She nodded.

'Has he asked you to?' Billie was slightly taken aback.

'Yeah, ages ago, and I said I needed my own place. I do, too, so I'll keep this house, but I'll move in with Sol. Actually' – she raised her right index finger – 'that reminds me. Mina in the bar up the street, she cleans there and she's from Syria. Her brother and his family are coming here next week, as finally they've been accepted as refugees. They could have this place.'

'Do you know them?' Billie asked.

Marilyn looked at her like she was crazy. 'They're from Syria! No, I don't know them, but they're going to need a house, right? They've got five kids, so they can have this one for free. The US government paid for it anyway – I bought it with my compensation.' She shrugged. There. Solved. 'And how about you? Are you going back to LA?'

Billie nodded. 'Yes, I'll catch a flight this afternoon. I need some time to think. It's so weird – I was running away from there when I came here, and now I'm running away from here. I feel like I've been running for so long. I'm tired, Marilyn.'

'I know you are. You've had a lot to deal with. But remember, adversity grows character. We should welcome it.' The older woman patted her hand.

'Do you think Pops knew about me?' Billie asked suddenly.

'No, he didn't,' Marilyn said with certainty.

'Well, that's something, I guess. At least he wasn't lying to me too.' She got up and stood in front of Marilyn.

The older woman fixed Billie with a penetrating stare and remained silent for a few long seconds before saying, 'You'll be fine. Your parents loved you, Billie. They loved your brother too, but not more than you or less than you – that's not how being a parent works. Don't get hung up on the trivial stuff and forget the big picture.' She moved towards the door. 'I'll leave you to shower, and I've left some clothes for you on the rail in the bathroom. Don't worry, they're not mine. They belong to a girl I know who stays here sometimes when she needs to. She's about your age, a little bigger than you, but they're clean.'

Billie felt a weight lift. Marilyn was right – this was only as big a deal as she wanted to make it. Her dad would always be her dad, but she was intrigued.

As she stood under the shower, she couldn't help her mind wandering. Did this Irish guy, Billy Joyce, look like her? Was he married? Had he other kids? She might have half-brothers or -sisters in Ireland. Suddenly, after what seemed like ages of pain and sorrow, followed by humiliation over the Rob situation, there were the beginnings of something exciting happening. She was nervous and worried and a million other emotions, but she was sure of one thing: She wanted to go to Ireland.

CHAPTER 8

The following afternoon, Conor and Ana arrived home, feeling refreshed and much more positive about the Artie situation. They'd discussed it at length and were in agreement that they would trust the school to handle it appropriately. Conor still didn't think much of Mr Bredin, but he had faith in Imelda to do what was best. Ana only agreed on the condition that if the school failed, they would take more drastic action. He didn't know exactly what she meant, but he could guess.

Conor had sent Imelda a text requesting a meeting the following Monday morning, and she'd agreed.

They found the house empty and everything locked up when they got there. Jamsie's car, a vintage Mercedes C-Class coupe, was a source of fascination to the lads, and it was also gone, so they assumed Jamsie had taken the boys off somewhere.

They were pleasantly surprised to find the place spotless. All the toys were neatly stacked in the playroom, and the kitchen counters were clean and devoid of the usual collection of books, toys, bills and newspapers. The washing machine was even running. Ana's parents were helping out at a church event that weekend – there was a conference of parish councils on, groups coming from all over Munster, and the Ennis Parish was the host that year, so Danika and Artur were highly involved – so it was unlikely they were responsible for the big tidy-up. There was a note on the table, in Artie's writing.

Hi, Mammy and Daddy,

We hope you had a lovely holiday without us. We cleaned the house with Granda, and now we are going to the funfair in Kilkee. We'll have chips and burgers, so don't worry about dinner. Granda says we will be home at seven thirty.

Love Artie, Joe and Granda. xxx

They had drawn a picture of a dog, like they did on every single note they ever wrote. It was an ongoing battle because they were desperate for a dog, but Ana was allergic to them, so it was a non-runner.

'Artie wrote the note,' Conor said as he chuckled. 'And Joe drew the dog.'

'I feel so bad for them. I know how much they want for a dog, but if you see what happen to me if I am near fur... I get all itches and everything. I tell you, it is horrible.'

'There's no fear of them. Haven't they every toy known to man? And they are off below at the funfair now, flying around on bumper cars and the rollercoaster. They have a great life, so don't you feel one bit guilty, do you hear me?' Conor said earnestly.

'I know they do, but for so long now, it is "Please, a dog". Every time we go to the park, the same – dogs, dogs, dogs. Every day the same.'

'Well, they'll have to get over it. When they are grown up and have their own houses, then they can have all the dogs they like, but you're allergic, the end,' he said as he lit the big wood-burning stove in the sitting room.

As he washed his hands, his phone pinged. He pulled it out of his pocket, read it and groaned.

'I'm so sorry, pet, but I need to get out to the hotel. Carlos texted – the new receptionist just quit. According to him, he did nothing, but I wouldn't put my shirt on that. He's impossible at the moment. I could choke him sometimes.' It wasn't like Conor to say such things, but all the stress that had been relieved by the weekend was quickly making itself felt again.

Ana turned to look at him. 'I could do it,' she said. She blurted the words, but it had been on her mind for a while to ask him for a job. She was cracking up just sitting around all day.

'Ah, not at all, pet. You take it easy. I'll manage. Thanks though. You're good to offer, but I'll sort it out.' He pecked her cheek and left.

* * *

ANA WENT upstairs and changed into pyjamas and slippers, trying not to feel hurt at how out of hand he dismissed her offer to help. She knew he just wanted her to relax, and it wasn't because he thought she wasn't capable, but still it stung. She needed to do something, and working at the hotel would be lovely. She'd be helping Conor, she could manage Carlos, she and Katherine were great friends, and she'd really enjoy it. She would not be physically able for a manual job, like she did before in the Dunshane, but working on the reception desk would be fine. Though, she reasoned, maybe her imperfect English – she'd resigned herself that it never would be perfect – wasn't good enough for that very fancy hotel.

Ana had seen the new girl the previous week when she went up to the hotel to drop off Conor's swim gear that he forgot, and she was so polished and perfect. Ana looked at herself in the mirror. She looked frumpy, she thought. Her blonde hair had grown back really curly after the chemotherapy and she hated it, so she kept it in a ponytail, and she had lost the curves she had. She was just thin and small. Conor was probably right – she wasn't what they were after.

The boys came home, disappointed their dad wasn't there to hear about all the adventures. They'd had a great time with their granda, and clearly he adored them too. They all sat on the couch in front of the fire, and it made Ana happy to see them both so animated and united again, finishing each other's sentences as they'd done since they were tiny. Jamsie made some herbal tea for Ana and hot chocolate for the boys.

Once they'd finished their drinks and Ana had read one of the Ukrainian folk tales they loved, Jamsie took charge again.

'Right, you two – shower, pyjamas, teeth and bed, in that order. No messing, right?' Jamsie grinned as he marched them upstairs.

They did exactly as he said, and so after kissing their mother, they were tucked up in bed and silent in record time.

Jamsie came downstairs. He looked like an older version of Conor; everyone said so. He was tall and muscular like his son, and even at seventy-six he got a lot of admiring glances. He played a lot of golf and went to the gym three times a week. One of the women who worked at the hotel told Ana she thought he looked like Sean Connery. Ana had no idea who that was, but when she Googled him, she realised the woman was right.

'They are exhausted,' Jamsie said. 'Did you have a nice time?'

'Jamsie, thank you so much, we really appreciate it. We had such a nice break. It is pity Conor had to work, but hotel is crazy always, and that Carlos, you know him? Well, he say something to one of the ladies in the reception, so now she go and don't come back.'

'He needs more staff.' Jamsie shoved his hands in his pockets. 'He'll work himself into the ground at this rate.'

'I know...' Ana thought before speaking. 'I offered, but he says no.'

'Offered to do what?'

'Well, he need receptionist. I thought maybe I could do it, but probably my English is not good enough. I make many mistakes now, even after all this years.' She shrugged.

'I don't know. I mean, you are charming and a pretty face for the front desk, and your English is fine. I know exactly what you're saying, and you understand everyone perfectly, so what more is there?' She smiled and he looked embarrassed. 'I don't mean to sound sexist or whatever, and Katherine O'Brien is a nice woman, but she'd frighten the dogs some days with the puss on her. He could use someone friendly and cheerful and able for it. I think you should apply.'

Ana laughed. 'Yes, send an application letter to my husband?'

'Well, yes. Put down all of your experience – use a different name, obviously – and then turn up for the interview in the suit and the whole lot. Tell him you were called for the interview based on your CV, and make him take you seriously,' Jamsie said, and Ana thought he might be right.

'What did you do? Before? For working?' she asked. It was something they hadn't discussed. The fact that he'd been on the missing list as a father since Conor was eight years old was still a sore spot, so they tended not to discuss it.

The relationship was still new, and Conor was reluctant to jump into it feet first. They had increasing contact, and Jamsie minding the boys on his own was a real sign of trust, but they had a way to go yet.

They knew that he had a daughter in England, but she and Conor had yet to meet. Once she knew Conor and Jamsie had reconciled, she'd written an email saying how pleased she was, and delighted she had a brother, and Conor had responded nicely. But he wasn't ready to meet her, and Ana didn't push him. She knew him well and understood he needed to come to things in his own time.

Jamsie had invited them all up to Dublin to his house, but Conor had declined. He knew there would be photos and things that he couldn't really explain to the boys yet – for example, the fact that they had an aunt they had never met – so he postponed visiting. Conor was very straight with his father: He forgave him for leaving them – him and his mam and his little brother Gerry – but he could not just jump into playing happy families. Gerry had died last year in their house, and that drew them all closer, but Conor still felt a loyalty to his mam and hurt at what his father had done.

'I had a few shops – they call them retail outlets now – and I rented the shop space,' Jamsie said.

'And you make lot of money doing that?' Ana asked. In the Ukraine, people were much more blunt and forthright in their speech; it was something she had not given up when she came to Ireland. It frustrated her that Irish people often didn't say what they meant, or mean what they said.

He smiled. 'I've enough. And a bit put by for a rainy day.'

'Good. My parents are happy now too, thanks to Conor. He brought them over from Ukraine, you know? Gave my dad a job, and they lived with us until they get visas and all of that, and now they love their little house. They would have a hard life back at home. The place where my father work closed, and the apartment is part of the job, so they were worried. It is good to have no worries when you getting older.'

'It is indeed.' Jamsie agreed. 'Ana, I wanted to ask you something, and feel free to say no, but the lads mentioned you are allergic to dogs?'

'Yes.' She rolled her eyes. 'I know it is all they want, but I can't. I get all...scratching and sneezing...'

'Yeah, they said. But I was thinking, how would you feel about a hypoallergenic dog?'

'They've made you ask this, haven't they?' She smiled.

'Well, yes and no. I took the lads to the park for a kick around yesterday, and I got talking to a man who was walking his dog, a Samoyed – you know, the big, white, fluffy ones? And he was saying he was allergic to dogs, but Samoyeds produce less dander, so he's fine with that one. And of course, the boys' eyes lit up. Told the man the whole story about why they can't have a dog and all the rest of it, and he said if you wanted to come over to his place someday, see if you react to his dog, you could. He breeds them, so they are all registered and treated properly and all of it.'

'I know that man. Often I see him walking the dogs. The boys always run to them, but I stay away.'

'Well, no pressure, but if you wanted to go over, he gave me his card.' He handed it to Ana.

'I want them to be happy, of course, and if I am not allergic, then I would do it. But these dogs are also very expensive. My friend tell me they are lots of money to buy pure puppy.'

'Well, if you want to, and only if you do, go and see if you're allergic, and if not, I'd like to get the dog for the lads' birthday. But only if you and Conor are OK with it, of course,' Jamsie added quickly.

'I can't let you do that! They are too much money...'

'Let's just see if it's a runner first, shall we? Talk to Conor, and if you think you want to check if you react, then call this guy. But please, I would love to get it for them, so if it's possible, please let me do that?'

'OK, I'll talk to him.' Ana said and put the card in her pocket.

'No problem.' He went to get his coat. 'I'll be off so, Ana, and thanks for asking me to mind the lads. I loved it, really. I had a great time with them. They are smashing little fellas.'

'But I thought you would stay? It is too late to go back to Dublin now? Please, stay...' She hated to see him go. From the moment he popped up out of the blue last year, Ana had been taken by his charm. In fact, it was she and Conor's friend Father Eddie who really put pressure on Conor to accept his father back – he hadn't wanted to initially. Jamsie was just an older version of Conor, and she loved him.

'Ah, well, I don't want to be in the way, and I'm flying to London on Tuesday. Liz is getting married on Saturday, so I'm going over for the wedding. She emailed Conor and invited you both –' Jamsie stopped, realising he'd said more than he should.

Ana was shocked at his news. Conor knew that his sister was getting married and never mentioned it? Ana felt a stab of something – she and Conor told each other everything, didn't they? She really wanted Conor to connect with his sister, but he said he felt disloyal to his mother. He explained that it might sound ridiculous to anyone else, but that while his father was putting all this energy into raising his daughter in England despite being separated from her mother, he'd had two boys at home that never heard a word from him. It wasn't Liz's fault, he knew that, but Conor just couldn't go there.

'I didn't know that. He never said. I wish Conor would make contact with her, but he...' Ana shrugged.

'I'm sorry, Ana. Me and my big mouth. I know, and he will, in time. He's a reasonable man. He knows it's not Liz's doing, but he has a lot of hurt still, and I don't blame him. I just need to be patient.' He sighed. 'I've said the same to Liz.'

Ana had an idea. She wasn't sure how Conor would feel about it, but he'd probably be fine, and anyway, she felt hurt that he kept the news of Liz's wedding from her. She went to the big sideboard where all sorts of things were kept. Inside was a large box that held a Waterford crystal dish. She'd bought this exquisite cut-glass bowl on a whim because she loved it so much, but she didn't dare put it out because with the boys, it would probably last ten minutes before being shattered by a football or a flying Dinky.

She also took a card from the drawer. It wasn't wedding themed; it was a Christmas card with a photo of her and Conor and the boys having a snowball fight.

Before returning to Jamsie, she took a pen and wrote,

Dear Liz,

Wishing you a beautiful wedding day and a wonderful life.

Conor, Ana, Artie and Joe xxx

She sealed the envelope and slipped it inside the large box.

'Is this too big to take with you?' she asked, showing him the box.

'No, but what is it?' He looked confused.

'It is a bowl made of Waterford crystal. I want Liz to have it as a wedding gift.'

Jamsie looked touched but apprehensive. 'Are you sure? Conor might not want...'

'Conor is not ready to meet Liz. He will be sometime, as you say, but not yet. But he would want to send her something nice for her wedding, of course he would.' Ana smiled.

'Well, then, thank you. She'll be very happy.' He paused. 'Can you tell Conor first though? I know it's fine, I'm sure it is, but my relationship with him is not as solid as yours, and I'd hate to think I was going behind his back or anything...' Jamsie looked uncomfortable. He didn't want to throw Ana's gift back in her face, but he needed to be sure it was the right thing to do.

'Of course. I would not do this without telling him, but it will be fine.' She smiled.

Jamsie left with the box, and Ana sat down with her laptop. She downloaded the application form from the Castle Dysert website and stayed truthful about all of her details except her name and address. She listed her experience honestly but changed the name of the hotel to one she made up. Conor knew everyone at the Dunshane. She felt a qualm about lying to Conor, but he would not take her seriously otherwise, and anyway, he'd lied to her about Liz and it stung.

CHAPTER 9

*P*ops looked at her like she was crazy as she FaceTimed him on his new iPad.

'No way, kid, not a chance.'

'Please, Pops, I'm really begging, and Marilyn says she'll come.'

Marilyn checked in with her every week – she had done so since the night of the big revelation – and Billie had grown really fond of Pops's kooky girlfriend.

She'd warned her, and Billie knew it would be a big ask. Her grandfather was not one for travelling. He didn't like flying and so had hardly ever left the state of Massachusetts since he got there, and the destination she was suggesting was a country he held in very poor regard for some reason.

'Then let Marilyn go with you. I'm not going to Ireland.' He seemed adamant.

In high school, she'd been friendly with a girl whose family were Irish and went there on vacation, and the friend said it was beautiful. She'd been about fifteen and had asked Pops why he didn't like the Irish. He had kind of closed down. She didn't know why, but she knew not to ask again. Now, though, it was different.

'I'm half Irish. Don't you like me anymore?' she asked, only partially joking.

He sighed, and it sounded like it came from his toes. He put his head back and leaned against the headrest of the chair in his office, now cluttered with Marilyn's stuff. They'd moved in together and were loving it. Pops was even getting used to her chaotic lifestyle.

'Look, Billie, I don't go on about it because it's all water under the bridge now, but the truth is the Irish didn't want Jews when we needed someplace to go, when Hitler and the Nazis were trying to kill us all, so they can sure as hell not have me now.'

All the years later, Billie could still hear the hurt.

'Why didn't they?' she asked, trying to make sense of it all.

'I don't know. So I don't buy all their crap about being a beautiful welcoming place. It might be beautiful, but underneath, they have an ugly past, and they've never even acknowledged it. At least the Swiss own up to storing Jewish treasures for the Nazis, or providing a haven for them after the war. They don't make any excuses for what they were. But the Irish…'

Billie was silent for a moment. Pops had every right to feel as he did, but it was all so long ago, and she really wanted to go and have him by her side. Feeling badly but desperate, she played her trump card.

'Would you come if I invited Mom and Marko too?'

Billie knew it was a low blow, but she also knew how much it hurt Pops that his daughter and granddaughter were at such loggerheads. She had been on the brink of calling her mother a few times but never did. They had not spoken since the night of Pops's birthday; there was too much to say. Donna had texted a few times, just asking if she was OK, and she'd replied as shortly as she could.

She'd flown back to California after the disastrous weekend and left directly from Marilyn's. Pops had come over, and she'd told him she was OK but needed time to process it all and that she'd be in touch.

In the month since she'd been back at work, she'd tried to research Billy Joyce on Facebook, Instagram, Google, everything. But nothing.

There were lots of people with that name, but they were either too young or had no photo on their profile. She guessed he'd be somewhere between forty-five and fifty. She'd probably know more if she spoke to her mother about him, but she wasn't ready for that yet. There had been some creepy guy during World War II called William Joyce. She'd never heard of him, but he was nicknamed Lord Haw-Haw and used to broadcast German propaganda on the BBC. He sounded like a total weirdo. Every Google search came back to him. And he had connections with Ireland. She hoped her father wasn't a relative of his.

She was true to her word and worked weekends and late nights for a month to make up for the extra days she took, and anyway, she had nothing better to do. Her work distracted her from the train crash that was her life.

Noah had stopped by her cubicle one evening when she was still working at 9 p.m. She was alone in the office.

'Debt paid! I'm not a total monster, you know.' He grinned, popping his head over the partition.

'I know. But I've requested time off for travel, so I want to get this project off my desk before I go.'

'Fair enough.' He held up his hands. 'Don't let me stop you.' He turned to leave and then stopped. 'Where you headed?' he asked.

'Ireland.' She smiled. 'You ever been there?'

'No, but my parents have gone there three times. They love the place. They're always telling me I should go, but y'know, no time… They found some long-lost cousins over there or something.' He shrugged. 'You going there for a reason, or just to see all the castles and green fields? Or maybe the booze?' he joked.

She coloured. He'd never raised the incident of her making an idiot of herself that night. 'Definitely not that. I think my days of drinking like that are well behind me.' She considered telling a lie, but something about Noah made her want to be honest. 'My birth father came from there, and I just want to see it.' It was the first time she'd said the words out loud.

'Oh.' He didn't look too surprised. 'I didn't know you were

adopted. I am too.'

She had come this far; she needed to clarify. 'No, I wasn't adopted. I just found out that the man I thought was my dad wasn't. He and my mother knew all my life, but she only told me a month ago.'

'Wow.' Noah exhaled. 'That must have been a shock.'

'It was.' She nodded. 'Me and my mom aren't close really anyway – long story – so it makes it super awkward, y'know?'

'I don't really. My mom and I talk every day, but I can imagine.'

'You're lucky to have such a good relationship with her.'

'I guess. We've always been close.'

Billie finished up what she was doing and logged out. They walked to the lift together.

'Well, good luck in Ireland. I hope it all works out.' He said as they approached the main door. 'Don't you have a car?' he asked as they were about to part.

'No, I don't get paid enough to have a car,' she joked. 'I take the bus, as it's not far.'

'Yeah, but it's late. Let me drop you off. Where do you live?'

'San Fernando Road. But honestly, it's fine...' she protested.

'No, I'm going that way anyway. It's not a problem.' He gestured towards his car, a Jeep Grand Cherokee that was parked down the street from the studio.

His car was nice but not flashy like Marko's. Noah was one of the best-paid executives in the industry and could probably afford something really showy, but he wasn't like that. They talked easily, and she was surprised at how chatty he was. He came across as a bit stiff in work sometimes but was actually funny.

'Tell me to mind my own business if you like, but did you ever consider finding your birth parents?'

He glanced over at her and observed her for a moment. Immediately, she regretted the question. He was her boss and was doing a nice thing giving her a ride home – she shouldn't have pried.

'Do you want to go for a coffee?' he asked, his eyes on the road.

'Um...yeah. Sure,' she replied, not sure what was happening.

'Or food? I guess you haven't eaten yet?' he continued.

'I had a sandwich at my desk.' She checked her watch. 'Ah…seven hours ago.'

'OK, food.' He accelerated through the traffic lights.

Over pizza, he told her his story. How his parents had adopted him out of the foster care system in Florida when he was five. He had a vague memory of his birth mother, but it was nebulous. She could have tried to see him once the adoption went through but didn't. Even when she was around, he was in and out of state care. His adoptive parents had saved him. He explained how he had no interest in meeting his birth mother as he grew up. He knew her name from his birth certificate but had no idea who his birth father might have been as nobody was listed on his paperwork. He got a call one day from his adoptive mother to say a woman's body was found in a public park in Tampa. The woman had the same name as his birth mother. He did a little investigation, and it was her. She'd died of an overdose.

When Noah finished telling her, Billie put her hand on his instinctively. 'I'm sorry. She had such a sad life, but she did the best thing for you, and I'm sure it wasn't an easy decision, no matter her circumstances.'

'I guess it wasn't.' He sighed.

The rest of the night passed companionably. They talked about music, movies, families. She ended up telling him all about her mother and Marko and Pops and Marilyn.

She admitted how angry she was at her dad for lying to her, and her fears that he didn't love her as much as her brother.

'Maybe he was afraid of you rejecting him rather than the other way around?' Noah said softly.

'But of course I wouldn't! He was my dad…' she protested.

'But if he were here now, maybe he'd be saying the exact same thing, that as far as he was concerned, you were his daughter and he didn't want anything to ever change that.'

She sat back and looked at him. 'Marilyn said the same thing.' She smiled.

'See? I've wisdom beyond my years.' He chuckled.

'Well, if you met Marilyn, you might not be equating your wisdom with hers. She's unique,' Billie said with affection. 'Every conversation with her leaves me smiling, though she is downright bizarre at times. Her latest thing is travelling next week to Quebec, Canada, to meet with a pack of wolves in a sanctuary there because she had a dream that one of them was the reincarnated spirit of her old hairdresser and she has an important message to relay regarding a family feud in Chattanooga, Tennessee. The management of the sanctuary told her she was more than welcome to visit but they could not facilitate any one-on-one meetings with specific wolves. But she saw that as a mere formality.' Billie could hardly get the words out as she was laughing so much, and Noah grinned at her amusement.

'I'd love to meet her. She sounds hilarious,' he said.

'Oh, she is. She signed a check last week using her Sanskrit name, Achara. The kid in the bank had no idea what she was talking about when he called to query it. But she's a sweetie, really, and so good for my pops. He adores her, and I love seeing him happy.'

'And your mom and this Marko guy, are they happy?' Noah asked, scraping the last bits out of an ice cream sundae he had insisted they share.

'I guess. He's filthy rich. They have an amazing house, and my mother looks like one of the Desperate Housewives, so I think so. I don't know… And to be frank about it, I don't care, either.'

She knew from his reaction how harsh that sounded, and she instantly regretted it. For some reason, it mattered that he thought well of her.

'Look, it's complicated, as I said…' she explained.

'Hey, not my business, Billie.' He held his hands up.

'But yeah, I want to go to Ireland,' she said, changing the subject away from her mother. 'I'm trying to convince my grandfather to come with me. Marilyn is totally on board, though what she'll get up to over there is anyone's guess. But Pops hates Ireland for a long and complicated reason, so he's refusing. I even suggested inviting my mother and Marko as bait – Pops is trying to get us back on good terms again – but so far, no dice.'

'If anyone can convince him, I'm sure you can.' He grinned, and she noticed he had a really nice smile. He called for the bill, and when she tried to pay her share, he waved it away, claiming it was a 'company expense'. He gathered his keys and phone, and she followed him out to the car.

He dropped her off and drove away, and as she waved from the sidewalk, she reflected on how she'd not had such a nice night in so long.

She let herself into her apartment, went into the tiny kitchen and flicked on the coffee machine. Her eyes fell on the framed photo on the windowsill. It was of her and her dad taken in Cape Cod; he was sick then but not as bad as he would get. He looked older, tired, but still the twinkle was in his eye. The reason she had that one framed was because of the way he was looking at her – just pure love.

She picked it up. Gazing at him, she wondered, did she really wish he'd told her the truth? Would it have changed anything? Was he afraid she'd reject him, go off looking for her real father?

She touched his face. 'You're my dad, no matter what happens, and I'll never stop loving you or missing you. I don't know why, but I want to go to Ireland. I don't know if I want to meet him, or if that's even possible, but I just want to…I don't know…make some kind of sense of it. I hope you understand. I'm not choosing him over you or anything like that.' She replaced the photo and made her coffee but continued talking to him.

'Dad, if you can hear me, try to influence Pops to come with me? I'll go alone if I have to, but I'd rather he was there.'

She gazed at the inky-black night sky as she sat on the sofa sipping her drink. She had no drapes. There was too much light pollution to see the stars, but after a long day, she liked just to sit and gaze out at the infinite blackness. Was he out there somewhere? It didn't feel like it. She remembered something Noah said when they were discussing life and death. Noah had been raised Baptist, and his parents were very devout. He told her about an episode of the Netflix show *Grace and Frankie*, and in it, one of the characters, who was gay and Catholic, was worried he was going to hell because he'd married a man. His friend, a priest, explained that heaven and hell existed in the way you lived on earth. Like Hitler, a truly awful man, was remembered with hatred, and so he was in hell and nothing would ever expunge his crimes. But people who were remembered fondly, with love, based on the kindness or compassion they showed on earth – that was heaven. Your legacy was the decider.

If that was the case, then her dad was definitely in heaven. So many people spoke about him in the days and weeks after he died, how he was such a good friend, such a good neighbour, such a great co-worker and boss. Her father was loved by everyone who knew him, except, it would seem, his wife.

It hurt her so much to think about her dad in a loveless marriage, particularly when he was so open with his feelings about Donna. But now it made sense. She married him to bag herself a man who could take care of her and her baby and pick up the bills. He loved her, but to her he was just a meal ticket. It was a horrible thought, and Matt Romano had deserved so much better.

She rinsed her cup and went to bed. She didn't understand people who said they couldn't sleep after coffee, but Pops said it was because she was young. She was only twenty-five but felt about eighty.

Billy Joyce. Who was he? Was he even still alive? What was he like? Did she look like him?

Eventually, as the light of dawn streaked across the sky, she fell asleep.

* * *

THE NEXT MORNING, as she showered and dressed for work, she heard her phone beep. A text from Pops.

OK. And believe me, I don't want to go, but I'll do it for you (and because Marilyn won't let it go), but only if you invite your mom and Marko and are nice to her for the entire trip. Those are my terms, non-negotiable. She's hurting, Billie, and you're the only one who can stop that pain. Pops

She felt a wave of relief – Pops would go to Ireland! And Marilyn too, which was wonderful, as she had a calming effect despite her wackiness. Mom and Marko... Well, if she had to, she would be nice.

She shot off two quick texts, one to Pops. *I love you.*

And another to Marilyn. *Thank you, I know it was you who convinced him. xxx*

The contact with her mother was going to be more complicated.

A thought struck her. Maybe her mother wouldn't want to go to Ireland. Billie hoped she'd say no. She'd invite her, and then if she declined, Pops would still have to make good on his word. She'd have to word the invitation carefully, warm and welcoming. If there was anything in it that suggested she was less than enthusiastic, Pops would pull out right away, and she needed him by her side.

Actually, she thought a phone call would be better. She needed to call her mother anyway – they'd not spoken since the night in the restaurant. Donna had texted repeatedly, and Billie replied but kept it brief.

Boston was three hours ahead. She scrolled for the number. Donna, not Mom. Most people would find that weird, but it was how it was. Dad was Dad in her phone, Mom was Donna. The irony that the parent she was closest to was no relative of hers struck her again.

She took a deep breath and pressed the call button. It rang a few times. Billie could imagine Donna in that huge mausoleum of a house, clip-clopping about in her designer shoes. Just as she was about to hang up, her mother answered.

'Hi, Billie.' Donna sounded happy but cautious.

'Hi, Mom.' A pause.

'How are you, sweetheart?'

'OK. You know…just working and all of that.'

'It's good to hear your voice.'

Billie could hear her mother breathing.

'I wanted to call, but Marko and Pops said you needed time. That was a shock to hear, I know…'

'Yeah. It was. But I guess you're right. Dad was my dad, and that's the end of it as far as I'm concerned.'

Billie thought she heard her mother exhale.

'Exactly. He loved you so much, you know that, and he never saw you as different from Gio in any way.'

Billie tried to ignore the stab of pain at the mention of her brother – well, her half-brother as it turned out. Pops said Donna had been going back to therapy, giving it another shot. Maybe that was why she kept mentioning Gio. She never used to say his name. None of them did. Not because they didn't want to, but because they couldn't. It was too hard.

Her brother's handsome smiling face flashed before her eyes – his warm, dark eyes and floppy dark hair that, in her dad's opinion, he wore too long. Her father was always threatening to give Gio a buzz cut, but the boy liked to gel his hair. Everyone said he was the image of their dad. He played basketball and had a wide circle of friends. He died in the second summer of middle school. He'd confided in her that there was a girl he liked but they were just friends. He'd called Billie a few hours before he died, asking her where her boogie board was, as their mom was taking him and two of his friends to the beach for the afternoon. She warned him not to lose it and told him where to find it. They'd had the usual jokey banter between siblings. One of her clearest memories was ending the call with 'Love you'.

'Love you too,' he'd replied.

It was a habit their father had got them into. Everyone in the family ended calls that way. Even if it was just a perfunctory call to pick up milk on the way home, they always ended with 'Love you'. She was so glad those were the last words she'd said to her little brother.

'I know he didn't,' Billie said to Donna. Mad as she was with her mother, she was dreading telling her about her trip to Ireland.

She took a deep breath. 'Mom, I've decided I want to go to Ireland. I don't know about tracking my father down – I'm still on the fence about that – but I just want to see the country, get a feel for it, you know?' She found, to her surprise, that she wanted her mother's approval, even after everything.

A pause… The silence crackled on the line. Billie found she was holding her breath.

'OK.' Her mother's response was hard to read. Was that a genuine OK or a guarded one, or did it mean it was anything but OK?

She carried on. 'So I've asked Pops and Marilyn to come with me, and I was wondering – well, hoping really – that you and Marko could come too?' She hoped she sounded sincere, as much as she wished her mother would refuse.

'To Ireland?' her mother replied, like she'd just been invited to a tea party on Mars.

'Yeah, to Ireland.' Something made her continue. 'A friend of mine here, his parents go often. They love it. It's supposed to be beautiful, green and loads of history and stuff, so at the very least, we should have a nice vacation.'

'But what about your job? You can't surely just take off for Ireland?'

'I'm due some time, so it's no problem. So what do you say?' She had no idea why, but she found herself half hoping her mother would agree.

'When do you want to go?' Donna sounded troubled.

'I don't know, April?'

'And for how long?'

'I can take a week? I found a reasonably priced hotel outside of Dublin for me, Pops and Marilyn. We can't afford something fancy, but you guys could stay somewhere nicer if you liked, and we could just meet up...'

'Leave it with me. Have you booked a flight yet?'

'No, not yet. I think there are two main airports in Ireland, one on the east coast and another on the west. I think the one on the east is for Dublin, which I guess is the capital there?'

'Can you give me until tomorrow? I'll get back to you.'

Billie heard herself say, 'I would like you to come, Mom, really.'

'Thanks, sweetheart, that means a lot.' Billie could hear the choke in her mother's voice.

'OK. Well, I better get to work. Talk later.'

'OK. Billie, I...I love you. You know that, right?'

Billie was nonplussed. 'I do, Mom.'

She ended the call and left her apartment, mulling over what just happened.

CHAPTER 10

*C*onor shook hands with the polished and glamorous young woman he'd just interviewed for the deputy manager position. There was no doubt in his mind she was the right choice. He would have liked Katherine to give her input – he suspected she might be more exacting in her questioning – but nonetheless, he was happy with her. She didn't have much experience but was keen to learn and seemed charming and approachable. Just what he was after.

He'd begun to give up hope. She was the fourth and final candidate on the list. The first three were a total washout; one had dirty fingernails, and another was a young man who muttered so much when he spoke that Conor had to ask him to repeat himself several times. The third obviously got the wrong job spec. Her dyed blonde hair fell in blowsy curls, and her shirt was open to reveal impressive but clearly synthetic bronzed breasts. Her make-up was totally over the top, and her skirt barely skimmed her bottom. She spoke in a breathy way, which Conor was sure she thought was seductive but she just sounded mad. She would be more at home in a strip club than on the reception desk of Castle Dysert.

He decided to have a coffee before the new receptionist candidates showed up. God only knew where the agency had dredged the next trio from. They didn't even look great on their applications, but he was desperate. There was one application from a woman called Liga Florek that looked promising though. She had previous hotel experience, computer skills and good English. She was in her thirties and was looking for part-time work. He'd asked Ana if she knew anyone by that name, but she didn't. She knew a lot of the Eastern Europeans through the women's refuge she'd volunteered at before the cancer. Her friend Valentina ran it and Ana translated. She also shopped at the Polish shop in Ennis to buy things unavailable near their home.

He'd more or less decided if this Liga was anyway half decent he'd give her a shot. The other three were too young and had no experience. The main question he wanted to ask the candidates was how they would feel about being spoken down to and snapped at by an annoying little eejit in a wheelchair, but he supposed he couldn't do that.

Carlos was driving everyone up one wall and down the other wheeling around on his chair and finding fault with everything. Katherine could manage him, and weirdly he liked Ana despite tormenting her for years when she was a waitress in the Dunshane, but those were possibly the only two women on earth who could put up with him.

The list of casualties so far included the new receptionist, who had left in tears, a head chef who explained to Conor how if Carlos Manner set foot in his kitchen again he'd find himself at the wrong end of a cleaver, a Nigerian barman who said he'd never experienced such racist remarks anywhere, and one of the household staff, a woman in her fifties who had walked out the door telling him to stick his hotel where the sun don't shine. Carlos was normally much better than this, but the pain and frustration of his injury were making him unbearable. Normally, Conor would ask him to sit in on the interviews, but in his current mood, that would be a disaster.

They were haemorrhaging staff and recruitment was so difficult. Ireland, thankfully, was at full employment and enjoying a meteoric recovery from the bad days of the economic crash in the early 2000s, but it meant service industries were all feeling the pinch. The country had tough immigration laws, so the people who would be most likely to fill positions of housekeeping, gardening and so on were just not there. Irish kids all went to university and expected to come out to prestigious careers with six-figure salaries. Manual labour was, in their millennial opinion, far beneath them.

Conor thought about how times had changed. He'd left school at sixteen to become an apprentice mechanic. He remembered how thrilled he had been to get his first job, learn a trade and work his way up. After years of working for his old friend and mentor, Joe, after whom his son was named, Conor got the opportunity to buy the garage for a very cheap price. That was how he had seen his life going, and he still had faint traces of oil in the grooves of his fingertips all these years later. But then his brother had taken off for America with Conor's girlfriend, leaving him heartbroken and with a diamond ring in his pocket.

He left Cork and got a job as a tour driver. He had enjoyed that life, and it was how he met Ana, but when he was bequeathed money in the will of a very wealthy Texan who'd come on a tour with him and subsequently became a friend, it allowed him to join Corlene in bringing Castle Dysert back from the brink of dereliction into the magnificent resort it now was. Conor was a self-made man; he wasn't afraid to get his hands dirty and never thought any job was beneath him. He'd vowed to Ana that once the boys were old enough, they would be getting part-time jobs at the hotel and would earn their pocket money. He was determined not to raise entitled children.

As he got up to leave, his phone rang.

'Should I send the first receptionist candidate in, Conor?' Sheila Dillon, head of housekeeping, was manning the reception desk though she hated the job and had a pathological terror of computers. But at least she wouldn't bite the heads off the guests.

'Right, do so,' Conor said with a sigh. *There goes my coffee break.*

He was checking his emails when Ana walked in.

'Hi, pet.' He was delighted to see her. 'I'm sorry, but I think Sheila is sending an interview candidate in to me now. I was hoping to take a break, and I'd have loved to have a coffee with you. Is everything OK?' He paused. 'You look different.'

Her blonde hair, which she'd always worn short, was now jaw-length. She said it was the only way she could bear the post-chemo curls, and he thought it really suited her, though she only took it out of a ponytail when going to bed. She'd been to the hairdressers – it was blow-dried straight, and she looked very sleek. She wore a little make-up, and the black trouser suit with a pale-green shirt underneath fitted her perfectly.

'Yes, this is my interview suit,' she said as she sat down opposite him and handed him a buff envelope. 'My CV and a reference from Ms O'Brien and another from Mr Manner.'

'What?' Conor wasn't sure if she was joking.

'I'm here to do an interview for the receptionist job.' Ana didn't smile.

'Ah, but, darling, I've someone coming in right now...' Conor's brow knitted in confusion.

'Yes, Liga Florek. I'm sorry, Conor. I applied using this name because I thought you would not take me seriously.' She swallowed. 'I know I asked you before and you say no, but I want to work. I have experience. I can do this. I want to do this.' She tried to keep the emotion out of her voice.

Conor stood and went around to her side of his large desk. He perched on the corner and took her hand. 'Sweetheart, I'd love nothing better, but you need to take it easy. This place... Well, you know how it is. It's mental here most days, and I don't want you to overdo it. And we don't need the money...' Conor said, trying to be reasonable without destroying her confidence.

She withdrew her hand from his and turned away from him slightly, facing forward. 'Can you please just ask me what you ask –' – she corrected herself – 'will ask the other candidates? I think you don't ask them about how tired they might be?' She was cool and calm but businesslike.

'But, Ana...' he tried again, going back to his side of the desk and sitting down.

She looked directly into his eyes. 'Conor, listen. Don't talk, just hear me. I am going crazy. All day, I sit at home, I wait for the boys. I'm fine. Yes, I get little tired, but I can do this. I think maybe my English is not perfect, but I can understand everyone, what they say, and they can understand me. And what more is there?' She echoed her father-in-law's words.

'I have worked before in hotel, you know that. I am hard worker, and I am nice to people, helpful. I know this place and where is everything. Please, Conor, let me try at least. I know we don't need it, but I want to earn my own money, to be a little bit...I don't know what is the word...like free?'

'Independent?' he suggested with a small smile.

'Yes, this. I don't have to ask you if I want to buy something, nothing like that, I know. Our money is ours, but it is all of it yours. You earn it, and I just... Well, I do nothing. Long ago, this is OK. For my mother's time, this is normal. But I am a young educated woman, and I need to be something more than just a mother and a wife. Can you understand?'

Conor looked at his darling wife, pleading with him. She was the toughest, bravest, kindest woman he knew. She had been the one to get their relationship going in the first place; he'd been reluctant, thinking he was too old for her. Then she was the one who encouraged him to be a father, something he cherished. She'd helped him manage his father's reappearance and his brother's death, all while battling breast cancer. She'd done so much for him, and here she was asking him to do something for her. He had to trust that she knew her own body and what she was able for. He had no qualms whatsoever about her ability – the truth was, she was just what they needed – and if anyone could handle the new and miserable Carlos, it was Ana.

'OK, let's give it a shot. Part time, though, not forty hours – maybe fifteen or twenty hours a week. And if it's too much, or you're too tired, you have to promise me you'll just say it, OK?'

She beamed. 'Really, I can have the job?'

'I don't see why not. I'll employ someone else for the hours you don't do.' He laughed as she jumped up and went around to his side of the desk and kissed him.

'Now, I'm interviewing this evening as well, so let's not set a precedent of kissing the successful candidate every time I give someone a job, OK?' He chuckled and put his arms around her.

Just as he was about to kiss her again, the door to the office burst open and a very irate Artur stood there. Ana's father was the most serene man Conor knew, so something bad must have happened to get him so riled up.

'I am sorry I interrupt you, but I cannot – no, I cannot – move all this shrubs to the other side of the driveway. They is sun-loving plants. I research long time on the internet what is best, and this is best for sunny side. I put other shrubs, ones for not dark... What is word...' He was frustrated.

'OK, OK... Artur, what's going on?' Conor asked.

'Carlos Manner say to me all these shrubs, only planted two week ago, must to come out and go to the other side. But I tell him this no good, will die there because is in shade – yes, that is the word, in shade. But he tell young men who work to do it anyway. I take Danika to hospital for check, and when I come back, they is all moved. I tell him no, it can't be, but he just...'

Conor exhaled, struggling to control his fury at Carlos meddling in things that were not his concern.

'Artur, I'm sorry about that. Please take as many staff as you can and move the plants back to where they should be. I'll deal with Carlos.'

Artur nodded and left.

'Are you sure you want to work here?' He looked doubtfully at Ana. 'Carlos is like a briar being stuck in the wheelchair, and he is wrecking everyone's head. I know he only came back early to help me out, but I swear he's causing more problems than he's solving.'

'Don't worry. I can manage Mr Manner. Remember, I had many times with him in the Dunshane. It will be fine, and besides, he likes me now.'

'OK.' He smiled.

'Can I start now?' Ana asked as he pulled out his phone to call Carlos.

'Please do. Sheila hates the computer, so she'll be only thrilled to get back to housekeeping.'

'Great.' She went to leave, but before she got to the door, Conor called her back quietly.

She turned.

'I love you.'

'I love you too.' She grinned, blew him a kiss and headed out to reception.

*   *   *

CONOR WAS RIGHT – the minute Ana said she was taking over, Sheila was gone like a rat up a drainpipe. And immediately after she left, the phone rang. Ana took a deep breath and answered it. 'Good morning. Castle Dysert, Ana speaking. How may I help?'

It was someone looking to book five people for six nights. She didn't know how to use the reservations system yet, so she made a note of the booking on a notepad by the phone. She would figure it out when it got quiet.

When she heard the surname she was surprised. 'Pavlovych? This sounds Ukrainian. I'm from Kiev.'

Immediately, the man spoke in Ukrainian to her and she responded. Both laughed at the coincidence. He explained that his wife and her adult daughter, as well as his father-in-law and his girlfriend, would make up the party.

Ana told him all about the hotel and the facilities, and discussed the myriad of things to see and do in the area. He told her that they were looking to do a bit of genealogical research and asked if there was any way to employ someone to help with that.

This was a common request. There were something like forty-five million Americans claiming Irish roots, so people looking for their family homes, graveyards and so on were a big part of the tourism industry.

Ana liked the man and remembered how often Conor had been able to assist those looking for their Irish ancestors.

She started to say, 'My hus –' but stopped herself. 'The owner of this hotel is a bit of an expert on that sort of thing. He's not a professional genealogist, but he's been helping people for years, so I'm sure he could meet you when you get here and see what can be done.'

Conor passed by, surprised to hear her chatting happily in Ukrainian. She pointed to the note she'd made, and he instantly understood. She leaned back to allow him access to the computer. He brought up the reservation screen and inserted the dates.

'We can do two doubles and a single room, or a double and a family room for a little cheaper.' He pointed at the screen, and Ana relayed the information.

She said something else, laughed a bit and bade the guest goodbye.

'He said his stepdaughter might try to smother him in his sleep, so best she has her own room.'

Conor rolled his eyes. 'More drama.'

'Well, he asked that they have the best rooms, price don't matter, so let's do what it is the man asks.'

Conor walked her through the reservation system and explained how the whole thing worked in between helping guests who came to reception.

Before they knew it, the other candidates for the reception job began to arrive.

Conor went into his office, and Ana had a wonderful time getting to grips with everything. The boys had hurling training after school – Artie had reluctantly agreed to go back when Joe begged him. They wouldn't be finished until five, so she worked until four thirty.

As she walked to her car, she got a text from Jamsie. *Well?*

She'd called him that morning for a bit of confidence.

I got it. Started today and I love it. Thanks for the idea. Ana x

Good woman yourself! Delighted for you. x

She drove to the school, feeling happier than she had for ages. She arrived as training was still going on, so she parked on the side of the pitch and waited. Joe was in full flight, but Artie was sitting, looking sullen, on the bench. She longed to go over to him, to put her arms around him, but she knew that would be social suicide for the boys, so she just waited.

As she did, she spotted three girls in the stand behind the dugout. They seemed to be saying something. Artie was studiously ignoring them, his bony shoulders hunched. She thought he was shaking, and realised to her horror, he was crying. Then one of the girls threw something and hit him on the back of the head.

Ana was furious. The trainer was at the other end of the pitch explaining something to the gathered team, and no other parents had arrived yet.

Without thinking, she got out of her car and marched over to where the girls sat. One nudged the other as she approached, and the two either side of the girl who threw something at Artie had the grace to look embarrassed at least. Artie was far enough in front so as not to notice her.

Ana marched up and stood in front of them. Blind fury pulsed through her veins as she looked into the face of her son's tormentor. She was tall for her age, with long blonde hair and what looked suspiciously like make-up on her small catlike face. She was ten years old, but there she was, brandishing the latest iPhone and dressed in a manner entirely inappropriate for a child. She wore black Nike skintight leggings and an expensive branded t-shirt that clung to her non-existent curves. To finish the look, she had a designer handbag flung over her shoulder. Ana knew exactly who she was.

'You two.' She pointed at the pair flanking Emma. 'Go. Now.'

They exchanged a quick glance but realised Ana wasn't joking, so they did as she commanded, leaving Emma alone. Ana waited until they were out of earshot, then moved forward.

She bent down so her face was inches from Emma Doyle's. 'I want you to listen very carefully, Emma Doyle, as I do not repeat myself.' Ana's voice was low and threatening. 'I am not Irish, so I do not behave like an Irish person when someone hurts my family. I do not do this Irish way, all talking and trying to see every sides. No, I react like a Ukrainian. So this is the only warning you will get. From this moment on, you and your stupid little girlfriends' – Ana jerked her head at the departing figures, now fifty feet away – 'are not to speak to or touch or even look at my son – either of my sons, in fact – or the consequences will be very bad for you. I know people, believe me, who can hurt you and your family much more worse than the way you are hurting Artie, and I will not show mercy. These people that I know, they do not talk. They act. Do you understand?' Ana stared into the terrified girl's eyes.

The child swallowed. All colour had drained from her face, and she had lost her confident swagger along with her two henchwomen.

'I – I'll tell my dad that you threatened me! I'm just a kid and you're a grown adult. We'll sue you...' Emma spluttered, her voice a combination of whining and fear.

'You can tell whoever you like, that is no problem. I will deny everything. I am respectable mother, I am on parents' association, my husband is the boss of most of the town, so try to damage me if you want. But remember this. You know how so many people, every year, they disappear? What you think happen, eh? They just walking down the road and one day' – Ana clicked her fingers dramatically – 'they are gone? No. People make people disappear. So you must decide. Is it worth the risk to bully my son again? I know it is not, but do you, Emma?'

Ana's eyes raked the girl's face, never once blinking. Ana knew absolutely nobody who would ever commit such a crime, but she also knew that her accent made people think of baddies. The boys loved James Bond, and the bad guys were always Russian. Nobody in Ireland could tell the difference between Russians and Ukrainians, or even Poles or Lithuanians. In their eyes and to their ears, they were all the same. She might as well capitalise on it.

'Do you understand, you stupid little girl?' Ana's voice dripped venom as her green eyes bored into Emma's.

The girl nodded slowly, and Ana could almost smell her terror.

'Good.'

As she walked back to her car, she was happy to note neither Joe nor Artie seemed to have seen her. She sat back in and thought about what just happened. She knew Conor would go mad if he knew – he was more into sitting down and talking it through, trying to come to a solution – but bullies only understood one thing, and Emma had got the message loud and clear. Ana knew she was just a child, but she was a nasty child and needed to feel a bit of the fear she was putting into poor Artie.

She didn't regret it for a moment.

A few minutes later, a muddy and exuberant Joe got in the car, followed by a pristine and subdued Artie.

'Were you here? Did you see my goal from the forty-five?' Joe asked excitedly in Ukrainian. It amazed people when they heard the boys switch effortlessly between English and Ukrainian, but Ana had never spoken to them except in her native language. And while her parents were coming to grips with English, her father better than her mother, they conversed exclusively in Ukrainian with the boys. They spoke English when Conor was there, though his Ukrainian was improving.

'No, *sérdénko.*'

He smiled at her Ukrainian endearment.

'I just got here.'

She tried to catch a glimpse of Artie's face, but he kept his head down.

All the way home, Joe jabbered on about the big match coming up at the weekend, but despite both his brother's and his mother's attempts to include him in the conversation, Artie stayed quiet.

Once they were home, they began their homework while Ana cooked dinner. She was rejuvenated by the new job, but also by the hope that her threats might have sorted out that little madam who was upsetting Artie so much.

Conor had texted to say they were meeting the principal again in a few days' time, which should give her a good idea if her quiet word with Miss Emma Doyle had done the trick.

Conor was in a jubilant mood as he came into the kitchen just as she was taking the lasagne she'd made out of the oven.

'Great, not too late. I'm starving,' he said, helping her by closing the oven door and getting a trivet for the hot dish.

Ana was delighted he was home so early and not looking as exhausted as he usually was. The boys heard his voice and came charging in, launching themselves on him. Within minutes, all three were on the floor wrestling, and Ana was glad to see Artie had perked up a little.

She called them to the table, and Conor supervised the washing of hands.

Just as Joe was about to tuck in, Conor stopped him. 'Don't we have something to say to Mammy?'

They both looked at Ana and chorused, 'Thanks for the lovely dinner, Mammy.'

'And?' Conor prompted.

The twins exchanged a look.

'And we'll wash up after,' Artie said with a smile.

Conor ruffled his son's hair. 'Good man. Now, we're celebrating because today Mammy got a new job. Did she tell you?'

'Where?' Joe asked.

'At the castle,' Ana announced. 'I'm going to work with Miss O'Brien on the front desk.'

'And who'll pick us up from school?' Artie asked, his eyes fearful.

Imelda had mentioned the problems Artie was having appeared to be happening before and after school more than during the school day. That was why it was so hard to catch.

'Oh, don't worry, I will be finish before you. I only working in the time you two are at school because I was so sad and lonely here with you two gone. Now I am happy.' She made funny faces and they giggled.

'Congratulations, Mammy,' Joe said. 'But you won't have to work in the evenings like Dad does sometimes, though, will you?'

'Well, funny you should mention that, Joe,' Conor interjected, and all three looked at him. 'Because I think I've found an assistant manager. I interviewed her this morning and offered her the job this afternoon, and she took it. Not only that, but she can start right away.'

'Really? That's great news. You were not hopeful after last time. So they send someone good?' Ana was relieved; he needed help.

'Well, she comes highly recommended. She managed a large guest house in England and now wants a break. She got a glowing reference, though, from her last place. Castle Dysert is a lot bigger, and she'll have a lot to learn, but she seems to have her head screwed on and is really excited about the move. She'll live on-site as well, in one of the apartments above the stables. She was happy to have that as part of her package, so it's looking good. We'll have to see, but I'm optimistic.'

'What's her name, Dad?' Artie asked.

'Olga Jakobdóttir. She's English but her parents are from Iceland, and she moved to the UK when she was a child.'

'That's a funny-sounding name,' Joe remarked.

'Well, she explained that in Iceland, you take your father's name as your surname. Her father was Jakob, so she is Olga, Jakob's daughter.'

'So if we lived there, I'd be Joe Conordóttir?' Joe asked, and Artie grinned.

'No, you would be Joe Conorson because you're a son not a daughter,' Ana explained.

'I think we'll stick with O'Shea,' the boy said, reaching for another slice of garlic bread. 'Sure that kinda means the same thing, doesn't it, Dad?'

'It does. O in Irish is "of", so you are of the O'Shea family, and the Mac names, like MacCarthy or McNamara, mean "son of",' Conor explained.

'So why are we not MacShea so?' Artie asked, suddenly interested.

'Well, some names are just traditionally O or Mac. They've been that way for years and years, so you can't go changing them now.' Conor explained.

'And what about names that have no O? Like Jack Sullivan in fifth class – he's got no O, but most of the others are O'Sullivan?' Artie asked.

'Well, they say that people who have no O in their names when there should be, like O'Shea, O'Donovan, O'Sullivan and so on, they say that they "Took the soup".'

'What does that mean?' both twins asked at precisely the same time. Ana and Conor were used to it – the boys often had the exact same thought at the exact same time – but when others heard it, it made them smile.

'It means that during the famine in Ireland, during the mid-1800s, they set up soup kitchens to feed the people who were starving. But they would only give you soup, the story goes anyway, if you agreed to drop the O out of your name, making you less Irish, I suppose. So people who have no O might have taken the soup.'

'But sure, it would be better to take the soup and not die surely and change your name if you had to?' Artie said.

'Or you could take the soup and tell them you'd drop the O, but then after the soup, not do it at all?' Joe said.

'That's my boy.' Conor grinned.

Once dinner was finished, true to their word, the boys loaded the dishwasher and tidied the kitchen. They even made Ana a cup of tea and brought it to her in the sitting room where she and Conor were relaxing on the sofa watching TV.

'So you think this Olga is going to be able to help you?' Ana asked, cuddling up to her husband.

'I hope so. She seems nice...well, a bit formal, you know the way. But the fact that she'll live in is going to be great. It means she'll be on hand in case anything happens, like Chef finally beheads Carlos with a cleaver, or Katherine uses that voice – you know the one that says "I cannot believe a person as stupid as you exists" – on one of the guests. She's huge though, like over six foot, I'd say, very Icelandic looking. Blonde hair, blue eyes, powerfully built. Carlos will have to think twice before he says anything derogatory to her – she'd floor him in a second.'

Ana chuckled at the thought. 'I'm glad you've found her. When is she starting?'

'That's the best bit. She's coming in tomorrow. I didn't even clear it with Corlene. She won't care, and anyway, she's never around.'

'So she moved over here and just tried to get a job then?' Ana thought that a little strange.

'Yeah, apparently. She's staying in the Ashe Hotel at the moment, so she's moving out of there this evening. Carlos is making sure one of the apartments is all in good shape, and she's reporting for duty at 9 a.m. tomorrow morning.'

He sighed deeply. 'Maybe if this works out, we could get a week away somewhere sunny before the real mayhem of the season starts?'

'That would be lovely, but I just start a new job, and the boss, well, he's not so nice...' Ana chuckled.

'Ah, I'm sure you could find a way to convince him,' Conor murmured as she kissed his neck.

CHAPTER 11

The plane was finally over land. Billie looked out the window. Far below were a patchwork of green fields and a rugged coastline.

'Good morning, ladies and gentlemen. This is your captain speaking. We are now approaching Shannon Airport. The temperature in Shannon today is fifteen degrees Celsius with a light south-westerly breeze. I'd like to take the opportunity to thank you for flying Aer Lingus and wish you a nice onward journey or a pleasant stay in the Shannon region. *Go raibh mile maith agaibh go leir.* Cabin crew, ten minutes to landing.'

Billie caught Pops's eye and reached across the aisle and took his hand. He was not a fan of flying and, in particular, landing. Marilyn, who was seated next to him, held his other hand.

The first-class cabin was the picture of sumptuous living: huge seats that reclined to flat, every imaginable entertainment and an endless supply of delicious food and drinks. When Donna had phoned back to say she was willing to go to Ireland, she also said Marko insisted on paying for everything. Billie hated being beholden to him, but then she thought about Pops's bad knee and how much of a sacrifice he was making coming with her in the first place, so she thanked them and accepted.

Of course, her mother and Marko also rejected the midrange hotel Billie had chosen in Dublin and had instead booked them into a five-star castle on the west coast. When Pops saw the price of the rooms, he'd been appalled, but Donna insisted once again. Billie had been annoyed – she didn't want to do this her mother's way – but when she looked on the hotel's website, she had to admit it looked absolutely amazing.

The hotel was mainly a big old castle on a craggy outcrop into the ocean. There were beautiful gardens that sloped right down to the water's edge, and the hotel had its own long beach. Behind the castle were newer buildings, a state-of-the-art gym and pool complex, stables with horses the guests could ride and a long forest trail around the huge grounds. It was like something from a storybook, and Billie could never have afforded it.

So this is my father's home, she thought as the plane made its descent. It sure looked as beautiful as everyone said. She nudged Pops; in a field below them, clearly visible, was a ruined old castle.

'Neat, huh?' she asked. For some reason, she was anxious that he enjoy the trip. He held deep-seated resentment, but they'd talked about it and she asked him to try to suspend his animosity and just see the country on face value.

He nodded, but she could see the dread in his eyes; they would land in the next few minutes.

Arrivals was small, and they found themselves out through the gates in a matter of moments. She felt a frisson of excitement. There was a man holding a card with Marko's name at the gate. The hotel must have sent him.

He was pleasant, though they had absolutely no idea what he was saying – he spoke so fast and in such an accent. They sped off from the airport, and the man driving prattled away, grinning and pointing things out. They nodded politely and laughed when it seemed expected, but they had no idea.

The scenery was spectacular. Ancient ruins dotted lush green fields. Rows of coloured houses sat in pristine villages, all adorned with flowers and brightly painted farm implements. There seemed to be a huge number of pubs. As they left the main highway and headed, presumably, to the coast, the landscape changed. There were single houses and tiny fields divided by dry stone walls. The land seemed less fertile, more hills and rocks, and sheep wandered everywhere, their wool dyed with patches of different colours. Billie wondered why and thought about asking the driver but thought better of it.

On their left was the azure Atlantic, gently lapping at the shore, and the colours were so vivid, the sky so blue, the land so green, that Billie thought it looked like a fairy tale. Her dad used to read her a book about a land far, far away, where magical things happened, and she realised this was what she had imagined. She felt a familiar pang in her heart thinking about her dad. He could never have afforded a trip like this. She felt so disloyal; she hoped he'd understand.

They were all entranced by the views. No matter where they looked, the country was like a postcard. The car had to stop at one point when someone was trying to move a herd of cows across the road. They waited, and there appeared to be no apparent hurry on the part of either the driver or the farmer. Cows surrounded the car. A small child, no more than six or seven, seemed to be in charge. There was an ancient-looking farmer leaning on the gate, smoking a cigarette, but the child was brandishing a stick and saying 'hup, hup' to get the cattle into the field.

Once the cows had been moved, the driver put the window down and had a brief mysterious conversation with the farmer. Billie wondered if they were speaking Gaelic. She'd been obsessively researching Ireland in the weeks leading up to the trip. And the more she thought about it, the more she wanted to find her birth father. So many things made sense now, like why, when she became a blood donor and tried to encourage her father to go too, he would drive her to the clinic but always refused to go in, claiming he was squeamish. Billie was AB negative, a rare blood group, and her mother was O, one of the most common. At the blood bank, a person's blood type was stamped on their file. Billie had always assumed her dad was AB negative like her, but he obviously wasn't. There were other things too: how she had pale skin when both her parents were dark, how she could sing while neither Donna nor Matt could carry a tune in a bucket. She couldn't believe that none of this had occurred to her before.

She speculated about her biological father and knew she was guilty of over-romanticising. He could be a drunk, or mean, or he might not want to know her. She'd discussed it with Noah – they'd gone for coffee after work a few times since that night. No big deal, just chatting, but he seemed to understand the turmoil she was going through. Though he was over his personal story, he got it in a way that someone else wouldn't.

Noah was the only one she told, and she felt bad that she hadn't mentioned anything to Emily. Emily was her best friend, and normally they shared everything, but this whole mess with her family… She just couldn't. Emily was from New York, and they'd started at Visionboard together, the two East Coast girls. They were close but Emily didn't know her family and anyway, she didn't really know enough about what was going on herself to try to explain it to anyone else.

Talking to Noah was easy. He wasn't judgemental, but he said what he thought at the same time. She respected his opinion and found she hung around work later than was necessary when he was there, hoping that he'd invite her for coffee. There was nothing in it; he was just being nice. He was the boss and ten years older than her, and she wasn't about to make a fool of herself again. They never discussed it, but they kept their meetings secret.

He'd texted when she was in the airport. *Hi, Billie. I hope it all goes well for you in Ireland, with everything. If you ever need to talk, give me a call. Noah*

She would love to call him but was afraid it might be awkward. He never used text speak or emojis. He wrote texts properly, with commas and apostrophes and everything. They talked easily face-to-face, but apart from a few texts, there was no other communication between them. It was so weird – normally nowadays, the reverse was true, with loads of digital chat and no face-to-face. She'd laughed out loud when he told her he didn't use any social media. No Snap, no Twitter, no Insta…not even Facebook, and even Pops was on that.

The car slowed down, turned in through ornate gates and drove up a smooth winding driveway. Either side, people seemed to be gardening, moving bushes from one side of the driveway to the other, and they waved as the car passed.

The gardens were so luxurious, nothing like what they'd seen on the drive here. They sloped gently to the seashore, a verdant lush green. Lots of purple rhododendron bloomed, intermixed with lilac and wisteria. One side of the hotel had a stand of blossoming cherry trees that swayed gently in the breeze. She put the window down. There was a sense of spring in the air. It wasn't warm, but the sky was bright and the air smelled fresh and floral, with a hint of sea breeze.

The car pulled up to the main entrance, where well-worn limestone steps, eroded from centuries of feet, led to a huge front door. It was ten feet wide at least, heavy oak, studded with huge black fixings, and it led to a circular lobby. On their right was an enormous stone fireplace, with lions' heads carved into the marble pillars either side of it, beside which stood two suits of armour. The hearth was filled with a luxurious flower arrangement, and what appeared to be a very old rug was in front of it, completing the look. Donna went in search of the ladies' room as Marko walked up to the desk where an attractive young blonde woman was assisting another guest.

Billie, Marilyn and Pops just took it all in: the stained glass windows, the stone flags on the floor, the suit of armour in the corner. The room had a huge staircase leading out of it and several doors off it. There was a cute little sign, like an old-fashioned signpost, indicating the spa, the bar and both of the restaurants.

To Billie's astonishment, Marko appeared to be laughing with the woman on the desk. They edged closer, and she realised Marko was speaking in his own language to the woman. Once she'd checked them in, she came out from behind the desk bearing three keys on large brass rings. She was tiny and curvy, no taller than five feet, with vivid green eyes. She reminded Billie of Tinker Bell from *Peter Pan*.

'Good morning.' The woman smiled. She had a foreign accent when speaking English. 'My name is Ana, and I want to welcome you to Castle Dysert. I hope you have a lovely stay, and please, if there is anything we can do to help, or if you need something, please, just call to me or any of my colleagues, and we will see to it right away.'

She pressed a bell on the desk, and a young man in a beautiful green and gold uniform appeared.

'This is Sean, and he will help take your luggage and show you to your rooms. Have a lovely stay.'

Marko asked her something, and she went to the computer to check. 'Ah, yes,' she said in English so everyone could understand. 'We have a table in either King's Restaurant or in our bar, Grenville's. King's is beautiful – Chef has a Michelin star – but it is formal dining, so if you rather something more relaxed, then there is a large bar menu also. I'll send both menus to your room, and you can decide and let me know.'

They nodded their thanks and followed Sean to the elevator, which was cleverly camouflaged with wood panelling.

The rooms were equally sumptuous. Billie's room overlooked the ocean on one side and, because she had a corner room, had a view of the gardens on the other. She just stood there for several moments, drinking it all in. She turned to tip the bellboy, but he was gone. She remembered reading somewhere that Ireland didn't have a tipping culture. The minimum wage was almost ten euro an hour, which was around twelve dollars, and labour was hard to get, so most service personnel were on a much higher rate. It was customary to tip in restaurants when service wasn't added, but not everywhere else. She was glad. Though Marko and her mom had been more than generous, she wanted to at least try to pay her way. She earned a reasonable salary – and she was going to go for a promotion when she got back – but it wasn't enough to cover these kinds of vacations.

She sat on the bed, a beautiful carved piece of furniture covered in a gold damask bedspread. The moss-green deep-pile carpet complemented the room perfectly. As she was admiring the bathroom, there was a gentle knock on the door. She opened it.

'Mom, hi. This place is incredible, isn't it?' Billie said.

'It really is, and the woman downstairs is Ukrainian – turns out she comes from Kiev – so she and Marko had a big conversation. I've never seen him so animated.' Donna smiled. 'Anyway, he wanted me to tell you that her husband, who owns this place, is good at finding people and so on, so if you wanted to try to track your father down, then he might be able to help.'

Billie could see the uncertainty in her mother's eyes, and a moment of empathy hung between them. She was sure the last thing her mother wanted was to go on a hunt to find her long-lost boyfriend of twenty-six years ago. For the first time maybe, Billie saw things from her mother's point of view. She'd had a lot of time to think since hearing the bombshell news, and she found she'd kind of mellowed. Noah had helped, as he was good at untangling things.

She invited her mother to sit on the sofa that faced an old bay window overlooking the expanse of lawn ringed by a bed of what looked like wildflowers.

Billie sat beside her and took a deep breath. All the way over on the plane she'd rehearsed this. 'I want to say something, and I'm not sure how to start.'

Donna looked like a rabbit in the headlights, probably preparing for another outburst. Billie felt so bad; her dad would be so angry if he thought she was treating her mother that way.

'I...I'm sorry. For everything. I shouldn't have put Dad before you these last few years, or treated you the way I did. And especially after Gio died, I just...I don't know. I kind of lost myself. And Dad was who I clung to. I see now that you were barely holding on yourself.'

Unshed tears shone in her mother's eyes, but she said nothing.

'I...' Billie went on. 'I was mean to you when Dad died, and I said some horrible things. I'm sorry. Marko makes you happy, I can see that, and you deserve to be happy. You've had enough heartache. And you don't need more from me, so I'm really sorry.'

'Oh, Billie, I'm sorry too.' Donna was crying now.

'You were a great mom to me and to Gio all those years before we lost him, and I forgot that. I should have tried more to understand what it was like for you.'

With her thumb, Donna wiped the single tear that slid down Billie's cheek.

'I just shut down after Gio. Your father had to be both a mother and a father to you, and he was heartbroken too. I just couldn't... I don't know what else to say. I blamed myself. I should have been paying more attention, as he was just a child. But I can't turn the clock back. Your dad never blamed me, nobody did. Over and over, he told me it would have been the same if he'd taken Gio and his friends to the beach, that he'd have been relaxing and not watching them every second. I know he meant well, but the thing is, him saying he didn't blame me only made it worse. I wanted him to rage at me, to tell me I'd killed his son, but his kindness was so hard to bear.' Donna's voice was barely more than a whisper.

'Matt was such a good man, Billie, such a decent, kind man, and he needed me. You both did, I know, but I just couldn't. I suppose over the years, the pain has dulled to an ache, and I feel I can at least breathe again, but by the time that happened, I thought I'd lost you too. Not in the same way, but I missed you, my darling girl. I missed you so much.'

Billie found herself in her mother's arms, both women sobbing. The years, the pain, the grief for Gio and for her dad all converged, and she let it all go. Her mother rubbed her back as she cried, just like she'd done when Billie was a little girl. When Billie felt she had no more tears, she sat up and gazed at the garden below.

'Dad would love this place,' she said quietly, remembering the hours her father spent in the yard.

'He would.' Donna agreed. An easy silence fell between them for several minutes, and then Donna spoke quietly. 'I did love him.'

Billie turned. She'd always wondered. 'You did?'

Donna nodded. 'And not just because he saved me when I found myself expecting you. I loved him very much. He was a really good man. Something changed in me when Gio died. It was like I was frozen inside or something. I couldn't feel anything but numb. We were both grieving, but we couldn't help each other. He wanted to talk about Gio, have a memorial, celebrate his life, but I just wanted to lock myself away. I couldn't bear it. I couldn't bear Matt near me...' She paused. 'Or even you. I just wanted to die with my son.'

Billie heard the raw anguish in her mother's voice.

'To have your child die, it's the hardest thing any mother could bear. But to blame yourself for it... It's...indescribable pain.' Donna's voice was choked with emotion. 'Matt went to counselling. He wanted me to go too, but I couldn't. For me, it would be like twisting the knife. I could barely stand the pain as it was. Having a stranger ask me questions about Gio, about how I felt... I just couldn't bear it. Matt begged, and when I refused, he even asked me to do it for you. He could see how I was pushing you away. Eventually I went once, just to stop him going on at me, but it was as bad as I feared – worse actually – so I didn't go back.'

Billie recalled those days after Gio's death. Her mother didn't get dressed, and they ate takeout all the time. Billie was a freshman in college, and she came home for the funeral. All she remembered was that her mother was in a blind fog of grief, fear and denial. If she refused to talk about it, then it didn't happen.

She remembered the pity in people's eyes. How Gio's little buddies didn't know what to say, so they said nothing, just stood there with their parents, looking uncomfortable in chinos and button-down shirts when all they normally wore were shorts and football jerseys. Uncomprehending why their parents were holding them closer.

For the first time in her life, she saw her mother as another human being, a woman whose child had died at twelve years old, a woman trying to salvage some kind of a life from the ashes.

'But Pops said you're going to see someone now?'

Donna nodded slowly. 'Yes.'

'And is it helping?' Billie asked gently.

Her mother sighed. 'Yes...I don't know. Maybe. It's hard to tell. Some days, I leave there feeling a little better, other days worse. Last week, I drove home from the therapist's office in the dark with no lights on in the car. Marko nearly had a heart attack when I pulled into the driveway.' She gave a small smile. 'How about you? Are you doing OK?' Donna ventured to ask, something she probably wouldn't have dreamed of a few weeks ago.

Billie felt the familiar hackles rising. She rarely spoke about Gio, she couldn't stop talking about her dad, and she never mentioned her mother to anyone.

'Yeah, I guess.' She thought for a second. Should she say it? She didn't want to, but if she were to have any kind of relationship with her mother, it would have to be based on honesty.

'I…I felt so upset when Dad died, and then you married Marko so soon. I know it's your life and you're entitled to be happy, and waiting wouldn't have brought Dad back, but still it hurt. It felt like you didn't care about him enough or something, like you couldn't wait to be rid of him. That's why I didn't go to your wedding.'

The words hung between mother and daughter. Despite all the rage and fear and pain, Billie realised she'd never actually said what was bothering her.

'I can see why you'd feel that,' Donna said. She didn't offer an explanation. She didn't seem as eager to please her daughter as she had been before; she looked tired.

'Was Marko on the scene when Dad was dying?' Billie asked, her eyes on the green carpet. She didn't want to meet her mother's gaze.

'Yes,' Donna replied.

Billie gazed out the window at the manicured lawns surrounded by wildflowers. Such an idyllic scene, and yet here she was, hearing her worst fears realised.

'Your dad knew. He knew about Marko, and he understood. Our marriage had been over for a long time, in the sense of what a marriage should be, and we had planned an amicable divorce. He couldn't bear to see me not dealing with Gio's death, and I couldn't bear him talking about our son. We grew further and further apart, but not in an angry way. We loved each other. We had two wonderful children and a lifetime of memories, but it was over. Our marriage died with Gio. We separated and were going to tell you when you came home for Christmas. Your dad had an apartment and he was happy. We met for coffee often, and he told me how he felt better, not walking on eggshells around me anymore. He joined a group, a support group for bereaved parents, and he made some good friends there.'

Billie was stunned. Her parents had split up and nobody told her? Her dad had called her almost every evening, and this news never came up? She struggled to come to terms with this new version of the man she thought she knew. He wasn't her biological father, he split from her mother, he was in a support group, he had a bunch of new friends, and yet he didn't think to share any of this with her?

'So what happened? When I got back, you were both...' Billie didn't want to hear any more of this story but knew she had to.

'Then he got the diagnosis. Pancreatic cancer. The cancer was so advanced, the doctors only offered palliative care. It had spread all over, and there was nothing to be done. I was with him when they told him. So I insisted he move back home. By then, I was seeing Marko and your dad knew that. He was seeing someone as well, actually, but he didn't want her involved in his illness, so he broke it off. He became so ill, so quickly – it was like he faded in front of our eyes. Marko was very kind to him. I couldn't have managed him at home on my own, as he was too heavy to lift, but within a few weeks of diagnosis, he couldn't walk.'

Billie remembered her visit home, the only one before he died. Her big strong father had been a frail, thin man, lying in a bed. His voice was weak and he was in pain, though he claimed he wasn't. Her mother nursed him to the end. They got the palliative care team to come into the house – her dad hated hospitals – to manage the pain. She'd wanted to stay, but he insisted she go back to LA, as she'd just started the job with Visionboard. She refused and he begged, tears in his eyes. He didn't want her to watch him dying. They said goodbye, knowing it was forever, and Pops drove her to the airport. She stood with her grandfather in departures, their arms around each other. She didn't think she could get on the plane, but she did. Three weeks later, she was back in Boston to bury her father.

'So Dad knew Marko, and knew you two were together, and he

was fine about it?' Billie could hardly believe she was saying those words.

'Yes, he was happy for me. Marko isn't as taciturn as he seems, Billie. He's quiet, and he's had his own troubles, and I think that's why we work. He had deep hurt too. I know the details but we don't discuss it, and he doesn't ask me about Gio. I know people say talking things out, getting things in the open is best, but that's not always true. Sometimes respecting another person's private grief is important. Marko has given me a new life, and it helps that he never knew Gio. I will have this pain in my heart till the day I die, but for the first time, I feel like I can live with it, that it's not going to consume me.'

Billie tried to process all of this information. It was overwhelming.

Donna faced her and took her hand. Billie couldn't remember the last time she'd had anything but the most perfunctory of physical contact with her mother. It felt strange but oddly comforting.

'I have one child left. And you mean everything to me, Billie. And since we're being honest, I don't want to be here – of course I don't – but you do. The idea of showing up at some Irish guy's door, when I haven't seen him for twenty-six years, and confess I never told him he had a child is enough to make me want to throw up, but if this is something you need or want to do, then I'm with you.' She squeezed her daughter's hand. 'I grew up without my mom, and Dad did a great job, but I missed her. I get it, kids and parents don't always have the perfect relationship, but you are my child and I'm your mother, and I love you. I want to support you – we all do. You've been through so much, so if you want to find Billy Joyce, then we'll do whatever it takes.'

Billie swallowed the lump in her throat and blinked away the tears that threatened. 'What was he like?' she asked at last.

Donna beamed, a real smile, not the sad little efforts Billie was used to seeing. She realised she'd not heard her mother laugh for years. She wracked her brain, trying to visualise her mother laughing. She must have done, years ago, but Billie had no recollection of it.

'Billy was wild, honestly wild. He would do anything. He loved life, and he loved what he called the craic. It's an Irish word that means extreme fun, not drugs.' She smiled again, seeing Billie's shocked face.

'He was gorgeous. You look so like him, sometimes it takes my breath away – same gorgeous red hair, same blue eyes. He was not tall. He was about my height and wiry, like a monkey. But he was a farmer's son, so he was really strong. One time, he wanted to take me to Coney Island, as I'd never been. We watched an old movie one day – we had both called in sick to work – *The Lords of Flatbush*. It had that guy, the Fonz. Remember him from *Happy Days*? And anyway, that movie showed the rides at Coney Island, and I said I'd love to go. But we had no money, so he challenged this guy, this huge Irishman who was working on the same building site, to arm-wrestle for money. You should have seen this guy – he was like a tank. But Billy set it up, and sure enough, he beat him, three times in a row. He won the money and we went to Coney Island.' Donna's eyes lit up at the memory.

'What else?' Billie prompted.

'Oh, he could sing, and boy, did he sing. In the shower, on the street, in bars. I was often mortified. He'd start singing in the grocery store, songs he'd make up on the spot about how beautiful I was. Everyone would hear it, and my cheeks would burn, but it just spurred him on. He didn't care what anyone thought. He was brave. But you know what he was more than anything, Billie?'

'What?'

'He was kind. He cared about people. Old guys, down on their luck, he wouldn't just throw them some coins – he didn't have much anyway. But we'd walk along, and suddenly I'd turn to say something to him and he's behind sitting beside some hobo, hearing his life story.'

'He sounds nice,' Billie said.

'He was. Very.'

'Did he tell you anything about his family here?'

'Just that he was from Galway, he grew up on a farm, and he had three sisters. Oh, one day, he was on the phone, talking to someone back home, I guess, and he was speaking Gaelic. He told me that only

Americans call the Irish language Gaelic, that it was Irish and that he and his family spoke it as their first language. He could play all sorts of instruments, and everyone loved him. It was a long time ago, but I have very happy memories of that summer we spent together.'

'That's OK.' Billie said. 'Thanks for telling me about him.'

'Now, the lady at the front desk said her husband is happy to meet us, and maybe he can point us in the right direction.'

'So we're doing this?' Billie held her mother's gaze.

'Well, we've come all this way. You even convinced Pops to come to the country he's been holding a grudge against for seventy years.' She smiled. 'I think we should at least try.'

'What if he doesn't want to know – Billy, I mean?' Billie asked, feeling like a child again.

'Then that's his loss,' her mother replied.

CHAPTER 12

*C*onor sat in his car, reading emails on his phone. He could do so in his office, of course, but he knew the moment he set foot in the hotel, the whole circus would begin again. Carlos was back at the hospital for the day, much to everyone's relief, and though Conor knew he was being mean, he half hoped the doctors would tell Carlos that he shouldn't be working.

Amazingly though, Carlos and Olga seemed to get on like a house on fire. She was often found with him as he explained some aspect of the hotel in what looked to be – for him at least – a state of animation.

The previous day, Conor had come on him actually laughing at something Olga said. And she seemed to be having a somewhat emollient effect on his temper too. Conor had not had a complaint from a staff member about Carlos in days. So far so good. Olga was worth employing even if all she did was manage Carlos.

Conor understood how frustrating recovery could be and was inclined to cut Carlos a bit of slack, but Olga was playing a blinder.

In the fire three years ago, when he'd had to go into the blazing wing of the hotel to get his twins out, he suffered a lot of burns. He was fine now – there was a little scarring but not too bad – but he recalled the frustration of convalescence, so he knew what Carlos was going through. But did the man have to take it out on the staff?

Ana was working this morning, and Conor wasn't surprised at how quickly she had the whole place running like clockwork. She was a capable lady, and while he was still a little worried she was over-doing it, she seemed to love the job. Katherine was back from her honeymoon, and he had been worried about how his old friend would take to a new person, but Katherine loved Ana and the feeling was mutual.

He'd texted her on her cruise to say he'd given Ana the job, and she'd texted back immediately. *A sensible appointment at long last.*

Praise indeed. He'd grinned. Katherine was not one for soft-soaping anyone, least of all him.

He dealt with all the urgent stuff and walked into the hotel. To his amazement, everything seemed fine. He passed reception: Ana was on the phone, the staff all seemed content, a large group were having tea and freshly baked scones with jam and cream in the orangery. The glass room was an addition, but it was proving very popular. It was circular and filled with plants and miniature fruit trees. Each morning it was full, but not just with guests at the hotel; local businesspeople dropped in for coffee, and lots of people joined the leisure complex, so groups of locals met for chats after spin and Pilates classes. Apart from the extra revenue, it gave the hotel a nice buzzy feel during the day, and it made Conor happy to see the guests intermingling with the locals.

Castle Dysert had always had a bit of a sinister reputation. The castle had seen a lot of sadness and tragedy, and there were rumours that it was haunted. Conor knew first-hand all about Grenville King, the child who died in the building in 1920 – he had the scars on his back to prove it. It was great to see that pall of suspicion lift from the local community. He regularly saw the families from around the locality celebrating birthdays and anniversaries with a meal in their multi-award-winning restaurants.

He gave Ana a wink and carried on into his office. It was the first day in weeks that he'd not been greeted by a wall of people with grievances.

As he sat at his desk, Ana popped in. 'Good morning, boss.'

He chuckled. 'If only I was. I know exactly who's in charge in my life, and it sure ain't me.'

She sat on the side of his desk. 'But I let you think you are, so that is what is important. Now, Eddie called. He wants you to ring him. And Carlos ring too – he say doctor put another cast on his leg. He was mad because doctor says he walk on it and now will take long to get better. He's not happy,' Ana said darkly.

'Does that mean he can't come to work?' Conor didn't dare hope.

'Well, doctor says no, but Carlos says he is back tomorrow. I say to him is bad idea, otherwise he must have operation to fix it again or something, but he just say no. He was like a cut cat.'

Conor burst out laughing. 'Like a cut cat, was he? Listen to my little Ukrainian with her Irishisms.'

'Yes, I have given in. I can't stop all this mad sayings, so now I do it too. I'm thinking I might translate some Ukrainian ones now to confuse people like Irish sayings confuse me.'

'Great idea. Further confusion is definitely what's needed here.'

She beckoned him closer and whispered, 'He is having dinner with Olga tomorrow evening. They want to sample new menu, and she said it is good idea to just dine in restaurant like guests to get whole experience. When she say this, he goes colour of the book there' – she pointed to a scarlet-red desk diary – 'and that is why he come back so soon. I think Carlos is a little bit in love with our new manager, and she listens to him like he has next week's lotto numbers in his head.'

'Are you serious?' Conor asked. Carlos had never been known to have a girlfriend or a boyfriend or any kind of friend in all the years he'd known him. And Olga was easily a foot taller and probably weighed twice as much as him. She'd told Conor in her interview that she was a cross-country skier at home but that she also enjoyed shot-put and hammer throwing.

Ana nodded but widened her eyes to put Conor on alert. Olga was at the door.

'Oh, hi, Conor. Could we have a quick meeting? Nothing wrong, I just had a few thoughts I'd like to run by you. I think I've got us on the minister's itinerary when he's down at Shannon later in the week.' She asked.

Conor replied, 'No bother, that would be brilliant.'

Liam Seoige was the minister for the environment, and Castle Dysert was a carbon-neutral building, so they were hoping he'd stop by.

They'd hosted lots of government people since they opened. The officials loved the luxury, and of course it was all on the taxpayers' money.

Ana went back to the reception desk, and Conor walked out with Olga.

'I need to make a few calls first, but how about I meet you in the orangery in an hour? We can have a coffee and a chat then?' As he spoke, two men crossed the foyer in working clothes carrying tool-boxes. Conor didn't recognise them.

'Sounds great.' Noticing his look, Olga explained. 'Oh, those are the masons. Carlos suggested that we open the French doors into the courtyard outside from the bar. Artur said they were closed because of concerns about the cracked flagstones, but I asked him to look into getting them repaired. I think it will be nice now that the weather is warming up to sit outside.'

Conor thought for a moment. That courtyard outside what was now Grenville's Bar was where two of the previous owners died, decades apart, having thrown themselves from the turrets high above. He hardly ever went out there. But Carlos and Olga were probably right. It was a lovely, sheltered, sunny spot, so they should use it.

In the ten days she'd been there, Artur said she'd asked him to take her on a detailed tour of the whole hotel, introduce her to everyone and explain how everything worked. He seemed very impressed with her; she was very interested in every aspect of the hotel.

'Righto, no problem. I'll see you in an hour so.'

He had a brief word with Katherine. She filled him in on what was happening with recruiting new office and housekeeping staff. With great relief, he'd passed over the job of interviewing junior staff to her.

Then he went back into his office and called his friend Father Eddie. Eddie had a smartphone but texting was beyond him, so he only did voice calls.

'Well, Conor, how's tricks?' Eddie answered.

'Grand altogether. How's things with you?'

'Oh, you know yourself. Saying masses to empty churches and dealing with young ones that want to fill the church with punk rockers for their wedding day but never darken the door of the place before or after the big event. Or people asking me to baptise their children names they made up themselves. Someone wanted to give a baby girl Kardashian as her Christian name last week! So the same old ding-dong.'

Conor chuckled. Eddie was a funny man. 'Well, you did a smashing job for Katherine and Jimmy. It was a lovely ceremony.'

Conor had convinced his old friend to have a church wedding. She was a spiritual woman, and he knew it was what she wanted, but she was afraid it would look foolish, two people of their age walking down the aisle like a pair of young ones. Jimmy was in his sixties, and Katherine, he imagined, was close to sixty but he'd never ask. Katherine had been left at the altar many years earlier when she was a young woman, and she'd put a protective cage around herself ever since. Jimmy Burns, an unassuming New York garbage man with a PhD in philosophy, came to Ireland on a vacation, and while staying at the hotel, hit it off with Katherine. Conor nurtured the relationship gently from the sidelines. They were both very unusual people, but he was thrilled they found each other. Watching his friend melt the years of humiliation and hurt and allow herself to feel was a privilege, and escorting her up the aisle was one of the happiest moments of his life. She told him in a rare moment of softness after the mass that she was glad she went with the church wedding in the end, though her new husband wasn't a churchgoer. Eddie had talked about love, loyalty and understanding, and he'd also had everyone in the church laughing with his gentle good humour.

'Well, if I haven't the hang of it by now, there's no hope for me, I suppose. But it was a lovely day. Is she back yet?' Eddie asked.

'She is. She came back to work on Monday, and it's like a magic spell. The drama is all dealt with, and the place is running like a mouse's heart again. Carlos is in better form too, thank God, because he was in very real danger of sustaining a few more injuries than he has if he kept on the way he was going. And I've a new young woman working as deputy, so I actually might get some time off for a change. You know Ana started working here?'

'I do. Sure 'twas Ana I was talking to before I could get to the head honcho. You'd need a papal letter these days to get to you.' Eddie chuckled.

'Go on out of that. Aren't you just back yourself from another junket out to Italy to see Declan and Lucia?'

'I am. Poor Father Otu was flat out here all the week, three funerals. Since our esteemed curate got the call to Rome, myself and my Ghanaian friend are flat to the mat. All unexpected deaths too, and he had to handle it on his own. He did a mighty job though. I'll tell you, Conor, he's a terrific help. It took the older congregation a while to get used to him – he's very "African" they'd be telling me, giving sermons about fellas hunting for lions and walking miles and miles and what have you. But sure as I tell them, they're sick to death of listening to me banging on week after week the same old rubbish – they're delighted with him. He had the place in stitches on Sunday with a story about some lad who stole another fella's goat or something. They prefer him now, and sure who can blame them? I could get offended, but I'm too old. Besides, it means I can play more golf.'

'Ah, I'm glad you've some help. 'Twas getting too much for one person. I had the same problems here with Katherine gone and Carlos laid up with a broken arm and a broken ankle and trying to be five places at once.'

'Great, does that mean we'll get a round of golf in this week?' Eddie asked hopefully.

'There's every chance of it. We are going to host the minister later on this week. He's down here pressing the flesh, you know yourself.

But Olga – that's the new lady I hired – seems to have it all under control, so we'll see. Leave it with me, and I'll see how things are going.' Conor opened up his planner for the week on the computer.

'Righto so.' Eddie was about to hang up.

'Before you go, how are Declan and Lucia getting on?'

'Not a bother on them. You'd swear he was making wine his whole life. Fluent Italian, that whole lot, but I suppose the priesthood taught him that. They are well settled there, and Lucia is delighted with life. Their three children are getting big now, God bless them, and they are lovely little people.'

Conor recalled the terrified Lucia Sacco who'd come to Ireland on a tour with her boyfriend, Declan Sullivan, a few years ago. Conor had known there was something odd from the start, but he had no idea just how strange it all was. Declan was a Catholic priest, and Lucia was the daughter of the infamous mob boss Paulie Sacco. Paulie was furious when he discovered his priest had become involved with his daughter, and to make matters worse, she was pregnant with Declan's child. Paulie was hell-bent on finding them. Hiding out on a bus tour of Ireland seemed the safest place for them.

'It's amazing how it all worked out, isn't it? Back then, with everything, FBI, witness protection, the whole lot. It seems kind of surreal now, doesn't it?' Conor said.

'It does surely. But you know, Lucia and her mother are so close now, and she realises how her father kept them apart all her life. He was such a jealous man that he couldn't even share his child with her mother. But it's lovely to see them all together now. And the little ones are mad about their grandmother. She moved into the vineyard with them a few months ago, and she helps taking care of the children while Lucia is out in the vines with Declan.'

'That's lovely. Sure they've invited us out there plenty of times. We should try to go,' Conor mused.

'You should – the boys would love it. They've a lake on the property that the kids can swim in, and Lucia is an amazing cook. I'll have to face the music next week in the doctor's when I've to go to get my bloods done. After all the pasta and cake and what have you, sure

Elaine Kinsella is going to eat the head off me again, I suppose.' He sighed. 'And to think I gave her her first communion and this is the way she treats me.' He chuckled.

Conor smiled. His friend was rotund and had a terrible sweet tooth. Doctor Kinsella was blue in the face trying to get him to lose a few pounds, but Eddie loved his grub and largely ignored her advice.

'Yerra, she knows what you're like,' Conor said with a chuckle. 'I'll give you a buzz later about the golf. Thursday afternoon might be OK.'

'Grand. God bless.'

Conor made another call and had a quick chat with Corlene. She was on the way to a lunch in Farmleigh House in Dublin with a bunch of politicians or something, so she cut the call short. She was really into this guy Colm MacEntire; he was the elected representative for Donegal and married. They made no secret of their affair, and Conor had seen several newspaper pieces on them. Corlene was sailing close to the wind as usual. She was getting a particular battering in the press because she ran a business providing courses that she said empowered women, but in reality, she taught them about hair and make-up and clothes and the like, and also how to pull their cheating men into line. Conor found her business ridiculous. Why should any woman struggle to keep someone who was cheating on her? But as Corlene pointed out, it was the domain of the wealthy. They didn't want to lose old Gerald – not because they loved him, but because they didn't want to lose the house and the cars and the villa on the Côte d'Azur.

'You saw what the *Sunday Herald* did?' Corlene asked dryly.

'I did.' She was referring to a particularly cutting piece in one of the Sunday papers.

'I suppose you're appalled?' He could hear the grin in her voice; she was incorrigible.

'Corlene, you live by your own rules, girl, you always have.' He was non-committal. Of course she should not be cavorting around Dublin with a married man, but at the end of the day, he was the one who made a commitment to someone else, not Corlene. If anyone should be ashamed of himself, it was Colm MacEntire.

'He's different, Conor, seriously. His wife comes across all sweetness and light, but she's a dragon, made his life hell. He's lived in Dublin for the last ten years, and they never speak.'

It sounded like an excuse to Conor. 'Sure why not get a divorce if that's the case?' he asked. He was concerned for his friend.

'He is. It's in the process, but it takes forever here, and that old crow he married won't play ball – she's deliberately dragging it out. This country has ridiculous divorce laws.' She sighed.

Corlene was right. There was no such thing as a quick divorce in Ireland.

'Marry in haste, repent at leisure, as the saying goes,' Conor replied.

'Exactly. Hey, have you heard from Dylan?' she asked, changing the subject to her son, whom she adored but drove insane in equal measure.

'Yeah, he and Laoise are coming home at the end of the month. They are playing here actually, so you should try to come down. No publicity, though,' he warned. 'It's just a quiet session for their friends and people around here. If the press find out, the place will be swamped. They played to thirty thousand a few weeks ago at some festival.'

'I know. They're taking the world by storm, those two.' She exhaled. 'Y'know he's threatening to make me a grandma?'

Conor laughed. 'I can just see you knitting bootees and baking.'

'Yeah, right. Look, I gotta go. Talk soon.' She hung up without ever once asking how the hotel that she owned sixty percent of was doing.

He popped out to the orangery to see Olga.

'So how are things?' he asked, joining her at a window table as one of the servers brought him a coffee.

'Good, I think. I went with Artur around the hotel. He introduced me to each head of department, and I met many of the staff also. I'm getting to grips with everything. Ana is going to talk me through reservations and so on this morning.'

'Righto, and you're getting on fine with Carlos?' He asked cautiously.

'Oh, yes. He came by my office the second day I was here, and I commended him on how well the logistics of the hotel were managed. It is the most streamlined I've ever seen. Very labour efficient. And I also like the environmental initiatives – this really is ahead of its time. He's a marvel, isn't he? You are so lucky to have someone of his calibre. We're testing the new menu tomorrow evening, and I'm looking forward to it.

'Now, on the subject of Minister Seoige. I know we are trying to get on his itinerary for the exposure, and that's a worthwhile idea certainly, but I was thinking a bit more than that. It was something Carlos said actually. People are interested in sustainability and are more aware of the impact we are having on our environment, and we here at Castle Dysert are way ahead of that curve. We recycle almost all our waste, composting and so on. The building itself is A rated, despite being very old. We have retrofitted all manner of energy-saving initiatives, we plant indigenous forests and wildflowers for bees and butterflies. Our restaurants specialise in locally sourced, ethically produced food. I think we should capitalise more on that, market ourselves as green and sustainable, emphasising our negative carbon footprint.'

Conor thought about what she said. She was right. And he was impressed at how she seemed to hit the ground running.

'What had you in mind?' he asked.

'Well, I thought we should pitch to host the European summit on climate change next year. Host it here at Castle Dysert. Minister Seoige's visit could be the jumping-off point. We'd need more than him on board, obviously, but it would be a start. If we pulled it off, it would mean international exposure, and the politicians get to look good supporting green business. It will show the world that it is not only cost saving to be environmentally aware but that you do not need to compromise on luxury.'

Conor thought she might be onto something. They'd hosted

conferences before but nothing on the scale of world leaders. But why not?

'OK, I like the idea in theory at least, but it would be a huge undertaking. Well done. How would you envisage we go about it?'

'I've done up a proposal. It's not complete, obviously, but I saw how you worked when you hosted the Special Olympics conference, and it was very impressive. I was here for that, as my brother is a Special Olympian. It was then I decided I wanted to work here,' she said.

Conor's face registered surprise. He'd assumed it was just a lucky coincidence that she'd applied.

'Oh, I didn't realise. So you came to Ireland specifically to work here?' he asked.

'Yes. I would have taken any job until something came up here, but it just worked out. So here is my proposal. There is a steering committee set up that organise such matters – we would need to pitch to them in Strasbourg. But I think you can convince them. We've hosted so many cabinet ministers here, we've been the location for party conferences, you know everyone by now – I have every faith in you, Conor.'

He took the cream folder she proffered and opened it. He nodded his thanks. She was enthusiastic, he'd give her that. He was used to meeting politicians and dignitaries now; it was part of the job. And it would certainly help their bid if the minister was on board. Currently, there was great pressure on businesses to become more environmentally friendly, and Castle Dysert was a great example. Hosting the European conference would really put the castle on the world stage.

A series of pages, each outlining the details of the conference, were there. It was a thorough job.

'OK. Thanks, Olga. I'll have a look and we'll talk again. If you can get the minister here, that would be fantastic. Now, anything else you need help with?' he asked, though he knew the answer.

'No, everything is fine. I spoke to the bar manager, Harry, and asked him to tighten up a little on the uniforms in there. One of two of the bar staff had tattoos showing, and one young woman's hair was hanging down in an unhygienic manner, so he is dealing with it. Chef wants to add a new entrée to the bar menu. He's sourced some local mushrooms and is anxious to see how it goes. He's doing them with shallots and smoked chicken, so that's on the menu this evening. And of course tomorrow night is the big launch of our summer dining menu. It looks very exciting, and I think people will be flocking. I'm trying to get the inside track on who the BiaSpy is these days. They did a review on the Chieftain in Galway last week and absolutely slated them, but I know the bar manager there, so I'm getting all the info I can. Even so, we'll need to ensure that all staff treat every single diner as if they were the BiaSpy.'

Conor was impressed. Bia was the Irish word for food and the BiaSpy was the dread of all eateries in Ireland. An anonymous food reviewer whose reports were syndicated to almost every newspaper and website in the country, the BiaSpy could make or break a place with one swipe of his or her pen, and not one person knew who they were.

'Best keep Carlos on a tight rein so,' Conor joked, but Olga just looked at him blankly. She had no idea what he meant.

She continued. 'Right, one last thing. I'm in negotiations with the supplier of our detergent. I think we can get him to go lower, as we are using so much more than was initially contracted for. And I have moved the staff smoking area from the kitchen door to behind the gardening sheds, out of view and further away from the building. I've checked – it can't be seen from any of the bedrooms. They have to walk a little further, but I've asked Artur to place the garden furniture we are storing out there to make it more comfortable, and he's going to set up a Perspex canopy so they won't have to stand in the rain if they want a cigarette. I think it's a reasonable compromise?'

Conor sat back. She was exactly what he needed. She saw what needed doing and did it without putting everyone's nose out of joint.

'Great. It sounds like you've settled in already. And your apartment is OK?'

'It's beautiful, thanks.'

'Right, well, I'll just take a walk around. I do that every day, just pop in to see everyone. It's a great way to keep communication open. I like to know what's going on with the staff, and we try our best to take care of them. So you know, if someone has a big birthday, or a new baby is born, that sort of thing, we make a bit of a fuss. Any issues, bring them to me if you're unsure, but for now, just keep doing what you're doing.'

She stood up. 'There is one other thing,' she began, less confident now.

'Shoot,' he said.

'Well, the new receptionist… I know you were under pressure because the last person resigned, but is she on a probation period?'

'No, why?' Conor asked, his voice betraying nothing.

'Well, I'm not entirely sure she's suitable. I overheard her speaking to someone on the phone, and she seemed a little overfamiliar for someone who just started here. A more professional approach would be best, I think. And also I think we could get someone with perfect English if we went recruiting again. I spoke to her and asked her how long she'd been in Ireland, and she seemed a little…I don't know…bemused?'

'Yeah, she can be a little bemused sometimes, but she's lived in Ireland for about thirteen years now and is excellent at the job,' Conor said.

'Well, yes, she seems like a nice person, but I –'

'Also, I can't fire her,' he said, supressing a smile.

'Why not?' It was Olga's turn to be bemused.

'Because she's my wife,' Conor said, enjoying the look of horror on his new employee's face.

'Oh, I apologise! I was just…'

Conor patted her shoulder. 'Don't worry about it. Ana just started last week, but she knows everyone and she's universally loved. Make a friend rather than an enemy of her would be my advice.'

'I will… I'm sorry… I…' Olga looked mortified.

'As I said, not a problem. Now, I'll let you get back to it, and I'll take a look at the proposal. Well done.'

CHAPTER 13

*T*hey all dined in the hotel restaurant the first night. Pops looked happy, and Marilyn was absolutely blown away by everything.

Once they'd finished eating, Marko cleared his throat to say something. His odd delicate gold bracelet was visible beneath his shirt-sleeve. It seemed a peculiar thing for a man like him to wear. He was dressed in a suit, an Armani Billie noted when he took off his jacket, and he seemed a bit more relaxed than usual.

'Please, I would like to say something.'

All eyes turned to him.

'I want to say to you all, I am happy we are here. This is a beautiful hotel, and I want everybody in this group to be here as our guest. Donna and I' – he looked at his wife with such a gaze of adoration that Billie was taken aback – 'we want to do this. So food, drinks, whatever you want, please charge it to my room and I will take care of it.'

Pops began to object. 'Marko, you've already paid for our flights and this amazing place. I insist on –'

Marko raised his hand. 'Sol, I thank you, but you see, I...I owe

146

Donna a great deal, more than you can know. And this I will do for her, for her family. Please, you must permit me.'

'Dad, please. We want to.' Donna laid her hand on her father's arm.

'But we can't expect Marko to pay for everything. This place is beautiful, but –' Sol argued.

'Yes, it is, and please, this is a special kind of trip, and let it be on us, OK?' Donna gave her father a pleading look.

'Well, if you're sure... Thank you both very much,' Sol said sincerely.

'Well, I saw a nice crystal chandelier in the airport. I think it was just a thousand bucks or something...' Marilyn joked to lighten the atmosphere.

'Only one, Marilyn, OK?' Marko retorted, and they laughed.

Billie wondered if she was wrong about this guy; he seemed to at least have a tiny sense of humour.

They retired to the bar for a nightcap, and the barman suggested they have Irish coffees. They were delicious. Billie had never had one before, but the combination of the cream and whiskey and coffee was really nice. She limited her drinking to one or two now since the Rob debacle.

They chatted companionably for an hour, and Marilyn explained how she was a Wiccan, the pagan witch organisation. She told them how she planned on going to a sacred place not far from the hotel one of the evenings and having a ceremony of thanksgiving and healing to the gods. Apparently, she had a particular connection to Freya, the goddess of witchcraft practitioners, shamans, love and healing.

'This is a very spiritual country, Billie. People don't dismiss psychic powers out of hand or speak disrespectfully of those who attend ceremonies, either publicly or privately. You're all welcome to join me in the ceremony if you want to.' She asked wide eyed and innocently as if she were inviting them to afternoon tea.

'When in Rome, I guess...' Billie replied with a smile.

Once back in her room, she found she'd had a text from Noah. She'd texted him when she landed in Ireland saying all was well.

Hey, Billie. Good to hear all going well. That place looks amazing. Enjoy it. Noah.

She found herself smiling, glad he'd thought of her.

Without allowing herself too much time to ponder it, she checked the time in LA. It was lunchtime. She video-called him, and he answered on the first ring.

'Well, if it isn't the intrepid traveller! How's the Emerald Isle?' he asked. He sounded happy, she noted with relief.

'Great. It's as beautiful as everyone says, and the people are friendly and the food is delicious, and you'd need an oil well to afford it,' she said with a laugh. 'This is where I live now.' She showed him around the sumptuous bedroom with two huge beds and a lounge area as well as a full-sized bathroom with a sunken marble bath. 'I think this room is bigger than my whole apartment.'

He whistled appreciatively. 'Wow, that looks amazing.'

'It is, and Marko is insisting on paying for it all. And he flew us over first class too.'

'Mean, horrible Marko?' Noah teased gently.

'OK, well, maybe he's not that bad...' Billie conceded.

'So have you decided what you're gonna do about your birth father?' Noah asked. It was another thing she liked about him – he didn't mince words.

'Yeah, we're meeting a guy – he owns this place apparently – and he's going to help us, or tell us how to find someone. I had a talk with my mom earlier...' She paused.

'And...how did that go?' Noah asked, sipping a cold drink and eating a sandwich at his desk as he spoke to her.

'Good... Actually, really good. Like, we said some stuff we never could say before. We were honest, and I apologised for being such an insensitive brat, and she said she was sorry for not being there...' She debated telling him the whole story of her dad, but it was hard on the phone.

'I wish you were here,' she blurted, instantly reddening. Where had that come from? Oh God, she was doing it again! 'Like, I just mean... Like, I...' She was tongue-tied. What on earth had made her say that?

He looked at her and said quietly, 'I wish I were there too, Billie.'

'You do?' she asked, realising she sounded so stupid.

'I do. You've been on my mind since you left.'

'Your crazy dysfunctional junior animator with a knack for getting herself into embarrassing situations? I'd have thought a break from all the drama would be very welcome.' She tried to laugh it off.

He didn't respond but held her gaze. 'I don't want a break from you. I...' He inhaled. 'I miss you, Billie.'

Panic flooded her mind. What did that mean? He missed her as in he liked her as an employee, as a kid who worked for him? Or did it mean what she secretly hoped it meant? She didn't know what to say.

'Look, I'm sorry. I shouldn't have said that...' he began. It was his turn to look uncomfortable. 'You don't need –'

'I...I miss you too,' she interrupted, lowering her gaze.

'Really?' He sounded like he wasn't sure.

'Yeah.' She said.

'Like a buddy or...?' he asked.

'Yes, like a buddy, but I don't know...' She didn't know what to say; this was so out of the blue. Noah was friendly with everyone at work. She didn't dare to think he felt anything special about her.

'I don't miss you like a buddy. I miss you like I miss this amazing girl I think about all the time. There, I've said it.' He exhaled.

Billie watched him on the small screen of her phone. She wished she wasn't so far away from him.

'So...' Suddenly, he didn't seem as together as he normally was.

'So...' she answered, allowing a small smile.

'I'd like to take you out sometime...if you wanted to...' He paused. 'On a date.'

Billie's heart sang, and she realised that she was really happy. For the first time in ages, she felt happy. Noah was asking her out, for real. She knew he wasn't one of those guys who dated loads of girls, and he wasn't on Tinder or any dating apps – Emily had scoured them for a trace of him – so him asking her out was a big deal. He'd risked a lot. In this current corporate world, work-related relationships were fraught with danger, especially when one person was the boss, but he was willing to risk it. The thing was, was she?

She started talking. 'Look, this might be a crazy idea... Actually, it *is* a crazy idea and I can't believe I'm even suggesting it, but...' She lost her nerve. 'Look, forget it. Sorry, I was... Don't worry about it...' She made herself stop talking.

'What? Let me decide if it's crazy or not,' he said softly.

'You could come over here – I mean, to Ireland...if you wanted to. But I guess you can't just drop everything...and it would be so expensive last minute. So look, it was a dumb idea. I'd love to go out with you, though, when I get back, and I can tell you –'

'I'll catch a flight in the morning,' he interrupted.

'What? You'd do that?' She was incredulous.

'If you'd like me to be there, I'd like to be there,' he said simply.

'But work and stuff...' she protested.

'Can wait. I am the boss, in case you'd forgotten, and I never take vacations, so...'

'Amazing! Really? You'll come?'

He chuckled, and a broad smile crinkled up his eyes and melted her heart. 'I will, if you want me there. See you tomorrow, or whenever I land. Oh, can you book me a room? I'll pay for it when I get there. And text me the name of the place.'

Billie bit her lower lip. This was so wonderful. She was over the moon. 'I will, sure... I'll text you the address. Fly to Shannon and just take a cab...or I'll meet you. Let me know.'

'OK. See you soon, Billie. I can't wait.'

'Me neither.'

He hung up and she stared at the phone. Did that just happen? He liked her, he wanted to go on a date, he was coming to Ireland.

Eventually, she fell asleep after gazing out at the starlit Irish sky.

* * *

THE NEXT MORNING, Billie and Donna sat together in the bar, waiting to meet the hotel's owner. Things were much better between them now. After the big conversation and dinner the previous night, there was much less awkwardness. Billie wondered how Donna was really feeling. She had said she was happy to help Billie find her father, but Billie wondered how it was affecting her deep down. It all seemed so much to deal with that she couldn't just blurt out her news. She hadn't even mentioned Noah to anyone, so she felt weird about announcing he was coming to join her. But she'd have to tell them at some point that day.

They waited in silence, just the two of them. Billie had spent so little time alone with her mother that it felt strange.

'We don't have to do this. Like, if it's too much for you…I could do it alone…' Billie began.

Donna turned to face her. 'Sweetheart, like I said, I… Well, I don't know how I feel about seeing him again, but I'm the link between you, and you deserve to meet your father. And y'know what? He deserves to know you.'

'It's only an outside chance we can find him anyway, so maybe this is all hypothetical,' Billie said, half hoping it was true as the moment of actually starting the hunt grew closer.

Soon a tall, powerfully built and very good-looking man entered the bar. He had olive skin and silver hair, cut short at the back and sides but longer at the top.

'Billie and Donna?' he asked as he approached them.

'Yes,' they chorused, Billie feeling a little foolish. The man's eyes were sapphire blue and matched his tie perfectly.

'Conor O'Shea.' He offered his hand for them to shake. 'Your husband mentioned that you were trying to do a bit of genealogy?' He sat down opposite them. 'Can I get you a drink?'

The bartender delivered his coffee without him asking for it, and he said, 'Hold on there a sec, Chloe, let's get these ladies something?'

'Oh, thank you. I'll have an herbal tea, please, any kind is fine.' Donna smiled at the girl, who looked confused.

'A what? Sorry?'

'An herbal tea?' Donna repeated.

'A herbal tea,' Conor explained, pronouncing the 'h'.

'Oh, right so! I just didn't know what an "erbaltee" was!' Chloe laughed.

'And I'll have a soda water with a twist,' Billie said.

'She means a –' Conor started to explain.

'Ah, Conor, come on, I'm not a total eejit. I know what a twist is,' Chloe said, rolling her eyes at the two women, who chuckled.

Conor shrugged good-naturedly as she went off to get the order. 'Now then, ladies, how can I help?'

Donna coloured, and Billie suddenly felt protective. She spoke. 'OK, well, we are looking for someone named Billy Joyce, and he was from Galway County. That's all we know. Oh, and that his family owned a farm. He would have been in Boston working construction in the early nineties, and was deported in 1993 for being an illegal immigrant.'

Billie expected him to say they'd need a lot more information than that, but he sipped his coffee and took out his phone. He winked at them and scrolled for a number, calling someone.

He waited and then said, 'Hi, Donal, how's things?' A pause. 'Ah, sure, grand altogether.' He listened to the man on the other line. 'She's flying it now, thanks be to God, all the treatment over and everything. She's really back to her old self.'

'Come here to me, Donal, you'd never check something for me, would you? There was a Billy Joyce deported out of the States in 1993, back here, illegal. Would Seanie know him?' Conor paused again. 'Righto, no rush. Sure give me a bell back if he does.'

He ended the call, and both women stared at him incredulously.

'So that's a fella I know. His brother Seanie had a kind of thing going there back along, getting lads into the States sort of illegally, if you know what I mean. Don't ask too many questions.'

'And you just happen to know this man?' Donna sounded sceptical.

'Well, I know his brother Donal, actually. He's a building contractor and did a lot of the work here. But yeah, if Seanie knew him, he'll let me know.'

They chatted for a few minutes, and the women mentioned to

Conor how beautiful the hotel was. He was in the middle of telling them about the history of the building when his phone rang.

'Hi, Donal. Oh great, good man yourself.' He paused, and then his face cracked into a smile. 'Sure it is, of course. I never thought of that. They're all at that caper these days, half-made-up loads of them. Well...'

He paused and listened again. 'Yeah, well, there'll be no bother with that. He's dropping by here later in the week actually.' Another pause and Conor laughed. 'I'm sure not. Wouldn't the papers love to hear that? Right so, Donal, thanks very much.' He ended the call.

'Now, I'd love to tell you it's always this easy, but it almost never works out like this. You were in luck. The man you're interested in is very well known here actually, but he goes by his Irish name. He's a minister of the government, your version of a congressman, and like a lot of them, he uses his Irish name. 'Tis a thing nowadays, to seem more patriotic or something.' Conor rolled his eyes. 'Anyway, his name is Liam Seoige. Liam is Irish for William, and Seoige is Irish for Joyce. He might well have changed it so that his brush with American immigration didn't follow him too, mind you!'

Billie found her hand was being squeezed very hard, Donna's nails almost digging into her.

'He spoke Irish as his first language,' Billie heard her mother say.

'Oh, right.' Conor paused. 'Tell me to mind my own business if you like, but is there a reason you want to track him down? Is he family or something? It's just that he's actually due to visit here in a few days' time, so if you wanted to, I could let his people know...'

Conor knew this was not just a story of two families with a shared great-great-grandfather, as would have been the norm.

'He's my father,' Billie said hoarsely.

'I see.' Conor said, waiting for her to explain if she wanted to.

'My mom discovered she was pregnant after he was deported. He...he doesn't know about me. I grew up with another man, my dad, as my father, but he died, and I... Well, I don't know what I want to do actually...'

'It's a big decision for sure. Um...look, he is the Minister for

Communications, Climate Action and Environment, but on top of that, he is being tipped to be the next Taoiseach – that's like the president – so he's a big name in Irish politics. So you could email his office maybe… Or if you wanted, I might be able to get you a private number.'

Conor looked at the two women, who were both shocked.

'Does he have a family?' Donna asked quietly.

'He does. He's married, and I think he has two if not three children, young I think, or young teenagers. I'm not too sure, to be honest with you. But if you Google him, you'll find lots of information on him.'

Billie looked up at Conor. Her father was a well-known person. She had never considered that as a possibility in all her speculation about what he might be like. This brought a whole other dimension to it. Would it destroy him if she showed up out of the blue? Would he wish her to never claim him? Would she destroy his career? Did she want that on her shoulders? She and Noah had talked a lot about that before she left. Was it a good idea? Once contact was made, her life would be irrevocably changed forever, for better or worse.

Conor sensed the hesitation. 'Take your time. It's a big decision.'

Suddenly, Billie felt a connection to this gorgeous Irishman; there was something deeply trustworthy about him.

'What would you do?' She looked directly at him, and he weighed up his answer before speaking.

'I'd have a good long think for myself, because once you open this can of worms, there's no going back.'

'Should I just leave it? Go back home and forget it? I mean, if the guy is going to be the next president of Ireland, he won't want me showing up out of the blue…' Billie said sadly.

Conor exhaled and ran his hand through his hair, thinking. 'Let me tell you a story, Billie.' He paused. 'It's not the same thing as you're facing, but it is about fathers and their kids. Long ago, when I was just a little lad, almost the same age as my boys are now, actually, my father upped and left. No explanation, no note, and we never heard from him again. All sorts of rumours were going around the place, but the truth was, he'd got a local girl pregnant and they had left together. My mam was devastated, as were me and my younger brother. We managed, but it was hard. There was no money, and my mam was kind of stigmatised, as if her husband leaving was somehow her fault. Then she got cancer when I was sixteen, so I looked after her as best I could, and then she died. My brother went off the rails and emigrated to America, taking my girl-friend, the person I'd hoped to marry, with him. So I was left alone. I was crushed, but I carried on because that's the only thing you can do.'

Both women were hanging on every word.

'So I worked and just, I don't know, lived my life, I suppose. And then one day, I met Ana. And after a complicated start, we fell in love and got married and now we have twin boys and all is great. But – and this is the part that I want to tell you about – last year, out of the blue, my father turned up. I was so angry. So much hurt and pain and fury were buried inside me, and I didn't know what to do with it. He was an old man and he was sorry. He brought my very sick brother home from America, who died soon after in my house. I could never have imagined a situation where either of them would be part of my life, but they are blood, and that really is thicker than water. Jamsie, that's my father, loves my kids and they love him.'

He placed his hand over her's. 'There's always room for more love in your life. It doesn't take from the love you had for your dad or anyone else. And maybe it won't work out, maybe any number of things could happen. But I know I don't regret reconnecting with my father, and he was a fairly irresponsible person at best. But he's changed, and he loves me, and I'm happy with how it's all worked out.'

He paused. 'Look, I don't know Liam Seoige at all really, apart from seeing him on TV, and I was at a conference last year where he was the speaker, but he seems like a decent man. There hasn't been any scandals or anything, and to say that about someone in politics is some achievement. He seems to be a family man. He speaks Irish, as you say – sorry for sounding a bit cynical earlier – and he cares a lot about the environment, so I think he's a good man. Whether or not he'll take kindly to meeting a child of his he never knew he had at this point of his career, well, I don't know, but that's not your problem.'

'So you think I should contact him?' she asked.

'Only you can decide that, but I know if it were me, and someone I had a relationship with years ago had my child, even if it was a shock, I'd still want to know about it.'

'Thanks. And thanks for telling me your story,' Billie said, her voice hoarse with emotion.

'The thing is, you know now. You know who he is, so it's up to you. Take some time. You don't need to make contact today. Let the idea percolate in your head for a while, and trust your instincts. You'll know in your gut the right thing to do if you just trust yourself. In a weird twist of fate, he's actually due to visit here this week, so if you wanted to...I don't know...make contact, then I could arrange for you to meet him in private. But as I said, take some time.'

Billie nodded. He was right. She needed time to think.

'So, Donna, I hear we have something in common?'

Donna, who'd not said a word since finding out Billy Joyce was an Irish speaker, looked confused.

'We do?' she asked.

'We're both married to Ukrainians?'

'Oh, yeah, sure. We are. Your wife has been so helpful to us. In fact, everyone we've met here is so friendly.'

'Yeah, well, we make sure Chef keeps them all supplied with lots of treats and plenty of coffee and tea, so they do a great job of keeping people happy, that's for sure. So what's your plan today?'

Donna shrugged. 'We're kind of taking it one day at a time, I guess. We thought the finding process would be a bit more protracted, so I don't know... We are too many for a regular rental car, and to be honest, I don't know how we'd fare driving on such little roads, especially in a big vehicle, but it would be neat to see some of the sights. The brochures in the lobby show some amazing places right near here. Is there maybe a bus we could take, or a train?'

Conor stood up and looked outside. The ocean was that lovely colour it got in the spring, azure and turquoise fading to the horizon of dark blue, and the sky was cloudless apart for a few small puffy ones scudding across the sky. The flowers were all in bloom now, the wild and the culti-vated, and it was hard to imagine a more perfect place on earth.

'Tell you what.' He turned. 'I fancy a bit of a skite myself. I was a tour driver for a long time before taking this place on, and we have a nice little minibus here. How about I take you all out for the day, show you the treasures of the Wild Atlantic Way?'

Billie and Donna couldn't believe his kind offer.

'Really? That would be so awesome. But aren't you busy?' Billie asked.

'Yerra, I am and I'm not. In fact, you know what? I'll spring my two lads out of school as well, give them a day out. They can come with us.'

'Oh my, that is so kind of you, Conor! Please just charge whatever it costs to our room.' Donna stood up. 'Should we go now? I'll gather the rest of our group.'

'No rush,' Conor said. 'Now, I'll swing by the school and pick the boys up. One of my lads, Artie – Joe is the other one, and they're iden-tical, so you probably won't tell them apart – has been having a tough old time lately. Some kid is bullying him. So he could use a break. And this is on me, no charge. You can buy the boys an ice cream, and we'll call it quits.'

'But we can't expect you to –' Donna protested.

'You're not expecting, I'm offering. So meet me outside in about' – he checked his watch – 'forty minutes, OK?'

'OK, if you're sure. Thanks, Conor,' Billie said, then ran off to tell Pops and Marilyn about the exciting day ahead. But Donna lagged back.

'Thank you for finding him, and for sharing your story with Billie. She's a great girl, and she's had some tough stuff to deal with, and I just want this to work out for her.'

'And you?' Conor asked. 'How do you feel about it?'

Donna looked a little taken aback. It was a personal question, but he'd found directness was not as frightening as people made out. Either people opened up or they didn't.

She paused and inhaled, as if gathering strength from the breath. 'Well, I guess I'm terrified, embarrassed and guilty. And the fact that he's a prominent person makes it more complicated. But funnily enough, I'm not surprised, as he was a very special kind of guy. Maybe I should have told him he was a father. But mainly I'm worried for Billie. What if he rejects her?'

'It must be hard. I can't imagine how awkward it must feel for you. I think you're very brave. Most people would chicken out. Like, who wants to stand on the doorstep of someone you slept with years ago and say, "Hi, I'm back."' Conor gave a her a reassuring smile. He guessed they were around the same generation, and he couldn't imagine anything worse. The past was best left there, undisturbed.

'Yeah, right. And how about, "Hi, I'm back, and here's the kid I had but never told you about."'

Conor put his arm around her as they strolled out to the lobby and gave her a quick squeeze. 'I think it will be grand. I do. Like, he might be shocked – I know I would be – but that doesn't mean he'll reject her out of hand. You know what I'd do, though?'

'What?' Donna asked eagerly.

'Email him first. Not Billie – you. I mean you were the person he knew. Tell him that you're here and that Billie wants to meet him. At least that way you're not catching him on the hop. You never know how people will react when they get a fright. He might say or do something he didn't mean. At least if he gets a bit of notice, he'll have some time to process it. Men aren't like you ladies, able to react to stuff quickly. We need a little time. I do, anyway. Like Ana will tell me something, and I need time to mull it over – it's just how I am. If I were in the same position as this Billy, I think I'd prefer advance warning rather than someone just showing up, you know?'

'That's a good idea. Nobody likes being ambushed, right?' Donna agreed. 'I'd better check with Billie though. She may not want...'

'It's not my business, but I will say this. This is as much about you as your daughter. You shouldn't totally disregard your needs in this too. I know you feel for her, of course you do, but this was your relationship, he was your boyfriend all those years ago, you do get a say, you know? You did the best thing you could do at the time, so maybe it's time to stop beating yourself up about it.'

Donna smiled. 'You're a very perceptive man, Conor.'

He laughed. 'Tell my wife that. Last week, I asked one of her friends when her baby was due, and it turns out the child is three weeks old.'

They both laughed.

'Now, I'll be back by ten thirty, so I'll see you then.'

Donna watched as he walked out of the lobby, stopping by reception to speak to his wife and give her a kiss on the cheek. Ana was a lucky woman.

CHAPTER 14

The green fields, each divided by tiny walls without any mortar to hold them together, fascinated them. Conor showed them the Cliffs of Moher, the tallest cliffs in Europe, and they marvelled at the way the Atlantic pounded the cliff face. Seabirds circled, cawing loudly. On the top of the cliffs was an old castle. It was idyllic.

He told them a funny story about the guy who built the castle. His name was Cornelius O'Brien, and apparently he had an eye for the ladies, despite being married. The story went that he built this fabulous new castle and took a young lady, not his wife, out there to show off his latest building. Word got to his wife that he was misbehaving, despite her warnings after the last time, so she took her soldiers and followed poor old Cornelius out to the castle on top of the cliff. She found him in a compromising position and took her revenge as she promised she would. Her soldiers did her bidding and threw him into the crashing surf below, and the castle forever more was known as 'the last erection of Cornelius O'Brien'.

As they travelled all morning along bouncy small roads, he told them stories about the ancient peoples who lived on this mysterious piece of land called the Burren. He showed them dolmens and stone structures thousands of years old. The landscape was not what they expected. It was 100 square miles of limestone, but it wasn't grey and bleak as Billie had imagined when Conor first mentioned it, because in between each of the rocks were the most incredible little flowers. He explained that Artic, alpine and Mediterranean flowers grew in the grikes because of the unusual soil composition. They saw trees that grew horizontally due to the unrelenting wind off the ocean.

They stopped at a huge stone structure called the Poulnabrone dolmen, which consisted of three upright stones holding up a large flat one. Conor explained that in Irish, Poll na mBrón means 'the hole of sadness,' and that when it was excavated, the bodies of over fifty people were found to be buried there. It seemed the Irish knew very little about the people who left these stone monuments, for two reasons. Firstly, according to Conor, there was a gap in the archaeology of some 600 years between 300 CE and 300 BCE, when there appeared to be no archaeological evidence to support a hypothesis of who lived in Ireland then. And secondly, because whoever they were, they were not a literate culture.

'Is that why we know more about the Greeks and the Romans than the Irish?' Donna asked, fascinated.

'Exactly,' Conor confirmed. 'Theirs was a written tradition. As well as that, they built large monuments, whereas the Aboriginal Irish, as they are referred to, tended not to. We do have some megalithic structures, literally big stone, in places like Newgrange and of course the dolmens that you see around you here, but they don't tell us as much as we would like. We traded for sure with other civilisations, but it wasn't until the invasion of the Vikings in the ninth century that we see a huge change in the demographic of the country.'

Billie wished Conor had taught her history; he made it so interesting and relevant. He was also gorgeous, this Irish man, standing beside an incredible tomb, built thousands of years ago, telling them about his culture. There was something very attractive about the whole thing.

'Is there an Irish language name for everything?' Marilyn asked, noting the bilingual signs explaining the archaeological significance of the site.

'Yes, there is. Most of our funny-sounding place names come about after a direct translation. When the colonisation of Ireland took place and the British sought to totally subjugate this country, one of the first things to be outlawed was our language. They sent over teams of people to change the place names from Irish to English, but they did it phonetically rather than on meaning. All Irish place names make sense if you translate them back to the original language. For example, the prefixes – bally means baile, which is town, kil means church, as in Kilkenny, cloch is a stone, as in Cloughjordan, dun or don is a fort, like Donegal.'

'Wow, I never knew that.' Marilyn was intrigued.

'And the Irish language is linked to ancient languages too, Latin and Sanskrit, for example. Take the word "father" – in Latin it's *pater*, in Sanskrit, *pitar*, and in Irish, *athair*. Or the word for "king". In Latin, *rex*, in Sanskrit, *raj*, and in Irish, *rí*. So we are more connected to the broader world through antiquity than we might think.'

'Is there anything you don't know, Conor?' Sol joked.

'Oh, I'm being selective, Sol, believe me. My wife could keep you here all day with the lists of things I'm clueless about. Last week, she told me to go upstairs and find a mauve scarf. I've no idea about that! I understand red and green, but peach and lilac and taupe? Are they trying to bamboozle us?'

The group laughed, and the men agreed that he was right.

'My Sanskrit name is Achara,' Marilyn told him.

'Well, in Irish, "a chara" is an endearment – it means "my friend". We'd start letters with "a chara",' Conor told her.

Marilyn was delighted. She nearly wept for joy and lay down face first on the large flat stone, murmuring some incantation or something.

Billie noticed Conor didn't seem remotely surprised. She guessed he'd seen it all in the years he was doing this job.

As Pops helped Marilyn down, she looked up at him, and Billie heard her say, 'Can you feel it, Sol, the tremors of the earth, of the mother? This is an amazing country. Thank you so much for bringing me here.'

Pops put his arm around her and whispered something Billie couldn't hear into her ear, which made her turn and kiss him fully on the mouth. Marilyn couldn't give a hoot about the people watching, and Billie noticed with surprise how her grandfather responded. She would have thought he'd have been embarrassed at such a public display of affection, but he wasn't. Ireland really was an incredible place.

As she walked across the uneven ground, her phone beeped. *Just landed in JFK. Couldn't get direct, but taking off in an hour. See you later. You still sure about this?* Noah ended with a funny emoji and a *#amireallydoingthisihopeso* hashtag. She giggled. They'd had a conversation about how his texts were quite formal, and so he was joking by adding in the hashtag and emoji.

I'm still sure if you are. B x

She'd never put a kiss on a text to him before, and she pressed send quickly before she deleted it.

A couple of seconds later it beeped again. *Xxx* was all it said.

She would tell them over lunch.

Joe and Artie, delighted to be taking an illicit day off school, were entertaining the visitors with explanations of how the Irish national sport of hurling was played. They even had Pops and Marko against Marilyn and Billie hitting the small hard ball called a sliotar with the stick they called a hurley. It seemed the pair never went anywhere without their sticks and a ball.

'Has this sport been played for long?' Marilyn asked the boys.

Their little Irish accents charmed the family, and they all tried to keep straight faces as the boys explained their passion so earnestly.

'Oh, ages and ages, like I mean ages ago before cars or houses or anything. Back in the time of Fionn mac Cumhaill, they were playing hurling,' Joe began.

'Even before history started. When everyone spoke Irish,' Artie interjected.

'Yeah, we had to change it 'cause of all the tourists. Like they can't speak Irish like we can, so they wouldn't have a clue what was going on if we were talking in Irish all the time, so we talk in English,' Joe explained.

'But the English made us too,' Artie clarified.

'Yeah, they were always making us do things long ago, but we got rid of them after loads of wars and stuff, and now we're our own country and it's way better. And we always beat them at rugby.'

'We can't beat them at soccer though,' Artie said.

'Ah, well, in fairness, they invented that. Like, imagine if another country started playing hurling and then we couldn't beat them. Sure that'd be a disaster.'

Marko and Billie shared a smile. This pair were like a comedy duo.

'But Germany beat them last Friday night.' Artie was always the one to stick with the facts; it was clear Joe was the showman.

Conor stood back and let the lads entertain the small group.

'Yeah, but anyway, we were talking about hurling,' Joe continued, warming to his theme. 'So ages and ages ago, there was a king up in the north somewhere, I don't know exactly, and anyway, everything has different names now. But anyway, there was this king called Conor Mac Nessa, same as my dad – well, the Conor bit anyway – and he had his kingdom in a place called Emain Macha.'

Joe stopped naturally, and Artie took up the story. 'This was in the time of mythology, you know? Like Oisín and Niamh and Tír na nÓg and all of that.' He registered their blank faces.

'Oh, those are all stories from long ago about different magical things. All Irish people know them. You could get a book, bring it home to any kids you know – they are great.'

Suddenly, to their total amazement, Artie broke into fluent Ukrainian and spoke to Marko.

Marko nodded and explained. 'He's saying that some Ukrainian folk tales are very like the Irish ones. He was giving me some examples.'

Not to be outdone, Joe then told Marko something in Ukrainian.

Conor interrupted. 'Marko speaks English, lads, so we'll carry on or we'll never get our lunch.' Conor gently brought them back to their story.

'Right, OK,' Artie continued. 'So anyway, this king was having a big feast and everyone was going. He used to have fantastic parties with loads of food and drinks and games and everything, and this black-smith, a fella called Culann who made spears and stuff, was going to the party, so he brought Setanta, a brilliant hurler, with him. Setanta was only a boy, but he was after beating a hundred and fifty other lads at hurling by then and so he was getting kind of famous.'

Without missing a beat Joe continued. 'And anyway, on the way up to the castle gates, didn't the blacksmith's wolfhound jump at Setanta and he got a desperate fright, so he pucked the sliotar – that's the ball you use for hurling, and to puck it is to hit it really far – and he was so accurate, the ball went down the wolfhound's throat and killed him stone dead.'

The boys had everyone's undivided attention as their green eyes lit up with excitement at the story.

'So' – Artie took it up again – 'the blacksmith was so sad about his poor dog, and Setanta felt very bad about it, so he said that he'd be the hound, or Cú in Irish, for the blacksmith until he trained another one. So that's what he did.'

'And that's the story of how Setanta became Cúchulainn, and he went on to be the greatest warrior that ever lived. He's famous, and all boys and girls in Ireland want to be great hurlers like him.'

To the delighted bemusement of the group, the boys delivered the last line in chorus. It wasn't rehearsed, but Conor explained as they ran off that they did that all the time.

'They are adorable. You and your wife must be so proud of them,' Marilyn said as they strolled along, a gentle breeze rustling her long grey hair.

'We are,' Conor agreed.

'Do you have other children?' she asked.

'No, just the twins.'

'Well, they are delightful. And they've been here before, you know,'

Marilyn said as Sol took her hand. 'They are old souls, especially Artie. He's a sensitive boy.'

Conor nodded in agreement with her.

Sol stopped to take some photos, and Marilyn fell into step beside Billie. The air was heavy with the sweet perfume of the canary-yellow gorse with its sharp dark-green spikey leaves.

'So what delicious secret are you hiding?' Marilyn murmured.

Billie looked guilty.

'It's OK. You don't need to tell me.' Marilyn winked.

Billie looked around. Pops was up on a small wall, focusing his camera on the landscape far below. Uneven little fields, colourful bushes and clumps of flowers, and bits of small ruined stone buildings all fell away down a hill to small dark cliffs. The water was covered in white surf – what Joe and Artie called white horses – and large seabirds circled everywhere.

A sign on a gate said 'Beware of the Bull', and Marilyn chuckled. 'Ain't that good advice for life!'

Billie laughed. 'I...I have a friend... Well, he's my boss, actually, and well, I've been telling him about everything...' Billie felt her face heat up.

Marilyn just waited.

'Well, he texted me to see how things were going, and I...well...I asked him to come over,' she finished.

'Over where?' Marilyn asked.

'Here...here to Ireland. He's in the air now actually.'

Marilyn let out a slow whistle. 'A friend, is he?' She nudged Billie playfully.

'Well, I thought it was – I mean, I like him, but I have a history of saying dumb things to guys I work with, and Noah, well, he's not like other guys, he's...'

'Go on, what's he like?' Marilyn linked her arm with Billie's.

'He's really nice, and he's kind and funny, and he... I know this sounds crazy, but he's wise or something, I don't know. He's been really good to me, helping me to get through all this stuff. He's got a way of seeing things clearly, y'know?'

Billie turned to face Marilyn. 'I'm dreading telling them. I'm afraid Pops will think I'm hooking up with loads of random guys, and I don't know if I'm ready for him to meet Marko and Mom, and I'm just...'

Marilyn placed her arm around Billie. 'Your pops wants you to be happy, that's all he cares about, and if he saw you with some guy like this Noah you describe, he would be so delighted for you. And as for your mom and Marko, they are the same. They are all worried about you, Billie, scared for you, and they all just want it to work out. So anyone or anything that makes that process easier would be welcomed with open arms. You've nothing to worry about.'

'I guess,' Billie said doubtfully.

'So is he hot?' Marilyn asked with a grin. 'Come on kid, spill!'

Billie laughed. 'Yes, he's hot. Well, I think he is, but not in the hipster way so many guys are now. He looks like someone you could take home to your grandma.'

'Well, this grandma has pretty racy tastes, so I'll be waiting to see if he's the eye candy you say he is!' Marilyn teased, and Billie found she now wasn't so nervous about telling everyone. Noah was easy to talk to; they'd like him.

They caught up to the rest of the group, which had stopped in the middle of a cluster of ruined houses, the tiny stone cottages gone back to nature, the roofs completely gone. Conor explained about how in five years, between 1845 and 1850, almost a million people died of starvation and another million emigrated, largely to the United States.

'Where they were welcomed, despite having nothing,' Pops said ominously.

'Indeed they were,' Conor agreed. 'And now they say there's forty million people in the US claiming Irish heritage. These houses would have been home to very large families, and survival was touch and go all the time, but when the blight hit the potato crop, the people starved. They couldn't pay the rent, and the landlords came and burned the thatched roofs and sometimes took a battering ram to the houses, leaving the people on the side of the road. The ones that emigrated were the lucky ones – they got away. Many more died in workhouses, or just in the fields where they lay, exhausted from it all.'

Billie and her mother exchanged a glance, and Conor noticed their looks of trepidation as they both looked surreptitiously at Sol.

'So you would think the Irish of all people would understand, would offer the hand of friendship to others in a similar situation, wouldn't you?'

Conor turned to face him. 'What do you mean, Sol?' he asked.

'Dad…' Donna began, but Conor interrupted.

'It's fine. I'm interested. What's on your mind, Sol?' He sent the boys off to play hurling in the adjacent field.

'During the Holocaust, much less than a hundred years ago, Jews were desperate to get out of Germany. They would have gone anywhere, and worked, and contributed to the society they lived in.' Sol's voice was quiet, but they could hear the bitterness there still.

'My family, we were German, we had a business, and my father and grandfather did a lot of trade with a company here in Ireland, owned by a Catholic family in Dublin. They became good friends. The Irish family visited us, and my parents went to visit them one time. We had photos of them having fun together sometime in the late twenties, I think. When the Nuremberg Laws were enacted, my parents were quick. They saw how it was going to go with Hitler and the Nazis, so they started trying to find ways to get us out. They tried everywhere to get a visa, any embassy they could get to. My father stood in line after line. He got picked up by the Nazis one day and was beaten up. After that, he redoubled his efforts to get us out. He never slept, he hardly ate – he was desperate. They took our business, they took our apartment. My father was a proud man. He didn't want to beg, but he had no choice. He kept telling my mother that his friend in Dublin would hear about what was going on and would offer to help, any day now, but no message came. He eventually contacted them. These people were not just business contacts – no, they were good friends. Christmas cards, presents for the kids, visits. So my father put his pride in his pocket and begged his friend for help. Asked him to find a way to sponsor our family into Ireland. Ireland was neutral. They could have taken us, they could have taken so many, but only a handful actually were allowed to come. My father's friend refused his pleas, essentially consigning us to the gas chambers. We got out, just in time, to China. But only my father and mother and their children. They had to leave everyone else behind – grandparents, aunts, uncles, cousins, the people who worked for us, friends, everyone. We fled to a country with which we had no affiliation, and because of the Chinese, and no thanks to this country, my parents, my siblings and I lived to tell the tale.'

Conor could sense the others were hearing this for the first time. Billie linked her arm with Sol's, and Donna looked stricken.

'Dad, I had no idea… I thought it was just a general thing you had about the Irish, not that it was so personal.'

'I don't like talking about it, honey. It upset my parents so much. They felt so let down… It made them see the world differently. They didn't make friends in the States, they kept to themselves, they didn't trust anyone… It was how they were.'

'I'm sorry, Dad,' she said, holding his hand.

He shrugged. 'It is what it is.'

'You are a hundred percent correct, Sol,' Conor admitted. 'I'm sorry to say. It is a great stain on our history that at the time when we could have helped people in dire need, we didn't. It's not an excuse, there is none, but by way of an explanation, I will say this. The Ireland you see now, the way we are, is nothing like the way we were. Ireland at that time was controlled by the Catholic Church – they honestly had the same power as law enforcement. You need only see the way they treated our own people, women and children particularly, with absolutely no checks at all. There has always been inherent mistrust of Jews by Catholics, and there were pogroms in Limerick in 1904, all led and encouraged by Catholic clergy. The hierarchy held such a grip that people were afraid to go against them. They were so indoctrinated, they wouldn't have wanted to either. On top of that, the state, which was heavily influenced by the Church, didn't encourage immigration either. As I said, I'm not excusing it – it is inexcusable – but that's why it happened.'

Conor wondered if giving more information would cause further hurt, but he decided to carry on. Sol looked like a man who would want the full story.

'There was an Irish legation in Berlin, and the head of that mission, a man called Leo McCauley, even went so far as to say, back in 1933, that as far as he was concerned, the Jews had brought the trouble they were experiencing at the hands of the National Socialists on themselves.'

Conor noted the other man's look of horror but felt he had a duty to tell him the truth, however badly it reflected on his own country.

'There was definite anti-Semitism here. There were public protests against admitting Jews, there was a military organisation called the Blueshirts, which had actually fought for Franco, would you believe, and they were backed by a group called the Irish Christian Front, who warned constantly of alien penetration of Irish industries. There was even a comment in *The Irish Catholic* newspaper in 1937 that Hitler had many admirers among Irish Catholics.'

Sol nodded.

'So the fact that one individual didn't help your family isn't that surprising. It was the culture of the country, I'm sorry to say.'

The old man gazed over the landscape, a picture-perfect postcard scene, as Marilyn held his hand. 'Seems hard to believe, doesn't it? That a whole country could be so heartless. Especially one as beautiful as this. It's at odds somehow, don't you think?'

Conor agreed. 'Yes, it is. But then it's hard to imagine Germany under National Socialism, or Ukraine in the grip of Stalin. But tyrants and their organisations are powerful, and people live in terror of falling foul of them. The Catholic Church wielded such power here, it's hard to describe. They effectively imprisoned girls who became pregnant outside of marriage, and sold their children. The men got away scot-free, by the way. Priests could destroy people's livelihoods, their reputation, by denouncing them from the altar. They interfered in marriages, refused to allow birth control though people were financially in ruins, they oversaw what was taught in schools, they ran the hospitals – the Church controlled every aspect of Irish life, from the cradle to the grave.'

'And now? What is the situation today?' Marko asked, hanging on Conor's every word.

'Now, well, we are still untangling it all. If you pick up any newspaper in Ireland, you'll read about excavations of the graveyards of these so-called mother-and-baby homes, or a trial of a paedophile priest. Ireland is becoming more secular, no doubt about that, and the priesthood is getting older and older with very few new recruits. But there are still people going to mass on a Sunday and the Church is still involved in schools, though to a lesser extent. We have some way to go yet in terms of separating church and state – they are fused together at the very core of our democracy – but we are working on it. So as I said, it's a slow process, but it is happening.'

Sol smiled and patted Conor on the shoulder. 'Thanks for your honesty, Conor. I appreciate it. And it does go some way to explaining why they wouldn't help. I don't think my father understood the context, or maybe he did. Who knows? He never spoke of his friend again, apart from saying that he wouldn't help. I guess if the control of the Church here was similar to the control Hitler had in Germany, people would have been endangering themselves by helping Jews.'

'Well, perhaps the Church wasn't that extreme, though the treatment of women and children was horrific, but they would have controlled a lot of life. They had such a strong hand in legislation. After centuries of rebellion, the Irish Free State came into being in 1921, but while it was built on very lofty ideals, the truth was, they hadn't a shilling. The British had paid for everything as the colonisers, so schools, hospitals and all the rest were now the responsibility of the new state. The Catholic Church, well able to afford to run such institutions, used their money and influence to not just bail out the government but to push forward their own agenda. They were big on morality and the lack thereof as they saw it, so basically in return for their money and organisational skills in the new state, they got to call the shots on a lot of things. We're dealing with it still. For example, in 1935 there was an act of parliament called the Public Dance Halls Act, which essentially outlawed anyone but the Church running dances. Dance halls were then monitored by priests, and all proceeds given to the clergy. Of course, these were temperance halls, no drink, as that only led to depravity.'

They all laughed, enthralled by his adept storytelling.

'Their tentacles were deep in every aspect of Irish life, and if that family you mentioned were in business...'

'They had a jewellery store,' Sol interjected.

'Yes, well, if it got out that they were helping Jews, it could certainly have damaged their reputation. It's horrible but true.' Conor sighed. 'Not all of our history is glorious, I'm afraid.'

Marko spoke up. 'I don't think there is a country on earth that can look at their past and say there were no dark days, Conor. Admitting it, moving past it, that is what is important for a nation. What the Russians did, for example, to their own people under Stalin was so barbaric, the treatment of black people in America, slavery, colonisation... Every country has a story.'

'I suppose you're right, Marko, but this never sat well with me, to be honest. The Second World War was never called a war here – we called it the Emergency. My father remembers it from when he was a child, rationing and all of that, before I was born. All we could see was how bad it was for England, and we were obsessed with staying out of it. We were definitely neutral on the side of the Allies, but still, helping England was seen as kind of sleeping with the enemy. But we should have seen the bigger picture, we should have been more compassionate, and we just weren't, and that's all there is to it.'

'Did your family make any contact with the Irish family after the war, Sol?' Marko asked.

'No, not to my knowledge, anyway. I think they felt let down, so...'

'I wonder if they are still trading?' Donna mused.

'What was it called?' Conor asked.

'O'Doherty's. Their place was on Henry Street in Dublin, I believe. They were gold merchants. That's what my father said, anyway.'

Conor thought for a moment. 'I'm not much of a shopper, and I'm not in Dublin much these days, but I'm trying to think... Hang on.' He pulled out his phone and scrolled for a number.

As he waited for it to ring, he said, 'A friend of mine does walking tours in Dublin – she'll know.'

'Hi, Elaine, how are you?' He paused. 'Great, you know yourself. Not missing the road at all.' He chuckled and waited as she responded. 'Listen, I've a group with me now, staying at the castle. Do you know, is there a jewellery shop on Henry Street called O'Doherty's?'

He listened again. 'There is? Great. Thanks, Elaine, and be sure to pop in for a coffee when you're passing.' He paused again. 'Righto, thanks. Take care.'

'It's still there.' Conor smiled. 'One of the oldest shops in Dublin, according to my friend.'

'Interesting,' Sol said, and they walked on.

They enjoyed lunch in a café beside a perfume place. Marilyn amused them all with her voracious appetite. She was a vegetarian, but she managed to polish off two slices of quiche, a portion of sweet potato fries and a baked potato. Once she'd finished that, she ordered three desserts for them to share: apple crumble, a chocolate cheesecake to die for and an odd-looking thing called bread-and-butter pudding that Billie had never had before. It was made with layers of bread with raisins and sultanas baked in a kind of custard and served with cream. It was incredibly good. The entire meal was delicious. Everything in Ireland tasted so rich and creamy, Billie was sure she was going to go home ten pounds heavier.

As they sat and lingered over coffee, chatting about the beauty and sadness of the country, Billie decided to make her announcement. 'So, guys, um… I have a friend…well, he's my boss actually. Noah Coulson is his name. And we've been, well, friendly for a while, and he knows all about the situation with my biological father and all of that. And, well, he texted yesterday to see how it was all going, and I… Well, he's on the way. He's going to join us, if that's OK?'

'Great!' Donna exclaimed immediately. 'He must really like you, Billie, if he's dropping everything to come to Ireland?'

'I…I don't know, it's early days. We're not… Like, we've never been… Well, we're just friends but we'll see.' Billie shrugged, glad she'd got this over with.

'If it makes you happy, then we are happy.' Pops laid his age-spotted hand on hers.

After lunch, they wandered around the picturesque village. The perfumery made scents using all of the flowers of the Burren, and Marko bought a bottle each for Donna, Billie and Marilyn.

Billie realised she'd never had an actual conversation with Marko. He was quiet and tended to stay in the background a lot, and her resentment of him meant she avoided his company. But as she looked back, she recalled the many kindnesses he'd shown her, even when she was so furious with both him and her mother, and decided she'd make an effort with the guy.

'Thanks, Marko, that smells amazing,' she said, spraying a little on her wrists and sniffing it appreciatively.

He gave a small smile and nodded in acknowledgement. 'You're welcome, Billie.'

As they strolled over to a really old church that had all kinds of carvings on the walls, Billie noticed Pops and Marilyn in deep conversation. She wondered what it was about but allowed them their privacy. Conor was explaining to Donna about the big crosses carved from stone, and Billie found herself alone with Marko.

'It's lovely here, isn't it?' she began as they sat on a mossy wall in the weak sunshine. Behind them in a little field, a donkey and her foal happily munched the lush green grass.

'Yes, very beautiful.'

'Thank you for paying for everything. I appreciate it.'

'Of course, it's no problem. I'm happy to help if I can.'

'Do you think I should contact him, my father?' She hadn't intended to ask him, but it kind of popped out.

He turned to face her, and as he did, she noticed for the first time a livid scar that peeped out just above his shirt collar.

His dark eyes met hers, and there was a moment of awkward silence. She regretted asking him such a question; she'd barely said two words to the man since she met him and then she launched into a really deep personal question. What was she thinking? She felt herself blush.

'I think you should. I know if I had a daughter, I would want to know about it. And also, if it doesn't work out, at least now you know. If you stop now, you will spend your life wondering.'

'Do you have family?' she asked, emboldened by his candour.

He shook his head. 'No. I came to America alone. I lived in Pripyat, the city that was abandoned after the Chernobyl explosion in 1986. I worked at the power station. My sister, Tetyana, also worked there, but she died. Acute radiation sickness. Luckily for me, I was at a rock concert in Kiev with some friends the night it happened.'

'I'm sorry,' Billie said, and he nodded.

'My father was killed in an accident when I was a child, and my mother, well...she wasn't... Let's just say she loved vodka much more than me or Tetyana. I don't know what happened to her. I assume she's dead.'

'How old was your sister when she died?'

'Twenty-five, two years older than me.' It was clear from the way he spoke that he still missed her. 'When she died, I had no reason to stay in Ukraine. Pripyat was evacuated, I had nobody there, so I went to America.'

'Is that her bracelet?' she asked suddenly, pointing to the delicate gold piece on his wrist.

He nodded. 'She asked me to take it to the jewellery shop in Kiev to have the clasp repaired. It is all I have of her. We were not allowed back after the explosion, too much radiation. It would have been too dangerous.'

Billie realised Marko was not a small talk kind of man. But big stuff didn't make him uncomfortable. It was an interesting combination in a person.

'And how did you get that scar?' she asked, pointing to his neck.

He ran his long fingers over the scar. Eventually he spoke. 'When I first arrived, I started up a security business, and some people felt it was not right that a foreign man would do that. I undercut them, offering proper security for nightclubs, bars, that sort of thing. What my, shall we say, competitors were offering was a protection racket.

They tried to convince me to close down. I didn't want to.' He shrugged. 'We fought about it.'

'Well, obviously you won.' Billie said with a chuckle.

'Yes, well. I grew up in the USSR, I did my military service, so that teaches you a thing or two about defence. Those people were just punks, all talk but soft underneath. Maybe their grandfathers were tough men, but these guys, raised in America, silver spoons in their mouths... But I don't do that kind of security now, and I don't mix with that sort of person.'

Billie looked up and realised her mother had been watching her and Marko talking, and she caught the look of love on Donna's face.

'Could I take a picture?' Donna asked tentatively.

'Sure.' Billie smiled and moved a little closer to Marko. He put his arm around her shoulder, and Donna took the picture. As she did, they both jumped – the donkey had pushed her head between them and let out a loud bray. Donna captured the moment perfectly.

CHAPTER 15

*B*illie got out of the taxi at Shannon trying not to betray the fact that she was a bag of nerves. Noah had texted to say his flight was landing at 7 p.m., and she decided to meet him. Her mother and Pops had offered to go with her, but she left them having dinner in the bar and took the twenty-minute cab ride alone. She was glad he was here – of course she was – but she was scared too. It was a lot of pressure for what was, in reality, a first date, and she hoped it didn't scare him off.

Pops seemed better, like telling his story had unburdened him, and Billie was glad. No wonder he held such a grudge. She was also glad he had Marilyn to share his life with. Pops loved her and her mom – she never doubted it for a second – but his life must have been lonely all those years. Now, whenever she saw him and Marilyn, they were talking animatedly or holding hands or even just sharing a glance of understanding. They got each other in a way that the world could never have imagined. They were nothing alike, but something clicked and it just worked.

As she stood in the tiny arrivals hall and read from the board that the flight from JFK had landed, she hoped she and Noah would have that too.

People started trickling out: tired-looking families rushing into the arms of those waiting, harassed-looking businesspeople, frantically fiddling with cell phones, and a few groups of college types on the holiday of a lifetime. She felt herself tear up as she watched a young couple emerge, him pushing their trolley laden with a stroller and other baby paraphernalia while she held her baby in her arms.

Someone was videoing it on a phone, and the man pushing the trolley, with a broad Irish accent, was telling his infant daughter to 'say hello to Nana'. His partner, whom Billie was sure was American, handed the child over tentatively as the man put his arm around her shoulders. The grandmother just gazed in wonder at her little granddaughter, tears flowing unchecked down her age-worn face. They were home.

So transfixed was Billie by the scene that she didn't notice Noah.

'So this is Ireland, huh?' he said to grab her attention, and she spun around.

'Oh, hi! You're here! It's great to see you.' Her eyes never left his.

'It's great to see you too.' He smiled, and she loved how it crinkled his eyes.

'I took a cab…so I guess we can just get another one outside. It's not far…' She felt so happy but also awkward. Should she hug him? Or kiss him? Or shake his hand?

'Great. I'm starving,' he said.

'OK. Well, the food in the hotel is amazing. I think the restaurant might have stopped serving, but we could get room service…' She stopped and felt her face flush.

'I mean you could…get room service in your room…' Oh no, that sounded even more dorky.

'The geography doesn't matter to me,' he said, pulling his suitcase behind him. 'I'm just happy to be here.'

'Oh, good. It's really lovely, and the history and the scenery…' She knew she was babbling and wished she could stop. Why couldn't she be all cool and ironic like women were in movies? Instead, she was acting like a fourteen-year-old at her first party.

They stood outside the terminal, waiting for a cab, the low sun setting in the sky. Close but not touching.

'I can't believe it's nearly eight o'clock and it's not dark,' he said.

'Yeah, Ireland is really far north, so in the summertime, apparently it stays light until ten thirty or eleven at night, and then it only stays dark for a couple of hours.' She was glad to have something sensible to say.

Within a few minutes, a taxi pulled into the rank and Noah lifted his suitcase into the trunk. Billie watched him. He had a normal build, she guessed, not super thin like all the vegan yogis she knew, but not heavy either, and about five ten. His dark hair was curly, and he kept it short. He was clean-shaven and wore a polo shirt with no logo and jeans. He was Mr Average she guessed, but there was something so attractive about him that when he smiled at her, her stomach flipped.

'Are ye here on holidays?' the young taxi driver asked as he pulled away from the kerb with alarming speed. His seat was so far back, the wheel was a full arm stretch away, and he had his seat reclined to a ridiculous angle. Noah made a funny face of mock terror, and she giggled. The driver had a tiny head and wore a baseball cap low over his eyes.

'Ah yeah, from the States,' Billie said.

'Jays, I'd love to go to America, to Las Vegas, y'know? Do ye know where that is? Out on the far side of America, not near New York or anythin',' he explained helpfully.

Billie and Noah shared a glance.

'I do know it. Have you been there before?' Noah asked him.

The lad's eyes lit up in the rear-view mirror. He had a spider's web tattooed on his neck. 'Las Vegas? No...I wasn't ever there, but I was in Barcelona once,' he said, as if that was an explanation. 'But Vegas...ah yeah, that's the place to be all right.'

'Well, there sure are a lot of casinos and bars and shows. It never sleeps,' Noah agreed.

'Well, I don't drink, never touched the stuff, or drugs either, wouldn't dream of it, and I don't want to go to any shows. I saw Elton

John by accident one night, and it was desperate altogether, pure solid torture, ja know what I mean?'

Neither of them had the faintest idea, but they nodded.

'Like, I'd only go to Vegas for one thing...ja get me?' He winked at them in the mirror once more while careering around a roundabout. Billie was shoved beside Noah as he turned, and then jolted when he jammed on the brakes to allow a cyclist to make it home alive. Noah put his arms around her protectively. When the car started moving again, he made no effort to change position and neither did she.

'Um...yes, I think I can guess...' Noah said doubtfully.

'MMA!' the boy confirmed, as if this was the most obvious thing in the entire world.

Their look of confusion caused him to explain, his face lighting up. By now, the entire conversation was happening with him looking in the mirror rather than at the road.

'MMA, like, ye know what MMA is, don't ye? Mixed martial arts! Ye've heard of it? It's a sport, the best sport actually, though some people in it aren't great now, I'll grant ye. But I want to be the best MMA fighter in the world, boy, like better than... Well, better than everyone...and I can do it, like, I totally can. I'm so driven! Eyes on the prize, buddy...eyes on the prize.'

Billie hoped his fighting was better than his driving as they weaved all over the road.

'Don't tell me ye never saw it? I could stop there if ye like, show ye a few moves? Like, I'll turn off the meter and everything. I wouldn't charge ye for that or nothin'.'

Before they had any time to react, he pulled the car over onto the side of the busy freeway. He mounted the grass kerb, jumped out and opened their door. Reluctantly, they got out and stood on the grass verge, traffic whizzing past.

'Maybe we shouldn't stop just right here?' Noah yelled over the noise of an articulated truck passing dangerously close.

'Ah, it's grand. The chief super is the granda of a fella in my class at school. I'm Bazza, by the way,' the young man yelled, brushing their fears aside.

'And the chief super is?' Billie asked, thinking of the guy who ran her building. What would a maintenance manager have to do with what was clearly illegal parking?

'Cops, the shades, y'know?' the young man said as he did some very vigorous stretching and leaping.

Without warning, he then did a combination of some kind of high kick and spin, missing Noah's head by inches. They jumped back.

'OK, maybe we'll just go now. That's very impressive...' Noah began, but his voice was drowned out by a siren and the blue flashing light of a police car. A female police officer got out and walked towards them.

'What are you doing?' she asked, as if speaking to deranged five-year-olds.

'I'm just showing these people from America my moves, Guard. We'll be on our way now...' Bazza attempted to skirt around her, but she stopped him.

'Do not move,' she said in a voice that brooked no argument. She said something into her radio, then turned her attention back to Bazza.

'Name?' She took out a notebook.

'Bazza Mac,' he said, with a smirk at Billie and Noah.

'Your full name,' she said firmly.

'Whatever ye want it to be, sweetheart,' he muttered as she glanced behind her where another police car was now pulling up, lights and siren also on. An older policeman emerged.

Without any further conversation, she grabbed Bazza and forced him to the ground, flipped him round and placed handcuffs on his wrists. His MMA skills had seemingly deserted him.

'Hey, I never done nothin'... This is police brutality! Video this, will ya?' he demanded of Billie, who was standing, not knowing what to do.

The officer none too gently dragged him up and attempted to shove him into the back of her police car. The officer in the other vehicle approached and helped her to get him in the back. Once he was safely secure, they had a conversation as a third officer moved from the recently arrived car to the one containing a now apoplectic Bazza. The older policeman approached Billie and Noah. He was in his fifties and burly.

'Names?' he said, in a not unfriendly manner.

'Noah Coulson and Billie Romano,' Noah said.

'OK, and what are you doing on the verge here?' he asked, and Billie imagined he was trying to suppress a smile.

'Well, that guy, the taxi driver, seemed a little...I don't know...'

'Off his head?' the cop suggested.

'Well, yeah. He picked us up at the airport and was driving a little erratically. Then he told us he was into this MMA fighting or something, and next thing we knew, he was pulling over to show us some moves,' Noah explained.

'Dropped on his head as a child, that fella, I'd say. Don't worry, we'll deal with him and get that car towed. That's not his taxi – it was robbed from Shannon a half an hour ago.' He nodded in the direction of the abandoned vehicle.

Billie shared a look of alarm with Noah. 'He stole that car?' she asked.

'Yeah, well, he kind of stole it. It belongs to his uncle. He is, as we say, "Known to Gardaí". We're well used to him – he's a nutjob. Only out of jail four days, and he'll be going back there later on now after that stunt. He's an awful eejit altogether. But anyway, we'll take care of that. Now, where were you headed?' he asked.

'Castle Dysert,' Billie said, hardly believing what was happening.

'Ah, Conor O'Shea's place? That's some spot, isn't it? My wife took me there for my birthday, stayed over and all, and we only live about five miles from it. But 'twas some experience. And Conor is a grand man, not a bit of airs and graces on him even though he owns the place.' He grinned. 'Right so, hop in, and I'll get you back there.'

'Er...OK...' Billie wasn't sure. Did he mean take them back to the hotel in the police car?

It appeared he did, so Noah grabbed his suitcase from the 'taxi' and got into the back of the flashing vehicle.

'Well, it's one way to meet the parents,' he said with a chuckle.

Billie sat in and took the risk of sliding over beside him as they had been with the unstable Bazza driving. He put his arm around her, and she relaxed against him.

The policeman was on his mobile phone, and Noah leaned in and kissed her gently on the lips.

'This is too good a story to miss out on, that our first kiss was in the back of a police car in Ireland,' he whispered.

She smiled and kissed him back.

CHAPTER 16

Conor and Ana sat in silence in Imelda O'Donovan's office the next morning as Kieran Doyle claimed that Ana had threatened his daughter with violence.

Artie seemed much happier these days and was back playing sports. And so it was with a sense of hope that all was solved that Conor had driven Ana and himself from the hotel to the school for the meeting.

Conor could see that Imelda wasn't buying it. Mr Bredin, the boys' teacher, sat listening impassively, his beige jacket and trousers, cream shirt and brown tie managing to give him the most ageless look. He was every inch a teacher, and he looked like he could have been transported to a classroom in the fifties as easily as one today.

Doyle ranted about how school should be a safe place for his child and how being accosted and threatened by an adult was a matter for the guards, but that he was showing courtesy by informing them and the school first. His wife sat silently, her face inscrutable.

'As if the lasting physical and psychological damage on my daughter after the wild attack by their son wasn't bad enough.' He pointed at Conor and Ana. 'But now his mad wife is threatening my child, telling her she can make her disappear and all sorts. Poor Emma can't sleep – she's terrified of her.' Eventually Doyle stopped, finally running out of steam after having repeated his allegations several times.

To Conor's surprise, Ana was quite serene. He'd expected her to be spitting nails at such slights, but she sat with almost a half-smile on her face.

'Well, thank you, Mr Doyle. I think we can now hear from Conor and Ana?' Imelda said, looking at them.

'Please, my husband talk... I don't...' Ana said in halting English.

Conor knew Ana, and understood she was deliberately taking a back seat. That was fine. He had this.

Conor's years of dealing with difficult situations and even more difficult people had taught him that first it was important to give the person with the grievance enough space to say their piece – they usually lost steam eventually – and to remain calm and friendly at all times. He'd read a book about 'tactical empathy', written by an ex-FBI negotiator, that he'd found fascinating. It was about getting what you wanted by making the opposition believe you liked them and were willing and anxious to hear their side. Conor realised he'd been doing a version of that for years, but to see it written down step by step was really interesting. He decided to employ that technique now.

'Right. Well, firstly, on behalf of myself and Ana, we would like to acknowledge Joe's wrongdoing and apologise to Emma and her family for what happened last week. Our son absolutely should not have hit her, and he knows that.' Conor said sincerely, and he noticed Kieran's wife, Tracey, responded with a small nod, an acknowledgement of his apology.

'And now, to come to the serious accusation that my wife threatened a little ten-year-old girl with violence?'

Kieran nodded, glad to have his point of view reiterated.

'But, Kieran.' Conor's tone was so reasonable. 'Why would she do that?'

Kieran spluttered, 'Because she's a nutcase I suppose, a foreign type coming over here...'

Conor didn't acknowledge the racism but kept on. 'But why, though? I don't understand why she would do that?'

'Because she thinks my Emma is bullying your son!' Kieran exploded.

'So Emma bullying Artie made my wife, an adult, threaten a little girl?' Conor knew he'd won. Kieran had said the words. Emma was bullying Artie.

'She did, she threatened her!' Doyle was incandescent now.

'Because of the bullying?' Conor asked mildly.

'Are you bloody deaf, O'Shea? Yes, because of the bullying, but it doesn't matter why. The fact remains that your mad wife is going around threatening little girls.'

'And have you any evidence of this? Because frankly, it's a little far-fetched,' Conor said with a sympathetic smile.

'My Emma told me and she doesn't lie,' Doyle said sullenly.

'But when she was asked by Mr Bredin and Mrs O'Donovan here if she was hurting Artie in any way, she said she had no idea what they were talking about. And we now know that was a lie, don't we?' Conor kept his voice neutral and caught Imelda's eye. Checkmate.

It was time to go in and finish it. 'So Emma is a bully, and we know she's told lies before, so I'm going to assume she's lying again now. That's reasonable, isn't it? So there are no witnesses, and only a child who has lied before said it happened, so I think we'll let that one go. Now on the other matter, I think we need to have another look at what you consider lasting physical and psychological damage. Emma has been bullying our son for some time. She's been making racist remarks about our family, which are very hurtful to both our sons but particularly to Artie. She has alleged that I am a paedophile, which is of course a very serious allegation that we will be dealing with legally, and she has physically assaulted Artie on more than one occasion. She knows she's been caught, and to counter-attack, she's accusing my wife of threatening her, which we've all agreed is just simply not true. Surely you can see this is just a child's way of lashing out? With respect, Kieran, I think Emma might need some help here. She's obviously in need of something.'

Conor found he was enjoying seeing Doyle's reaction. The man had no idea what to say.

'You can't say that! My daughter is a perfect –' Doyle exploded.

Mr Bredin reached into his jacket pocket and pulled out an envelope containing several notes. 'I confiscated these notes from Emma Doyle,' he said simply. He pushed the notes across the desk for them all to see, and Conor picked them up.

One by one, Conor read aloud the poisonous content, pausing for effect on the ones about his own sexual proclivities. It was hard to believe a child of ten would even know about such things let alone be so vitriolic in her hatred, but it was there in pink sparkly pen for all to see.

The group were stunned to silence except for Doyle, who was spluttering that this was a setup.

Imelda stood and addressed the meeting. 'I think Mr Bredin can verify that this is in fact Emma's writing and it is from her copybook?'

'Emma Doyle wrote them,' the teacher again said simply.

Conor thanked his lucky stars that Eddie had rung him to say Bredin would be helpful. He couldn't say exactly how, only that he would be on the O'Shea side. It turned out that Colin Bredin was a reader at mass and was on good terms with Fr Eddie. Conor had mentioned to Eddie his problems with Artie over golf, and Eddie had taken it upon himself to approach the teacher as a friend. It must have paid off, as the man was being uncharacteristically helpful.

Bredin went on. 'I have noticed that all is not well there, and she's making life difficult for Artie.'

'Get my daughter in here,' Doyle demanded. 'Then we'll see who's lying.'

'Kieran, let's just go...' His wife stood up, her cheeks blazing in embarrassment as everyone saw what kind of person her daughter was.

'No way! This Russian, or whatever the hell she is, is threatening our child and I won't have it,' he spat.

'Very well, take a seat again, please,' Imelda said, then went in search of Emma. The Doyles, the O'Sheas and Mr Bredin waited in silence.

'Daddy, she threatened me!' Emma blurted as she came in the door, immediately bursting into tears and pointing at Ana.

Kieran Doyle moved beside his daughter, comforting her.

'Oh, for God's sake, Emma...' Tracey tried to intervene, but her husband spoke over her.

'See! I told you!' Kieran shouted at the principal, incensed at the turn the meeting had taken.

'I think we'd better stick with one thing at a time,' Imelda said smoothly. 'Mr Bredin confiscated these notes from you, Emma, is that true?'

'No, Daddy, I swear, I never saw...' Emma tried to say, though the fact that she was lying was obvious to everyone.

'I confiscated those notes,' Mr Bredin said quietly but firmly. 'Emma was passing them to another girl in the class. I also witnessed her throwing pebbles at Artie O'Shea in the yard, and when I took her to task, she used very inappropriate language. I reported the incident to school management as soon as I became aware of it.'

'Emma? I'm going to ask you once more, did you write these notes about Artie and his family?' Imelda asked gently.

The girl was sobbing now, an Oscar-winning performance in Conor's opinion.

'She said that she would get me kidnapped!' She pointed at Ana, her face red and blotched from crying. 'That she knew people who would make sure I would disappear! Russians!' she added for effect.

Ana looked completely bewildered. 'What she is saying? What I am suppose to do? I don't know Russians, I am from Ukraine.'

'When did she say this, darling?' Kieran asked. His wife was clearly mortified now.

'At training the other day. I was sitting behind Artie, and she came over and threatened me... Chloe and Aoife were there as well.'

'Get those girls here now,' Doyle demanded. 'If that refugee or whatever she is thinks she can go around threatening Irish children...

You probably bought her off the internet. We all know those places – Russian brides, was it?' he snarled at Conor.

'They didn't hear her, Daddy. She made them go away...' Emma began.

Conor addressed the meeting that was now getting very heated. He'd had enough of the Doyles. 'Look, I don't have any more time to devote to this. My wife didn't threaten anyone. And I'd suggest you change your tone when speaking either to her or about her, Kieran. Now, I think we can all see what went on here.'

He turned to Emma, still sobbing theatrically into her father's chest. 'Emma.' She turned her head to face him, and Conor bent down to be level with her. 'If you say you are sorry to Artie for being so mean to him, and Joe says sorry to you for hitting you, do you think we can all let this go?'

'She most certainly will do no such –' Doyle began.

But Tracey snapped. 'Kieran, sit down and shut up, for God's sake, and don't be making a bigger show of us. She did bully that boy, you know she did.'

Emma looked in horror at her mother, and then made eye contact with each one of the adults, who were all looking at her, waiting for her answer. She knew when she was beaten. She nodded, her face sullen.

'Right, let's get Artie and Joe in here and get this finished up for once and for all.' Imelda sounded relieved. 'Well done, Emma. It's hard to admit when you make a mistake, but you did it, and I'm proud of you.'

Conor caught Mr Bredin's eye. In no court of law would a surly nod be considered an admission of guilt, but it was as close as they were going to get.

The teacher followed the principal out to fetch Artie, and the four parents and Emma waited.

'I think you should say something to Mr O'Shea too, Emma,' Tracey Doyle said, ignoring the glares she was getting from her husband.

'It's all right, pet,' Kieran said, soothing his daughter and rubbing her hair.

'No, Kieran, it's not all right. What she said about him and his family is not on. Say you're sorry, Emma.'

It was clear that Kieran Doyle might have been all bluster and threats but Tracey was the one in charge.

Emma barely looked up as she muttered, 'Sorry.'

Conor paused a moment longer than was strictly necessary, then replied, 'Apology accepted.'

When the twins appeared, they were wide-eyed and nervous. Artie ran to Ana, and she put her arm around him. Joe stood beside Conor.

Imelda addressed the gathering. 'I've explained that Emma is going to apologise to Artie and nothing like this is ever going to happen again. And then Joe is going to say he is sorry for hitting, and he is also going to promise that he won't ever do that again. So you first, Emma.' Imelda gently took Emma by the hand and led her out of her father's arms to stand in front of Artie.

'I'm sorry,' she said, her eyes on her shoes.

'And what else?' Imelda prompted.

'And I won't be mean to you anymore,' Emma conceded.

'And Joe?'

Joe looked up at Conor, who gave him a slight nod.

'I'm sorry for hitting you. I won't do it again.'

Conor saw Ana visibly relax.

'Right, you three, back to class now. It's almost lunchtime.' The principal shooed them out the door. She turned to the four parents, shaking hands in turn with each one. 'Thank you all for coming. It's great to get things sorted out, and I'm sure that will be the end of it.'

Imelda was purposefully bringing the meeting to a close before Kieran Doyle could start up again.

The parents went out two separate doors, not saying a word to each other, and it wasn't until they had pulled out of the school gate and were driving back to the castle that Conor spoke. 'I'd say you scared the bejesus out of her.'

Ana smiled and gazed out the window. 'You have your Irish way, I have my Ukrainian way. Together, we get what we want.'

CHAPTER 17

*T*he following morning, Billie and Noah sat in the sunny glass-walled orangery that jutted into the gardens on the eastern side of the castle. The profusion of flowers outside delicately fragranced the room through the open windows. She watched Pops and Marilyn at the counter, deliberating over cakes, but they hadn't seen her and Noah yet. Marilyn loved sweet things and seemed determined to try every confection the hotel offered. Though they were not long after the most sumptuous breakfast – Billie had been blown away by the array of choices – that did not deter Marilyn. How the woman stayed so slim was a complete mystery considering how much she ate.

The previous night, after the stolen car/MMA debacle, she and Noah had ordered room service, which turned into a nightcap and ended up with him falling asleep on one of the beds in her room. They were dropped off at the hotel in the police car as Conor was on his way out. Initially, he'd looked a little taken aback, but the officer who returned them, a man called Dan, had a chat with him when they arrived and explained everything. Turned out Conor knew of Bazza as well; the guy was notorious. There had been an incident during the reconstruction of the castle with him requisitioning a forklift, which he proceeded to drive down the narrow country lanes around the hotel. Billie and Noah had gone up to her room, chuckling about the absurdity of it all.

Luckily, the family had all turned in so she could wait until the next day to make the introductions.

When Noah fell asleep, she'd wondered if she should wake him. He was fully clothed and there was another room booked, but in the end, she just put the covers over him and got into the other bed. She'd woken that morning to him kneeling beside her on the floor, his face inches from hers.

'Good morning, Billie,' he had whispered.

She opened her eyes and had to orientate herself for a moment. She pulled herself up, and he sat on the bed beside her, showered, shaved and dressed in fresh clothes.

'I conked out last night. I'm sorry. I was so jet-lagged and I pulled an all-nighter the night before to tie stuff up. And then there was the excitement of almost getting arrested. I'll be more lively today, I promise.'

'Good morning.' She managed.

He leaned over and kissed her, and she hoped her breath didn't smell bad.

On and on they kissed, and she wrapped her arms around his neck.

'When I woke up, it took me a minute to figure out where I was,' he said when they moved away from each other.

'Well, you're in Ireland, with a member of your junior animator staff, who is just about to enter into an emotional storm that may or may not end in tears, so that's all good, right?' She chuckled.

'I could think of nothing I'd rather do.' He replied.

She got ready. They had missed breakfast so decided to just have coffee in the little glass café downstairs. She'd tried calling her mother and Marko's room, as well as Pops and Marilyn's, but both rang out. She guessed they were taking it easy today. She knew Marko and her mom planned to visit the spa and Pops wanted to take some photos around the grounds. They were allowing her to take the lead on everything, and she appreciated it.

The orangery was busy. While they waited, he leaned over and took her hand.

'Is this OK?' he asked.

'What?' she replied, not moving her hand.

'This, me holding your hand, me being here, us...whatever this is?'

'It's OK with me – more than OK – if it's OK with you.' She said.

'It's more than OK.' He smiled in return. 'We never really talked about this. I mean, we talked about loads of things, but I honestly had no idea if you just saw me as your boss, or as a friend or anything else. I was on the brink of saying something so many times, but it felt wrong. It still does a little bit.'

'Why?' she asked.

'Just...' He ran his hand over his jaw and exhaled. 'I don't want to mess things up between us. Like, you are vulnerable right now, some pretty heavy-duty stuff going on, and I don't want to take advantage of that. Like, I don't want you to wake up one morning and think I preyed on you when you were down. And there's the age gap.' He said the last sentence in a rush, like he needed to get the words out.

Though he was older, and more successful, and more experienced at almost everything, she felt protective of him. He was such a decent person, a good man. A man like her dad actually, hard-working, fun, kind. She thought for a second. Was that why she liked him so much, because he reminded her of her father? She observed him and said nothing for a few seconds, trying to formulate her thoughts. What she said next was going to be important; she didn't want to mess it up.

'I really like you, Noah, but I was nervous too. I thought you might feel I was behaving like a silly middle schooler with a crush on the teacher, so I convinced myself there was nothing but friendship between us. But the truth is, I wanted more... I've never had a boyfriend. When my little brother died, I was kind of messed up, and then my dad passed. I guess I was never in the right frame of mind. But you're not like other guys – you're one of a kind, and I'm so happy you're here.'

She looked at him and saw the relief there.

'So am I your boyfriend now?' He chuckled and she blushed.

'Well...I didn't mean...' She was flustered; she shouldn't have said that. Why was she so horrible at this? People didn't say 'boyfriend' and 'girlfriend' anymore – they saw lots of people and were not exclusive. Emily was always dating a few guys at once.

"Cause I'd love to be, if you'll be my girlfriend?' He made a funny face that caused her to giggle.

'Really?' she asked.

'Really,' he confirmed, taking her hand to his lips and kissing it.

'So this is the famous Noah?' Marilyn burst into their moment. 'Or if you're not, you better beat it, 'cause some guy named Noah is on his way.' She winked and placed the laden-down tray on the table.

Billie moved over to make space for them and made the introductions. 'Noah, this is Marilyn and this is Pops.'

Marilyn kissed him on the cheek and winked at Billie behind his back as he shook hands with Sol, mouthing, 'Very cute.'

It was immediately like they were old friends and Billie and Noah had been together forever. They joked and laughed, and Billie was so proud of him. She could see that Pops approved, and that mattered so much to her. Despite the turmoil she was in about everything else, she felt really happy. Inevitably, the conversation came round to her birth father. Billie assured Pops and Marilyn that Noah knew everything, and so they discussed her next move.

'It's hard for your mom, especially since the guy is famous over here,' Pops pointed out.

'I know.' Billie sighed. 'I know this is about her as much as me – more than me really, as she was the one who knew him. I get all of that, and I'm lucky. Most people would run a mile, but she's sticking by me and facing down her ex-boyfriend of decades ago. I guess it's just a case of waiting to see if he responds.' Billie shrugged.

After a discussion with Billie the previous afternoon on the bus back to the hotel, her mother had emailed the address given on his website, explained who she was and the purpose of the visit and received a two-line reply.

That evening, Donna had forwarded it to Billie, who had read it and reread it about a hundred times.

She showed Pops the email, and he read it aloud.

Dear Mrs Pavlovych,

Thank you for your message. I am Minister Seoige's private secretary. I will pass your correspondence to him.

Kindest regards,

Angela O'Leary

He looked up at her and Billie shrugged.

'That was yesterday, or last night, I think, and so far nothing. Mom gave him her cell and my cell as well as where we're staying in the email. I think you'd either call right away or not at all, right?'

'Not necessarily. He might not have read it yet or –'

Billie interjected. 'I know you're trying to be nice, Pops, but if your long-lost child shows up out of the blue, I think that might be worthy of a phone call. Especially considering he's due to arrive here in this hotel tomorrow.'

She'd spoken at length to Noah the previous night as they ate chicken sandwiches and drank coffee in her room. He was rational and told her that there were any number of reasons why he might not get in touch immediately. Maybe he never told his wife and kids about Donna and America, maybe he wasn't ready to have this out in public as it was a big deal, maybe he thought she was after money... It could be anything. She explained that Conor was hosting him for a coffee morning the following day, arranged long before they ever got there. Noah was blown away by the coincidence, but Billie was getting used to the idea that everyone in Ireland seemed to know everyone else. It wasn't like back in the States where there was zero chance of bumping into a congressman by accident. People here knew their elected representatives, as they attended family events in their constituencies and they held clinics where the public could come and voice their concerns. Apparently this Liam Seoige was big on sustainable energy and the hotel was a shining example of green development, so he was coming to check it out.

'I read about him last night. He seems like an impressive guy,' Pops said, sipping his coffee.

Billie looked guilty. After Noah went to sleep, she had searched for Liam online, something she had promised herself she wouldn't do because if he didn't want to know, it would only hurt her more. But she couldn't stop herself.

Over and over, she had watched him give a speech about the future of green energy, and he seemed so sincere, so genuine. But then politicians worked hard to come across that way. She paused the video where he talked about the responsibility his generation had to their children, and then to their children, and she thought ruefully, *You don't mean me.*

She had tried to see any resemblance between them, and it was undeniably there. He had the same colour hair, the same lithe build, the same eyes. She'd always thought she had her dad's eyes and she did – just not the dad she thought.

His voice sounded strange to her; he had such an Irish accent, with those soft vowels and not pronouncing 'th'. Conor had told them that Irish people didn't know what Americans were talking about when they said Irish people said 'dis', 'dat', 'dese' and 'dose' instead of this, that, these and those. As far as they were concerned, their pronunciation was perfect.

'You look very like him,' Pops said quietly.

'I know. It's so weird. I honestly don't know how I feel. Mom said in her message that we were not trying to make trouble and didn't want anything from him, but I guess he's going to be wary. It's natural, right?' She was so conflicted, disappointed, worried, guilty, nervous.

'She's not wrong,' Marilyn said, spooning the last of a lemon meringue mousse into her mouth. 'Especially if this guy is running for president.'

'Maybe I need to face the fact that he doesn't want to see me.' Billie sighed. The hurt went deeper than she cared to admit even to herself.

'Maybe, but there could be other reasons too. Let's give the guy a chance.' Marilyn was upbeat. 'Now, Sol, are you going to tell Billie and Noah about our little side trip?'

'What's this?' Billie asked, glad to have something else to focus on.

'I... Well, Marilyn thinks I should visit that jewellery store in Dublin, tell them who I am...' Pops turned to Noah. 'Has she told you my story?'

Noah glanced at Billie.

'I did, Pops. He knows.'

'OK, so Marilyn thought if I went there... But I don't know... What are they supposed to say? It was years and years ago, nobody even alive now would remember. They'd probably call the cops.'

Billie's heart went out to Pops. He'd borne that hurt for so long, it was a part of who he was. She remembered her mother saying how her grandfather never really got over the fact that he survived and so many others didn't. It blighted his life, the survivor's guilt, and he was not an easy man because of it. Pops's mother too was apparently a very sad person and became hard as a consequence. They survived, but it seemed they got no joy from life – it was just something to be endured – and that must have been a tough house to grow up in. No wonder Pops felt so strongly about it all.

'I think it's a good idea. You never know – maybe someone there will remember, or there might even be a relative if it's a family business. You can say your piece, and maybe it would put those ghosts to rest for you.'

Sol gave a sad smile. 'That's what Marilyn said, but nothing can ever change it. Sure, we survived, and we went on to live a good life, first in China and then in America, but my parents lived all of their lives with such deep sadness. My father didn't like to talk about it – he was determined that we would make a success of America – but he would say Kaddish for his family, and us kids could see it there, the loss, the grief that never went away. They never smiled or laughed, even on family occasions, weddings, babies being born. And one time I asked him – I think it was when Diana was born – and he said that a new baby, new life, just reminded him of all the lives that would never be. I'll never forget his face. He just turned to me and said, "If I could have got them out, if only someone would have helped. But it turned out that my friends were not my friends."'

Billie put her hand on his. It was unusual to see him so cut up. Mad yes, and frankly racist towards all Irish people certainly, but this sadness was deeply unsettling.

'So will you go?' she asked. 'Conor said it's only a few hours' drive from here.'

Her grandfather looked up and fixed her with a gaze. 'I will if you'll come with me,' he said.

She'd given him the exact same ultimatum weeks earlier. 'Of course I will.'

After coffee, they all walked in the grounds, the salty breeze cool on their skin. Castle Dysert really was the most remarkable place. Marilyn told them the story of the castle that she'd heard in the bar the previous evening from one of the plumbers who'd worked on the reconstruction. To Billie and Noah's amused surprise, Marilyn seemed to know all the staff by name and they her. They waited as she spoke to a young woman in a housekeeper's uniform. Marilyn held her hand and extracted a small glass jar from her jacket pocket. It contained ointment of some kind, and Marilyn gently put some on the girl's hand.

'What was that about?' Pops asked as she rejoined them.

'Oh, that's Marta, she's Polish. She burned her hand yesterday on the press for the sheets, so I told her I had something for it,' Marilyn explained. 'Her grandmother was a witch,' she added, as if she was telling them that the girl's grandmother was a shopkeeper.

'I won't ask how you knew that,' Pops said with a smile.

'We can see each other, Sol. It's simple.'

Noah seemed delighted by Marilyn, and Billie was pleased. The older woman came across as a bit kooky, no doubt about it, but she was a wise old soul and had such a refreshing view on life. She talked openly about her time in prison, though she never again mentioned her son. Billie thought often of the advice Marilyn had given her on that first day after her mother broke the news, about how a person's character is grown by adversity, not by ease. It was a comforting thought, that there was a point to all the suffering, that she would be a better, kinder, more empathetic person because of it. Perhaps that's why people her own age kind of annoyed her sometimes; they were so obsessed with stupid stuff, their image, their Insta feed, how many times they got something retweeted. And it was because, in the case of most people, luckily for them, having someone make a derogatory comment on your selfie was the worst thing they could envisage happening.

Noah held her hand as they walked. He was much more affectionate than she would have imagined; he had always been so proper before. He was different, older, and not bothered by the stuff that her friends worried about. He was great, and she was falling harder for him as every minute went by.

She would introduce him to her mother and Marko as soon as they emerged from the spa. She could never envisage her dad going to a spa, but she realised that the constant comparisons were not doing her any good. Matt Romano, the man she would always think of as her dad, was one kind of person, and Marko was another. They were different in every way, but in the end of his life, Marko was kind to her dad, he made her mother happy, and that was all that mattered to her. She vowed to give him a chance.

As they walked around the enormous castle with its limestone walls, red sandstone reveals and latticed windows with heavy oak shutters inside, she tried to imagine what life would be like if the place were a private house.

As she looked up, she saw Marko and her mother walking towards them, looking like a couple from a cruise brochure. Her mother's hair was blow-dried to perfection, and she wore snow-white jeans and a pink sweater. Diamond earrings completed the look. Marko looked equally suave in dark trousers and a Yves Saint Laurent polo shirt. The logo was subtle but there nonetheless.

'How was the spa?' she asked.

'Lovely.' Donna glanced over to where Marilyn, Pops and Noah were examining a very unusual plant. 'So is that him?' she murmured.

'Yeah, that's Noah. Come on, I'll introduce you.'

Marko and Donna followed her over to where the others stood. Donna kissed her dad on the cheek, who in turn put his arm around her shoulders. Billie had a flash of realisation – Pops was to Donna what her dad had been to her. The feud between her and her mother must have upset him so much.

'Mom, Marko, this is Noah Coulson. Noah, this is my mother, and at the risk of having so many fathers I don't know what to do, I guess this is my stepdad?' She caught Marko's glance and was relieved when he smiled. Everyone chuckled, and it felt good to make light of the situation.

They both greeted Noah warmly, and just like with Pops and Marilyn, the conversation flowed effortlessly. They all strolled around, admiring the surroundings. A little sailboat bobbed about on the glittering sea, which lapped gently on the hotel's private beach.

They passed through a beautiful cobbled courtyard, which was lined with stables. A few half-doors were open, and several horses' heads appeared at the sound of their voices. Billie went over to a large bay and rubbed its nose. Another one nuzzled Marko's pocket.

'If you've mints in there, she can smell them,' a voice called from inside one of the stables. A girl of about seventeen emerged bearing a shovel full of horse manure. She wore her extremely long hair in coloured dreadlocks and had a lot of piercings.

'Can I give her one?' Marko asked, taking the packet from his pocket.

'Do of course, though she'll roar the place down if you only give her one. You have been warned,' she said with a grin, emptying the shovel into a wheelbarrow.

The horse munched all of Marko's mints happily as they looked around.

'I wonder who lived here?' Billie asked, placing her hand on the smooth stone.

'The King family,' the girl answered. 'And they had a tragic life in lots of ways. I can tell you the history of the place if you like? I'm Olivia, by the way.'

'We'd love to hear it if you've time,' Donna said.

'Any excuse to take a break from shovelling that stuff.' She grinned, glancing at the wheelbarrow full of manure.

Olivia was animated in the telling of the tale. 'The house was in the King family for generations, old English landlords, and everyone round here worked for them. My granda and his father too worked here, back in the day, labourers like. But the IRA burned the whole thing back in 1921, during the War of Independence. They burned all the big houses – they saw them as symbols of British imperialism. Anyway, everyone got out except a little boy. His name was Grenville King, and that's why the bar is called Grenville's. Anyway, his twin brother came back years later and rebuilt it. He made a ton of money in Australia, mining opals or something. There are all kinds of stories, but the truth is this brother, the one who survived, built a playroom in the castle and filled it with old toys, because it was in the playroom the little brother died. He was a little eccentric it seems, this guy, and eventually his wife left him, taking his two daughters with her. She was Australian and a brilliant gardener, so that's why the range of flowers and shrubs here is so diverse.' She waved her hand in the direction of the gardens beyond the stables.

'Anyway, the two sisters inherited the castle when their father killed himself years later, and they came back to live here. They hadn't seen him for years, not since their mother took them back to Australia when they were kids. They never married or anything and lived like recluses here for decades until one of them threw herself off the top of the castle, exactly as her father did. The other sister moved into a home and eventually died too, and that's when Conor and his business partner bought it. Everyone locally said they were crazy, that it was haunted – the ghost of the little boy who died was said to roam about – but they went ahead anyway, and now it's a thriving success.'

Sol laughed. He lived very much in the land of the living, and ghosts and hauntings and such were nothing but old codswallop to him despite Marilyn's love of the weird and wonderful. 'That's some shaggy dog story,' he said.

Marilyn eyed him. '"There are more things on heaven and earth, Horatio, than are dreamt of in your philosophy",' she said quietly, without a hint of a smile.

'The Bible?' Billie asked.

Marilyn shook her head. 'Shakespeare. Hamlet says it to his friend Horatio after seeing the ghost of his dead father.'

Sol put his arm around Marilyn and gave her a squeeze. 'You would not believe how well read this lady is, Billie. There is nothing she hasn't heard of. Makes me feel like a real dodo sometimes.' He kissed the top of her head.

'Not much else to do for fifteen years in prison.' Marilyn shrugged. Then, changing the subject, and noting the look of surprise on Olivia's face, Marilyn said, 'But that's not all – wasn't there a fire?'

'A fire here?' asked Billie. The little group were hanging on the Irish girl's every word.

'You're right. There was.' Olivia nodded. 'Though Conor doesn't like us going on about it, so you didn't hear this from me. There's always been a problem on the third floor – the heating would not work and it was so cold up there. They got engineers to come from all over to see what the problem was, but it was useless. The playroom where Grenville died was up there. The story goes that they maintained the playroom as it was, full of antique toys, out of superstition or something. Though some say they tried to pack it all up, but every time they did, the next day it would all be back, exactly as it had been. So a few years ago, two years maybe, someone set a fire here maliciously, and Conor's two sons, Artie and Joe, were up in the playroom. How they even found it, nobody knew. It was out of bounds to everyone, but somehow they'd sneaked up there unknown to Ana during a party. Once the fire was discovered, and Ana realised the boys were missing, Conor knew somehow where to look for them. I wasn't here then, but my mam works here, so she told me how Conor had to run into the burning building, smoke everywhere and poor Ana screaming her head off. But he found them in the playroom and had to get them to the first floor window, in the ballroom now. He broke the windows and managed to throw the boys out to safety. He got out himself as well but only just, and he had a lot of burns. We're lucky he survived.'

They could all tell how highly the staff regarded their boss; it was nice to see.

'Now, I'd better get back to the mucking out or there'll be trouble,' Olivia said with a grin. 'This lot get fierce cranky if I'm late with the grub, don't you?' She patted one of the horses, who gave a snicker.

'You're welcome to ride them if you want to – that's what they're for?' she offered.

Noah and Billie exchanged a glance.

'I'd love to try, though I've never ridden a European saddle before,' Noah said.

Olivia gave him a flirtatious glance, which Billie noted.

'I take a hack out every morning at eight. We go along the beach and around by the ruined abbey and back through the meadows there beyond. You're welcome in the morning if you like.'

'Great, we'd love to, right, Billie? Anyone else?' he asked, putting an arm around her shoulders.

That little gesture, that sense that she was his and he was hers, warmed Billie's frozen heart. Olivia saw the lie of the land too and quickly changed her tone.

'The more the merrier.' Her smile was genuine.

'Sure, we could do that before we go to Dublin?' Billie replied, and turned to the others. 'What about you guys? You want to play cowboys?'

'Not for us, Billie,' Marilyn said. 'I think horse riding is not elder-friendly.' She giggled and Pops nodded in agreement.

'I don't really have anything I could wear...' Donna began, and Billie wondered if she was refusing because she thought that Billie wanted her to. Her mother used to love horses.

'I've got some leggings or something you can borrow. Come on, it'll be fun,' she coaxed. 'You'll come, won't you, Marko?'

He looked at Donna, a questioning eyebrow raised. 'Well, I am mostly Cossack, so I should be able to ride a horse, shouldn't I?'

'OK, OK, you guys win. Horse riding it is.' Donna held her hands up in mock surrender.

'Well, you would be very welcome. There are two others booked in as well, Germans I think, and we might get a few more. I can take ten. So I'll see you here in the morning. Just wear something soft, track pants or something. No jeans, as the seams will chafe, and if you have shoes or boots with a heel, not flat like sneakers, that would be good. But don't worry, we won't be galloping – it's all very gentle and sedate!' She laughed as she pushed her wheelbarrow away.

They continued their walk, chatting, and Billie noticed how they felt like a fairly cohesive group. Anyone looking on would never guess the complicated dynamics.

They explained the planned trip to Dublin to Donna and Marko, who offered to change their plans to tag along, but Pops insisted they go ahead with the medieval banquet they'd booked. Donna seemed disappointed that Billie didn't want to join them at the nearby castle for the festivities when they suggested it, but Billie wanted to give them some space as well. She and her mother were not used to being in each other's company all day every day.

'So we'll meet you guys for dinner?' Billie suggested. 'Ana said there was a nice pub along the bay that's famous for their fish and chips. It's only a twenty-minute walk, and we can plan our trip to Dublin? I can arrange a rental car for tomorrow if you like?'

'Well?' Marilyn turned to Pops, who had still not agreed to the trip.

'OK.' He sighed. 'I guess.'

They strolled back inside, and Billie was disappointed to see that Ana wasn't on the desk; instead, she had been replaced by a really severe-looking middle-aged woman in a dark suit. Billie left Marko and Donna talking to Noah. The four of them had decided to have a drink at the bar while Pops and Marilyn took a nap before dinner.

'Yes, may I help you?' the receptionist asked.

'Um, yes… I'd like to rent a car, please,' Billie said.

'Of course. To be delivered here?' The woman looked up from her computer.

'Yes, please.'

'Are you over twenty-six?'

'Er, no, I'm twenty-five,' Billie replied, wondering what that had to do with anything.

'Oh, then I'm sorry, you cannot rent from the company we normally use. They only insure over twenty-six and under seventy.'

'Oh, right. But could I use another company then?'

'Certainly, but they won't deliver the car to the hotel. Perhaps if you went back to the airport at Shannon, then you could get one there?' The woman still did not smile.

Both Pops and Marilyn were over seventy, and she was under the age. Noah had not brought his driver's licence, thinking he wouldn't need it. Donna and Marko were due to be at the banquet.

'And how would I get there?' she asked.

'I could arrange a taxi?' the woman suggested.

'OK.' Billie realised there was no other way. She didn't want to bring this complication to Pops; he'd just say it was too much hassle and call it all off.

The woman busied herself on the computer making the arrangements, and Billie waited. As she did, Conor emerged from the back office. 'Ah, hi there, Billie. How are you today?'

'Good, thanks. And thank you again for yesterday – we had a wonderful day.'

'Glad you enjoyed it. The lads were full of ideas of where I could take you today, hoping of course that they'd get to tag along and doss off school again. They're a pair of chancers, so they are.'

'They're adorable.'

Conor came around the front of the desk as the woman was on the phone to a taxi company. 'So how's everything else?' he asked quietly.

Billie shrugged. 'My mom emailed him, but that was yesterday morning, and I haven't heard anything, so...' She tried to keep the edge of disappointment out of her voice.

'Would you like a coffee?' Conor asked. 'I was just about to have one myself.'

'Sure, if you're not too busy.'

He led her to a quiet corner of the orangery and ordered two coffees.

'So there's not much else I can do, right?' Billie said as she stirred her frothy latte.

'I suppose not. That's a pity, though. How long more are you here?'

'We leave on Monday. Tomorrow I'm trying to rent a car to take

Pops and Marilyn to Dublin. He wants to meet the family who refused to help his father. Well, he doesn't really want to meet them, but Marilyn thinks it would be good for him. He's held this in his heart for so long, it might help him or something. Mom and Marko are going to some banquet in a castle, so it will be just us four.'

'Yes, I noticed you'd got company.' He winked and Billie was mortified. She had booked another room for Noah, but since he'd stayed in her room the previous night, she had cancelled it. They should probably be paying more now that there were two in the room.

'We'll pay whatever extra...' she blurted. 'And I'm sorry about booking and then cancelling last minute...'

'I didn't mean that. It's grand, whatever suits.' Conor waved her discomfort away. 'No, I'm just glad you have some support, as it's a stressful time. When my father turned up last year, I don't know what I'd have done without my wife. She was an oasis of calm, and I can talk to her in a way I can't talk to anyone else. So I'm happy for you.' He paused, thinking for a moment and then said,

'I need to go to Dublin this week for a meeting. I was going to go on Friday, so if it would suit you all to hold off on visiting Dublin until Friday, I could drive you to save all the hassle and stress of renting a car?'

'I can't ask you to do that! You've done enough for us already...' Billie began to protest.

'Well, first of all, you're not asking, I'm offering. And secondly, I need to go anyway. We are bidding for a big European conference, so I need to speak to my business partner to talk about how best to go about it.'

He paused. 'Liam Seoige will be here tomorrow. I don't know if you want to be here or not, but if you don't, I could arrange for the shuttle bus to take you into Ennis and you could maybe potter around or take a day tour, go to Galway maybe?'

Billie thought. She wanted to see him in the flesh, but only if he wanted to see her. And anyway, even if she was going to meet him, which wasn't looking likely, that would not be how either of them would want it, with cameras and reporters everywhere.

'No, I think I won't be here. Don't worry, Conor, you've enough to do. We'll arrange something. I kind of hope he gets in touch. My mom told him we were staying here. What a coincidence, eh?' She shrugged sadly.

'It is. But that's Ireland for you. Everyone knows everyone. You know yourself what's best. Have a think about it. In the meantime, honestly, it's no bother to take you to Dublin. I find that kind of thing interesting anyway. Over the years, I've been lucky enough to help some people finding others. I enjoy it.'

'So if he does, he does. I'm not going to hang out here like some creepy fangirl.' She grinned. 'But if you could take us to Dublin, if you're sure, and Pops got to meet those people, the trip would have achieved that at least.'

'I think this trip has achieved a lot already. You're getting on well with your mom and Marko, and now this guy is mad about you. And your grandad is romancing Marilyn around every bakery in Ireland.'

She laughed. It was true.

'So I'll arrange to meet my partner in town. I shouldn't be more than an hour. That way, your mother and Marko could go too if they wanted to?'

Billy thought for a second. 'Well, that would be so cool if you don't mind. But...' She paused. 'The lady on the desk might have it all arranged now,' she said, not relishing the idea of cancelling everything.

'Don't worry about Katherine. I'll explain.' He stood and drained his coffee. 'Her bark is worse than her bite,' he whispered with a wink.

She left too and found Noah and the others in the bar. They were finishing their drinks, and she suggested she and Noah go to the pool. They parted, agreeing to meet the others for dinner. As she left to go, Billie turned back, gave her mom a hug and kissed Marko's expensive-smelling cheek. 'Thanks, you guys, for everything,' she whispered, and followed Noah to the elevator.

The spa and leisure centre were incredibly designed. The end of the pool was a glass wall, and so it looked when you were in it that you could swim to America, as if there were no barrier between the end of the hotel and the vast expanse of the Atlantic beyond. The pool area was lined with heated loungers, fluffy blankets, magazines and a hot and cold drinks machine. Billie was glad she'd brought her nice bikini, and the appreciative look on Noah's face as she emerged made her smile. They swam for a bit and then wandered out to the outdoor hot tub on the stone patio to the right of the complex. The tub looked like something a Greek Goddess might have lounged in; all around it were trellised panels weighted down with flowers and foliage. The air was cool but the bubbling water hot, and as Noah lay back, he opened his arms. She leaned against him and sighed deeply. So much had happened, and yet nothing had.

They had the place to themselves and so they talked about her birth father again. She tried to focus on his advice to just be patient.

'Maybe he won't contact you before you go home, but we can come back. It's not like it's now or never, you know?' Noah said gently.

'Would you come back with me?' she asked.

'Well, it's total torture. I mean, this place is a dump and the food is gross and there are no drinks, but I guess I could endure it,' Noah teased.

'Well, on my wages, we won't be staying here, sunshine, so you better enjoy it while it lasts. And my boss is a tyrant, so there's no hope of a raise.' She turned in his arms to face him.

'I heard about him. Apparently the only way to get anything out of him is to seduce him,' he murmured, lowering his lips to hers.

* * *

As she stood in the shower, getting ready for dinner, she felt the familiar pain of grief. Sometimes it blindsided her, like now. She was happy for the first time in ages, and then this stabbing pain of loss. She longed to have her dad back; she had so many questions. She'd felt herself move through the phases: incredulity when her mother first told her the truth, then fury that he lied her whole life, which turned into sadness that he felt he couldn't trust her, and now she was still all of those things but also curious.

She knew her dad hadn't loved Gio more, and she was positive he never saw her as anything but his daughter, but she still had so many questions.

She dressed in a white lace minidress and gold flat pumps – it was the nicest outfit she'd brought with her, being mainly a jeans and t-shirts kind of girl – and blow-dried her hair. She applied a little make-up but decided against a jacket so her sleeve of tattoos was on show.

Noah was lying on the bed, ready. He looked so handsome in navy chinos and a cream shirt.

He saw her and gave a long low whistle. 'Wow!' was all he said.

'Do I look OK?' she asked, suddenly worried it was over the top.

'You look sensational. Don't ever wear that to work – nobody could concentrate.'

She laughed and threw a cushion at him.

'Show me your tattoos,' he said.

She sat down beside him. He'd seen her arm before, but now he examined all the artwork. Betty Boop, Mickey Mouse, Bugs Bunny, Pokémon, villains, princesses, woodland creatures and cute insects all cavorted around her slim arm.

'This is amazing work,' he said appreciatively, and she knew he meant it. He was good at his job.

'Well, I knew what I wanted. I designed it and did the drawings and then found a tattoo artist who could do it.'

'I love it. It's so quirky and cool, just like you.' He kissed the inside of her forearm.

'Thanks, I love it too. I don't often show it off, as it's kind of for me or something. But it's nice when I do that people like it.'

He stood up and put his arms around her. 'You're an amazing woman, Billie, you know that? Really special.' His eyes never left hers.

'I wouldn't have gotten through these last months without you,' she replied, allowing him to pull her closer.

* * *

'Nothing?' Donna asked tentatively as they gathered in the lobby.

Marko, Pops and Noah were investigating a suit of armour.

'No, nothing for you either?'

Donna shook her head sadly, but then smiled, nodding at Noah. 'He's nice. I like him.'

'I do too. I've never really dated anyone seriously though, so it feels a little strange, but good strange. I just hope I don't mess it up. I made a complete idiot of myself with a co-worker a while back so...' Billie found herself telling her mother the whole sorry tale, and she even ended up laughing at herself. Somehow, it didn't seem such a big deal anymore.

'Well, I'm sure it wasn't as bad as you think, and I'm glad he was nice about it.' Donna said kindly when she'd finished. 'I know you cringe now, but try showing up at some guy's door twenty-six years later to say you just happened to forgot to mention that you'd had his child.' Donna laughed and Billie joined in.

'I can't imagine. I really appreciate it. Most people wouldn't dream of it.'

'I should have told you years ago.' Donna sounded sad.

'Look, it's all done now, the past, everything. Let's let it go. You've got Marko now, and your life is good again at last. You deserve it,' Billie said sincerely.

Her mother reached out and smoothed Billie's hair, a gesture Billie remembered from her childhood. 'And you've got Noah now. He's crazy about you, I can tell.'

'I...I really like him. Over here, it all seems so easy, but when we get back, I don't know... I can't imagine it or something. He's kind of like the adult in the company, you know? Like, all of the people on the animation team are my age, and it's that kind of vibe. Like, we have slides instead of stairs and beanbags and big plasma screens showing old cartoons on a loop for inspiration. Meanwhile, he's got an office and wears a suit, so he's different.'

'But he strikes me as someone who doesn't care what people think.'

'That's true. I think that's one of the reasons I like him. He reminds me of Dad in lots of ways, like he's nice to everyone but he's his own man. Everyone is so taken up with image and what they wear and what they eat and all of that nowadays. Noah isn't.'

As they spoke, her phone buzzed in her hand – an incoming call from an Irish number.

She swallowed. 'You answer it,' she said, thrusting the phone at her mother like it was on fire.

Donna paled but pressed the green button.

CHAPTER 18

*C*onor got the call to say the minister and his entourage would be at the castle by 8:30 a.m. and gone by 9:30. It was a flying visit, but that suited him just fine. He had a lot to get through if he was going to be away the next day; he'd finally managed to pin down a time to meet Corlene. He'd not seen her for months, but if they were going to pull this huge conference off, she needed to focus her attention.

The minister's private secretary had called many times, finalising arrangements. RTE, the Irish national broadcaster, would be there, as well as several radio stations. The plan was for Conor to walk him around and explain how the castle had been retrofitted with every conceivable eco-friendly system available, how they recycled the rainwater, how the pool was filtered sea water, and so on. The garden was completely organic, the wildflower meadows around the grounds attracted bees and butterflies, the hotel's heating and lighting system was fuelled by a combination of solar and wind energy, and almost all of the building materials were locally sourced. Conor was proud of what they'd achieved and excited to show it off.

He'd addressed the staff in a meeting at 7:30 a.m. that morning. 'Good morning, folks, and thanks for coming in early. I see several faces in front of me I know for a fact are not on duty until later today, so I really appreciate you making the effort. Now, as you all know, today is a big day for the castle, or at least this morning is. Minister Liam Seoige is coming here, ostensibly to see how a zero-carbon-footprint hotel is run, but what we are trying to do is throw our hat in the ring to host the European summit on climate change early next year. If we can impress the minister, then that's one step in that direction. It's a long shot obviously, but if we can pull it off, it means a major boost in visibility for the hotel internationally, and that's good for all of us.'

He glanced around at the gathering and realised, not for the first time, what a great staff he had. They were from every corner of the world, as well as home-grown, but almost to a man and woman, they were loyal to the place and to him, and he was really thankful to them.

'So if we can just do what we always do, everything will go well, I know. The success of this place is down to you all. I'm always saying it, I know, but it's the friendly face in the bar, the immaculately cleaned bedrooms, the amazing food, the relaxation of the spa, the colours in the gardens, whatever the guest experiences here, that is down to each of you. That perfection and attention because you all take such pride in your work.'

'And 'cause Carlos would skin us alive if we didn't,' joked Ivan, the pastry chef, to a ripple of laughter.

Carlos was outside overseeing the car parking with the minister's security people.

Conor grinned. 'Well, that too. But as a thanks from myself and Corlene, and in line with every other year, there's going to be a free bar and barbeque for staff on Saturday night at the Wild Atlantic Tavern to kick the season off. If we manage to not poison anyone, or burn the place to the ground, we'll do it again at the end of the season. For those of you new to the castle, these events are great craic and a chance for us all to relax. As usual, bring the family.'

That news was greeted with applause. Conor knew he was one of the best employers in the industry, and even though he had trouble recruiting staff, his problems were much less than some of his fellow hoteliers who paid minimum wage and treated staff badly. The employees he had were paid top of the scale, but then at Castle Dysert, they charged top-end rates.

'So if everyone can get to where they need to be, ensure everything is in perfect shape, myself, Carlos and Olga will be around for any questions.'

Olga had already briefed him at 6:30. After the tour, the minister and his entourage would have tea and scones in the orangery, which she had temporarily closed to guests. Morning coffee for everyone else was relocated to the library.

Once back in his office, he picked up the phone and asked to be put through to Billie. He wanted her to know the schedule so that no surprises happened for either her or the minister.

'Good morning, Billie. It's Conor,' he said. 'Sorry if I woke you. I just wanted to let you know he'll be here at 8:30.'

'Thanks, Conor. You didn't wake me. We're going horse riding with Olivia this morning, and then we're going to Ennis today and maybe to a castle for a look around afterwards.'

'Great stuff, enjoy it. Olivia is great – she's like your man the horse whisperer. They are all calm when she's around. I don't know the front from the back of a horse myself.' He chuckled. 'So have a great day, and I'll see you tomorrow for the big trip to Dublin, all right?'

'Great, we're looking forward to it. And thanks for the concern, Conor. He hasn't called and I guess he won't. I got a call on my cell yesterday from an Irish number, but it was just the airline advising us that the flight home was going to be delayed by two hours. Mom and I were staring at the phone like it was radioactive, afraid to answer it.' She sighed.

Conor hated to hear the sadness in her voice. 'I'm sorry, Billie, but maybe he will in the future. I have a half-sister in the UK that I've never met, and I will make contact sometime, but I'm just not ready now. It's complicated, but sometimes people need a bit of time to get used to an idea, you know?'

'Yeah, I guess. Thanks, Conor, for everything.'

'Not a bother. Now I better get myself organised. Enjoy the day.'

He hung up and thought about his sister. Liz had got married a while back, and Ana told him that she'd sent a gift over with Jamsie. Initially he'd felt a bit – he didn't know – weird about it or something, but in hindsight, it was a nice gesture. Ana had been understandably annoyed that he'd never mentioned the wedding invitation. He should have told her, he supposed, but he didn't want to go and he didn't want her trying to convince him to. They'd had an argument and then a reasonable talk, and now it was all OK again, but he'd promised not to keep things from her in the future. He had no reason not to like Liz, or even to want to meet her, but something – loyalty to his mam probably – was holding him back. That was stupid, though; he knew that.

He checked his watch. 7:50. Everything was ready, and he had forty minutes to go. Ana was out on the desk with Katherine. Olga and Carlos between them had every conceivable thing under control – they were a force to be reckoned with. Ana told him the staff had nicknamed them Bert and Ernie, and he had to admit, they did look an odd pair. She towered over him, but there was a softness in Carlos in recent weeks that astonished and kind of unsettled everyone. He was transformed. They were both pernickety in the extreme – everything had to be just so – though she had better people skills, and they seemed to click. It was an unfathomable relationship, but like so many others in life, it worked.

He had nothing to do but wait. Then he had an idea. He scrolled through his emails, finding the one he'd received from his sister, and read it again.

Hi Conor,

Dad told me he'd found you and all you did for Gerry. It means the world to him to be reunited with you. He told me about you growing up, so I always knew I had two brothers, though you never knew about me understandably. I would really like to meet you sometime, but I won't push it. Here's my number, and if you ever want to get in touch, please do. Dad tells me you're married to a lovely woman and have two little boys. I'm getting married myself in the spring. His name is Damien and he's from Belfast. If you and Ana wanted to come, you'd be more than welcome.

All the best,

Liz x

Taking out his phone, he punched in the phone number.

'Hello?' a very cultured British voice answered.

Conor hesitated; he could just hang up. 'Hi, Liz, this is Conor.' He exhaled. 'Your brother.'

'Oh my God, Conor, I'd given up on ever hearing from you! How wonderful! How are you?'

Conor couldn't help but smile at her enthusiasm. 'I'm grand. I...I'm sorry it took so long. I just...'

'It's OK, I get it. Dad explained it to me, and I know it must be weird. I'm the reason he left and that would be so hard to reconcile. And then with your mum passing away... I'm so sorry for everything, Conor.'

'Not your fault. But yeah, the emotions were complicated. But I don't know... All of a sudden not seeing you or even speaking to you seemed so stupid. So here I am,' he finished, unsure what to say next.

'Well, I'm so glad you did. And thank you for the beautiful bowl. I'm actually looking at it right now. It's in the middle of our dining room table.'

'Well, that was Ana, if I'm honest,' Conor admitted.

'Oh, I know. Damien is the same. He admired a painting in his parents' house at Christmas that we'd bought them. He has no idea about that stuff.' Liz laughed, skilfully normalising what was much more than an oversight on Conor's part.

'So how did the wedding go?' Conor asked.

'Great, it was lovely. Well, there's a bit of tension, shall we say, between my mother and Dad. She's an incurable snob, if I'm honest, and she can't stand it that Dad and I are close. But we are, and that's all there is to it. Her husband is OK, a bit of an eejit as Dad might say, but he's fine in small doses. But Damien's gang are mad, typical Irish, up till all hours partying and singing. We went on our honeymoon to Mauritius and South Africa and had a great time, but it's back to reality with a bang now, I'm afraid.'

'And what do you do?' Conor asked, warming to the bubbly girl.

'I'm a radiographer and Damien is a cardiac surgeon. We met at work. Dad tells me you have an amazing hotel?'

'Well, part owner, but yeah, it's fairly special all right. Ana, my wife, works here too.'

'Dad has told me all about you, about Joe and Artie – he's crazy about those boys. He was so happy when you asked him to take care of them a while ago. He rang me right after he got off the phone from you – he could hardly talk. Last year, he was so nervous approaching you, and with good reason, I might add, but I'm happy it's worked out for him.'

Conor could hear the love she had for Jamsie in her voice. 'I wasn't exactly thrilled when he showed up, to be honest. My mam had a very hard life, and so did Gerry and I after he left us, so I had a lot of years of resentment to work through. But my wife is very persuasive, and she really encouraged me to bury the hatchet. Though at the start, I'd have been happy to bury it in his head.' He chuckled.

'I don't blame you. What he did was appalling. Leaving your marriage is one thing, but never saying why or ever contacting your children again, that's... Well, he's so sorry.' Liz was loyal as well as pragmatic.

'Would you and Damien like to come over for a weekend? You could stay at the castle, meet Ana and the boys?' The words were out before he had time to think about it. Life was too short for silly feuds. This business with Billie and her birth father and all the hurt that family endured over the years made him realise. Liz was his sister; it was time they met.

There was silence on the line, and he wondered if the call had dropped. 'Liz?' he prompted.

'I would love that, Conor, thank you.' He heard her exhale. 'I'd really love that.'

CHAPTER 19

*C*onor hung up and went out to the front desk, calling Ana into his office. Quickly, he told her what he'd done.

'Oh, Conor, I am so happy! And she seemed nice?' Ana was delighted.

'She did, very bubbly and chatty. She's got quite a posh accent, which I wasn't expecting, but reading between the lines, I'd say her family are very well-to-do, and she doesn't get along with her mother – she's a snob according to Liz – but she's very close to Jamsie. So she and her husband are coming over for a weekend next month to meet us all.' He was surprised at how good he felt.

'Wonderful.' Ana grinned. 'And you know what? Today I am dropping the boys, and Artie is just like himself again. Lots of boys playing football in the yard before school begin. I watching them, not so he can see, but he is back. Our boy is happy again.'

'That's brilliant. Such a relief, and all achieved by sitting down and talking it out rationally. Isn't that right, Ana?' he asked, a note of scepticism in his voice, as he put his arms around her.

'Mostly that, yes.' She winked and planted a quick kiss on his lips.

'I'm glad you're on my side, Mrs O'Shea, do you know that? Because I sure would hate to have an enemy like you.' He let her go.

'Be careful then,' she joked. 'Oh, what time you going in Dublin tomorrow?'

'Not sure. I've to meet Corlene, and take that girl Billie to meet a family in Dublin. I'll sort all of that once the bigwig guest is out of the way.'

'OK, darling. Good luck with the minister. You can charm the squirrels from the trees, so it will be fine.'

Conor looked up as she went out the door. 'Birds,' he said with a grin.

'What?' Ana was confused.

'Charm the birds from the trees, not squirrels.' He was laughing now.

'Well, that is stupid. Squirrels lives in trees, not birds...' She left, shaking her head.

Within seconds, Olga was at his door, saying the minister was on the way up the drive.

Conor straightened his tie, the sapphire-blue one that Ana bought him because it was the exact colour of his eyes, and shrugged on the jacket of his navy pinstriped suit.

'Showtime.' He winked at Olga.

'Good luck, Conor. You'll be brilliant.'

Carlos was hovering around the reception area, his eagle eyes darting everywhere. He was down to one crutch now, and considerably less ratty. The staff were busy, going about their business, and the guests of the hotel were beginning to mill about the breakfast room. Ana and Katherine were on reception and everything gleamed. A specialist company from Belfast had been called in to clean all the suits of armour, swords and artistic heraldry that dotted the castle.

Apart from running a thriving business, Conor got huge personal satisfaction from the hotel. It had such a tragic history, but to see it now, a hive of activity, providing quality employment for the area, buildings and grounds of exquisite beauty, made him immensely proud of what they had achieved. The third floor was now the same temperature as the rest of the hotel, and all of the unexplained events that had dogged the building for so long seemed to have been resolved the night of the fire.

People always asked him about the rumours of hauntings and sightings, and all the stories had legs and arms by this stage, but he would never be drawn and just laughed it off as old stories. He'd warned the staff not to get into it, though he knew they did, and theories and conjecture abounded. But Conor would never tell the real story of what happened that night to anyone.

The story of how Corlene's ex, Dylan's father, had tried to burn the place to the ground, how he attempted to assault poor Laoise, Dylan's girlfriend, and how Conor had fought with him, resulting in Conor being knocked unconscious in the process, was one everyone knew. It was also common knowledge how he came to and ran into the burning hotel once he knew his boys were in there. But the bit in between – how Conor woke in the stable yard to a little boy in Edwardian clothes pleading with him to wake up, this little long-haired boy telling him where Joe and Artie were – that was a story that Conor would take to his grave. Maybe people would believe it, or maybe they wouldn't. Perhaps they would say it was because of the blow to the head that he had imagined things, but Conor knew what he saw, and nothing would ever convince him that the little boy who saved his sons was anyone other than the ghost of Grenville King, the child who died in the 1921 fire.

The hotel had risen like a phoenix from the ashes. Luckily, the insurance paid out, and the castle was, in fact, better now than ever. He loved the place and wanted others to see how special it was too. Bringing Castle Dysert to an international audience by hosting the EU leader summit would take them into a whole other league if they could pull it off.

The hour flew by. The minster was a very affable man and clearly impressed with the castle. Conor felt a little awkward, knowing something so intimate about a man he'd only just met, but he managed to put it to the back of his mind. The relationship between Liam Seoige and Billie was not his business, but he wished for the girl's sake that Liam would reach out to her, as they were so fond of saying now.

The coffee break took a little longer than originally planned, as the minister wanted to see everything. He was excited by the environmental initiatives they had put in place and spoke with authority on the subject of renewable resources. He quizzed Conor about the castle, and it was 9:45 before he left, parting with assurances that he would back the hotel's bid for the summit. He seemed a very genuine kind of man.

As Conor escorted him back to his car, he noticed several guests had gathered in the lobby to see what all the commotion was about. TV cameras and several reporters with fluffy microphones pointed at the minister filled the entranceway but were shepherded back by the minister's minders. Conor waved him off, and within ten minutes of his departure, the hotel was back to normal once more.

Olga and Carlos were waiting at the desk.

'My office?' he said, ushering them ahead of him.

'Well done to both of you! It all went like clockwork. Thanks for all of your efforts. He seems to think we'd be the perfect venue for the summit, so we're one step of the way there.'

The glee on Olga's face was touching. Even Carlos looked pleased.

'Now, I've to go to Dublin tomorrow, so can you two hold the fort till I get back?'

'Of course.' Olga beamed and blushed. 'I'm so happy it all went well.'

'Thanks to you two and all the staff here, it did.' Conor smiled as the two left his office and locked the door so he could change his clothes. Five minutes later, dressed in dark golfing trousers and a polo shirt, he reappeared.

'Now I'm going to play a round of golf, and then when she's finished her shift, I'm taking my wife to lunch. And after that, I'm picking my children up from school and going home. Only contact me if it's really an emergency. I need a break, and you two are more than capable.'

He walked past them, ignoring their looks of astonishment. Conor hardly ever took time off, so they were not used to it.

CHAPTER 20

*C*onor really enjoyed his round of golf with Eddie, and he filled the priest in on his sister's upcoming visit and how the whole situation with the boys had been resolved. Eddie confided in Conor that he had developed type 2 diabetes, and so whether he wanted to or not, the diet would have to be taken in hand. Poor Eddie was allergic to the idea of living on the what he called rabbit food the nutritionist had restricted him to, but the alternative was horrible.

As Conor lined up his ball at the ninth tee box, he said, 'When Ana was sick, she researched all kinds of diets – you know, to support the chemo and all the rest. And she discovered that cutting out sugar made a huge difference. She found it tricky at the start, but you know, now we are all on it. The boys don't eat sugar and neither do I, and I used to have a desperate sweet tooth. Ana makes a chocolate cake, no sugar, just dark chocolate and eggs and butter, I think. Like, this is a treat food now, mind you, a sliver now and again, but I'll get her to make you some. You can do it, Eddie, and we all need you, so we'll help whatever way we can.'

'Ah, sure the scones and sweets had to catch up to me, I suppose,' Eddie said mournfully. 'They don't leave us much in the way of pleasure in the priesthood, so some lads hit the bottle and others hit the cakes. Either one will take its toll eventually.'

Conor laughed and patted his old friend on the back. Eddie had told Conor years ago that there had been a woman, someone Eddie cared about, but he was a priest and it couldn't be. It was a lonely life, but Eddie was resigned to it.

They finished their game, and afterwards, Conor picked Ana up and took her to a nice café for lunch. He thought she was looking a little drawn.

'Are you sure you're not doing too much? You look a bit tired,' he said, concerned.

'No, stop worrying. I'm fine.'

But he knew how ill she'd been, and he wanted to keep her well. He decided he'd ask Katherine what she thought.

Joe and Artie were delighted to see him – he hardly ever got to pick them up – and they dashed out of the schoolyard and ran towards him, schoolbags and coats trailing. Conor knew they wouldn't always do it, so he was enjoying it while it lasted, and seeing their delight made him realise how much of their childhood he'd been missing. He promised himself that whatever happened, he would make more time for his family.

* * *

THE NEXT MORNING, feeling refreshed and happy, Conor made the boys breakfast while Ana had a shower. They dropped them to school before heading into work together. It was a beautiful day, and he found he was looking forward to going to Dublin and helping Sol put some old hurts to bed for once and for all. One of the best things about being a tour driver all those years was the connections he made. He'd been fortunate to find himself in the middle of people's personal dramas, and he'd made some great friends, many of whom stayed in touch by email.

Ana was FaceTiming her sister back in Kiev, speaking such rapid Ukrainian that Conor was lost after a few seconds. So he reminisced as he drove. He thought of Ellen O'Donovan, who had passed away now but managed to find her family in Cork after over eighty years, and the friends of Bubbles O'Leary, a larger-than-life bar owner in New York whose friends scattered his ashes under a rainbow off the coast of Kerry. Images flooded his mind. The lovely old couple who knew the wife was terminally ill and who died on his bus, peacefully, one summer's day in Kilkenny. Anna and Juliet, two lonely women, decades apart, but who formed a friendship that suited them both. Anna was pregnant but married to an awful man, and Juliet was mourning her husband, Larry, but had come on holidays with the domineering Dorothy Crane in the absence of any better ideas. There had been all kinds of ructions, but in the end, Anna and Juliet set up house together in Florida. They were best friends, and now that Anna had remarried and had two other children, Juliet was a de facto granny. They sent a card every Christmas.

Ana finished her call as he rounded the bend, the entire vista of the bay before them.

'What you thinking?' she asked. 'You look happy.'

'Oh, just about all the people I've met who came here looking for one thing but ending up with something else. I was lucky to get to meet such interesting characters.' He reached over and held her hand.

'Do you miss it, driving the tours?' she asked.

'Sometimes, but not really. I get to do more or less the same thing sometimes in the hotel, and I get to be at home every night with my lovely family. So no, I wouldn't go back. But today I'm taking that Ukrainian guy Marko and his family to Dublin with me. They have something to do there, so I'm going to help them.'

He told her the whole story of Liam Seoige and Sol and the war, knowing she wouldn't breathe a word to anyone.

When he finished, she turned to face him. 'You're such a good man, Conor, so kind. I love you.'

He smiled as he pulled into the hotel carpark. 'I love you too,' he said.

Billie and the others were ready when he arrived. They'd finished breakfast and were enjoying the weak morning sun outside the castle.

'Morning, folks. I'll be with you in a few minutes. I just need to sort one or two things here, and we'll be off.'

'Take your time, Conor. We're enjoying the morning,' Sol said. He was reading a brochure while Marilyn practised yoga on the lawn, quite oblivious to all the hustle and bustle around her as people came and went into the castle. Donna and Marko were telling Billie and Noah all about the banquet the previous night, where they were chosen as the chieftain and his wife and got to sit at the top table and decide about putting people in dungeons and all sorts. They drank mead and ate ribs with their fingers, and it sounded like a lot of fun.

Conor had a quick meeting with Carlos and Olga – they seemed to come as a set these days – and they briefed him on every department and what was on that day. Carlos was in much better form as his injuries were almost healed, but the adoration of Olga being the main reason, Conor suspected. He was relieved to see him less prickly, and the man seemed to be getting on better with the staff as well – Olga was a wonder. Ana was on the front desk and Katherine was due in later. Everything was under control, and he felt confident leaving them in charge.

He loaded his little group on the sleek black Mercedes mini coach and set off for Dublin, giving them commentary as they went, pointing out ancient ring forts, castles and buildings of interest as well as regaling them with stories and interesting bits and pieces about Irish life. They shouted questions at him as they drove, and the miles flew by.

Conor noticed that Billie, Noah, Marko and Marilyn chatted but Sol and Donna seemed lost in thought. He stopped for fuel halfway to Dublin and gave the group a chance to stretch their legs and grab a drink. Donna stayed on the bus, so he went over to where she was sitting.

'Donna, is everything OK?' he asked, concerned.

She looked at him, and he could see the uncertainty there of whether she should confide in him.

'I'm fine, Conor. I just wish he'd call. I feel so bad for Billie. She's trying not to let it hurt, but I know she feels rejected. I know I can't do anything else, but I feel responsible and just wish I could fix this for her. I guess we feel our kids' hurt more acutely than our own sometimes, right?' She sighed.

Conor thought about how upset he was when Artie was being bullied and empathised completely. 'I know what you mean. It's a hard one. I spoke to him yesterday, and obviously he doesn't realise that I know anything, but he seemed like a decent kind of man. Maybe he just needs some time? It's a tricky one for anyone, but for him, at this point in time, it must be especially worrying. The current Taoiseach is very close to retirement age, and everyone had Seoige tipped as the new leader. He's squeaky clean, not a whiff of scandal, happily married, kids, no dodgy dealings, so there are plenty in opposition who'd love nothing better than this story.'

'He's not going to want a scandal,' Donna finished for him.

Conor shrugged. 'Maybe not.'

'Funny, I'm not surprised that he's so high up. He was a good guy, you know? Cared about people, and would do anything – I mean literally anything. He was fearless...' She paused. 'He would love her. They are so alike in lots of ways.'

Conor looked out the window to where the others were approaching the bus, Marilyn laden down with snacks of all kinds as usual, the others just holding coffee cups.

'Well, they are on the way back now. Why don't you get through today and let it be about your dad and his story first, and try to put the other stuff to the back of your mind? You told me that your relationship with her was a bit...I don't know...tense?'

'She hated me for marrying Marko, for not being there when my son died, for neglecting her and Matt... Take your pick of reasons...' Donna said sadly.

'But you are getting on so much better now, aren't you? And look at that.' He pointed out the window. Billie and Marko were joking around, trying on a leprechaun hat that had a red beard attached. 'I bet you never thought you'd see that, did you?'

She laughed. 'No, I certainly did not. I think you're right. Thanks, Conor.' Donna said as the others boarded the bus.

As Conor sat into the driver's seat once more, Sol approached him. 'I called the store yesterday, and they told me that there was nobody there at the moment who could help me, but I just got a call while we were in the gas station. One of the sons of the family is still alive. His secretary just called. She asked that we go to the house. He's elderly and in a wheelchair now, but he wants to meet me. She gave me the address.' Sol handed Conor a napkin. 'Sorry, I was waiting for Marilyn to get a sandwich, so I wrote on the first thing I could find.'

'Righto, Sol, that's no problem. It's Howth, a lovely part of Dublin, but it's a bit out of town, and I won't be able to get you there before my meeting. How about I drop you all in the city centre – you can do a bit of sightseeing or whatever – and I'll take you to meet this man when I finish? I shouldn't be more than an hour or so.'

'Are you sure?' Sol asked. 'You've been so kind to us, but I'm sure we could take a cab.'

'Ah, sure it's fine. I find these kinds of stories fascinating to be honest with you. I've been fortunate enough to be involved in lots of stories like these in my career, so I never turn down the opportunity. I might write a book of my exploits someday.' Conor winked and chuckled. 'But seriously, it's no bother. That's North County Dublin, so well outside the city, but we'll find it.'

'Thank you, Conor,' Sol said sincerely. 'For everything. You and your staff at the hotel are changing my perception of Ireland as an unwelcoming place.' He smiled.

'Well, we couldn't have been much worse in your estimation, so I'm glad I'm able to redeem at least some of my countrymen,' Conor joked as he turned the key.

He stopped at St Stephen's Green with instructions on where to go to see the sights of the capital. There was so much to see and do in Dublin that he'd had to restrict his suggestions to a few key places, but he was hoping they'd get at least a flavour. As they got off the bus, he spotted a former colleague and tour guide in the middle of a walking tour.

'Elaine, the very woman,' he called as she stopped mid-speech and embraced him.

'Conor! Great to see you. Are you back to us? The high life got too much for you?' she teased.

'Not exactly. I'm still playing lord of the manor. But here, would you do me a favour? These guests are friends of mine, and I've to leave them out in Dublin for about an hour and a half. Could you take them under your wing?'

She smiled. 'Of course. This group are all one family as well.' She turned to her gathered group. 'This is Conor, a friend of mine, and these people are wondering if they can join us. Do you guys mind if these folks tag along?'

They had no objection. A few seconds of conversation showed them as being from Boston too, so Conor left his group in Elaine's capable hands and drove off to park the bus before meeting Corlene.

She had booked a table for lunch at the Westbury, a very lovely hotel off Grafton Street, but she was late as usual. Conor read the paper and texted Ana while he waited. Eventually, Corlene turned up, all apologies and reeking of expensive perfume.

She was a far cry from the impoverished divorcee on the prowl for husband number five that she was when he first met her on one of his tours. In those days, she was all too-tight leopard skin, bottle-bleached hair and fake diamantes. She came to Ireland with her long-suffering teenage son, Dylan, to find a man, but she ended up finding a friend and a benefactor in an old Texan called Bert, who, when he died, left her a large legacy – and he left Conor one too. He was an unusual man, Bert, kind and shrewd in equal measure, and he saw an inherent goodness in Corlene that she may not even have known she had herself. She was now a wealthy woman, dressed to the nines every time Conor saw her, expensive designer clothes head to toe. But underneath, she hadn't changed. She was still an incorrigible flirt, but her heart was in the right place.

'Conor, I swear you get sexier every time I see you,' she purred into his ear as she kissed him hello, running her hand down his back. 'Mmm,' she murmured appreciatively.

'And you don't change a bit.' He grinned and sat down.

'So Ana and the kids are fine?' she asked in a perfunctory way.

Corlene was not a fan of family life, and children, by her own admission, bored her.

'Grand altogether.'

They ordered lunch, and he filled her in on everything that had been happening at Castle Dysert.

'You're doing such an amazing job, Conor, truly. And I know I haven't been there much. To be honest, you're probably as well off, and I know Ana can't stand me. But I have a proposition for you.'

'Oh yeah?' Conor raised a sceptical eyebrow. He wasn't going to contradict her about Ana, as she was right. He was cautious about what she was going to suggest. Corlene was a great one for madcap schemes.

'Don't be like that. It's not that kind of proposition, though the offer is always there.' She winked and grinned.

It was exactly that kind of remark that made Ana want to punch her, and Conor didn't blame her. If someone spoke to Ana like that, he'd be furious, but Corlene was an incurable flirt and would never change. Conor knew he didn't need to assure Ana that he would never look at another woman; she was totally confident of his fidelity as he was of hers. But he knew she liked it when he pointed out that if he were single, Corlene would most certainly not be his type with her fake everything from boobs to hair.

'OK. I'm taking a back seat in my business up here. I've a fabulous woman running it now, and she, like you, is spectacularly good at her job. Women are waiting months to do our courses. Who'd have thought there were so many straying husbands? But anyway, they are really more self-confidence courses now – most of the women gain so much in self-esteem that they often don't want their cheating, lying rats back.'

Conor was constantly amazed at how successful Corlene was in business. She'd set up an agency helping women of a certain age kind of liven themselves up a bit or something, he wasn't exactly sure. The idea had sprung from a woman she'd met when Corlene was on tour searching for a new husband. This lady, Cynthia, was a lovely person but looked like a scarecrow. Cynthia had fallen for a big Irish-American cop, also on the tour, but they were a bit bumbling in getting together. So Corlene decided to apply her not inconsiderable cosmetic commando skills to Cynthia and turned that caterpillar into a butterfly. The transformation was nothing short of miraculous. The cop, Patrick, was blown away, and Bert, an old Texan billionaire, saw a kindness in Corlene and offered to back her in setting up a business doing for other women just what she'd done for Cynthia. The generous offer meant Corlene didn't ever need to rely on a man again, and her son, Dylan, got to stay in Ireland with the music and the girl who stole his heart. It was a win-win. Corlene's business had expanded into a huge thing, advising older women not just on clothes and make-up but on careers, health and lots of other things, and it had become a serious movement.

'Well done. I saw the feature in the *Sunday Times* last week – very impressive,' Conor said as he cut into his salmon.

'Well, thank you, but that's not what I want to talk about. I want to sell you my stake of the castle.' She sipped her merlot and maintained eye contact with him over the glass.

Conor laughed. 'Oh right, no bother. I'll just use the fifty million quid I have stashed under the bed, will I?'

'No, hear me out,' Corlene said and lowered her glass. 'You know I'm seeing someone, right? And for the first time in my life, it's good, Conor. I know everyone thinks I'm a home-wrecking harlot, but it's not what it seems. Colm is not contesting the next election, his marriage is over, and he's leaving his wife. We plan on buying some-where, maybe Spain, and getting out of Ireland. It will be a bit hot for a while since his wife is the founder of that charity Cherish and on TV and all of that...'

Conor's brow furrowed in concern. 'Ah, Corlene, are you serious? I knew you were knocking around with him, but he's going to leave his wife, the nation's darling, Bláth MacEntire, for you? Are you sure about this?'

Conor wasn't easily shocked. Corlene had pulled some stunts in her life, but this took the biscuit. Bláth MacEntire was a bubbly red-haired chat show host who had founded a charity that helped very ill children. She spoke Irish and could play the harp, and she was universally adored.

'Look, she's not as sweet as she makes out. That so-called children's charity nets her a nice profit each year, and apparently she's all sugar and spice on that insipid TV show she does, but she's a horror to work for. She knows about us and couldn't give a damn. Men are not her thing, if you know what I mean. It was a political marriage, and she made him miserable. They stayed together while he was in office, but now that he's resigning...' She shrugged.

'Well, it's your life, but...' Conor wasn't sure. 'Does Dylan know about this?'

'Not yet. He's flying in next week from Australia, so I'll tell him then.' She hesitated. 'I know it looks bad, but honestly, we love each other, and, well, I just want to share my life with him in peace. Colm and Bláth have genuinely not lived under the same roof for ten years. They don't have any children because, well, they never had an intimate marriage. Her father was high up in the party and needed a pet politician. Colm's face fit, but he hadn't a dime when he started out, so Bláth's old man bankrolled him, and believe me, he got more than his money's worth. But he's dead now. Bláth MacEntire is a vindictive witch who delighted in making Colm miserable, and he's paid his debt. Neither of us have ever been really happy in a relationship before, and we just want to live out our lives quietly together.'

Something about her, an unexpected vulnerability, melted Conor. She'd had a hard life, and of course she deserved some happiness at long last.

Before he could say anything, she went on. 'So here's my proposal. The hotel would be hurt by association with me once the papers get hold of this, so you buy me out and the castle is unscathed by the inevitable media storm that's coming. You own forty percent already. My stake is worth about fifty million, but I'll sell to you for ten. I don't need any more.'

Conor was stunned. His first thought was Corlene's son. It was his inheritance she was essentially giving away.

'But what about Dylan, Corlene? What does he have to say about this? If you are giving your share to anyone, surely it should be him?'

'I knew you'd say that, but don't worry about it. I've spoken to him, and he's fine with it. He and Laoise have just signed a huge deal with their record company, so they are very wealthy young people. He was the one who told me to sell to you.'

Conor sat back. Corlene's asking price was ridiculously low considering what she was walking away from, and he appreciated it, but it was still impossible. There was no way he could get his hands on that kind of money. He said as much to her.

'You are thinking about the bank lending to you, Conor, but that's not the stake here. You need to think about the hotel as the asset. The place is thriving and you're going to host the European summit – I'll get Colm on board with that too before he bows out – so the bank will lend it to you.'

'And at fifty-five years old, I'm in debt up to my eyes? I don't know, Corlene, I –'

'Look, think about it, talk it over with Ana. But be quick. I'm going to sell my share either way, Conor, I'm sorry.'

The bombshell that he would have to deal with a new partner, and a senior partner at that, was a horrible one, but Corlene was entitled to do what she wanted. If she put her share on the open market, she could get 50 or even 60 million for it easily. The hotel was valued at over 100 million for insurance purposes, so she was really taking a huge hit by offering it to him for only ten.

They settled the bill and walked out onto the street together. Corlene had a hair appointment, and he needed to pick up his group again, though the last thing he felt like now was making small talk. His whole future was on the line, and he had some big decisions to make.

'It's a great opportunity, Conor, not one that will come around again. As Bert used to say, the opportunity of a lifetime has to be taken in the lifetime of that opportunity. The clock is ticking. I hate to pressure you, but this thing with me and Colm is a tinderbox ready to blow.'

'OK, let me think about it,' he said. He kissed her quickly on the cheek. 'And mind yourself. You know where we are if you need to escape.'

'Thanks, Conor. I just might need a few days lying low when this breaks, which could be any day to be honest. Don't take too long making your decision though, OK?' she replied as she tottered down Grafton Street on her ridiculously high heels.

Conor picked the group up at the appointed spot and did as he had done many times before – put his personal issues to the back of his mind and put on his professional face.

Sol was nervous, he could tell, and Marilyn sat next to him, holding his hand.

He found the house they were looking for easily. It was a large and imposing Georgian mansion at the end of a long driveway. The house enjoyed magnificent views over Dublin Bay, and Conor estimated that they must have been a very successful family to own such a property. He parked the bus in the large area to the side of the house.

A uniformed butler emerged and escorted them into a sumptuous living room with five beautiful bay windows overlooking the sea. They all stood and took in the huge room, the walls lined with grill-covered book cases. Several overstuffed sofas and armchairs dotted the room. There was an incredibly ornate fireplace, capable of burning whole tree trunks, Conor imagined.

He had offered to wait in the bus, but Sol asked that he join them. Sol wanted Conor to hear whatever the man had to say, and perhaps he could help them interpret it as well. Sol admitted that he found some Irish accents difficult to decipher.

They waited nervously, Donna sitting with Marko on one of the sofas and Billie and Noah standing and examining the bookcases. Marilyn and Sol sat beside the enormous cream and red marble fireplace, holding hands but saying nothing.

'This place is amazing, isn't it?' Noah murmured. 'I don't know why, but I never thought of these kinds of places being in Ireland.'

Conor nodded, deliberately keeping his voice low. 'Yes, the cottage is more the image Americans are familiar with, and I suppose most of the people who emigrated did so out of very poor houses. But there was always plenty of money in this country.'

After a few minutes, the butler appeared again, this time assisting an elderly man in a motorised wheelchair.

'Good afternoon. You are all very welcome. Thank you so much for contacting me.' The man turned slowly towards the butler. 'Brian, could you please arrange some refreshment?' He turned back to face them all once again. 'What would you like? I think we have most things.'

The man was in his late eighties, Conor guessed, and gaunt. A few wisps of silver hair grew from his balding head and his skin was wrinkled with age, but his voice was strong. He wore a suit and tie and had a canary-yellow handkerchief in his breast pocket. His accent was Irish but not like Conor's; it had a slight English intonation, common among the gentry.

'Coffee would be lovely,' Conor responded when nobody spoke.

The family all watched Sol for his reaction as the butler disappeared.

'Thank you for seeing us.' Sol stood. 'My name is Sol Bermann, and my father was Amos Behrman. He was a –'

The man in the wheelchair held up his hand. 'I know who you are, Mr Bermann, and I have a message for you, something I hoped I would get to deliver personally in my lifetime.'

The family were stunned.

'What do you mean?' Sol asked.

'Well, Mr Bermann, my name is Charles O'Doherty. My father and yours were friends, I believe.'

'Well, at one point they were...' Sol said darkly.

'Indeed.' Charles wheeled his chair over to an ornate bureau and opened a drawer. After rifling through several papers, he extracted a sealed envelope. He wheeled back to Sol and handed it to him.

Bemused, Sol extracted the single sheet. In copperplate script on the envelope was written, 'To any member of the Behrman family'.

Sol's hands trembled as he opened it. You could hear a pin drop in the room. He read aloud.

To Amos, Sofia or any surviving member of the Behrman family.

I have tried in vain throughout my life to find you. I owe you an apology, and my excuse is not worthy of mention. I am deeply ashamed of my actions, and not a day of my life has gone by without my thinking of you and your family and praying you survived. I am an old man now, and I have tried to uncover what happened to your family. I went to Germany in 1947. I found your house, but someone else was living there. They claimed to have no idea who you were or what had happened to you. I searched the police records and so on, but it all came to naught. I made several inquiries through connections we had here and in London, but again, in the vast ocean of human suffering brought about by Hitler, it was like trying to find a single shell.

I should have helped you. I could have tried harder and I didn't, the only reason being my personal greed and fear of loss of standing in my community. These are pathetic reasons, I know, so I won't dwell on them, not to ease my own discomfort, as that is impossible, but for fear you would think I was making excuses. I am not. My rejection of your pleas for help was then, and remains now, unforgivable. All I can offer is my most heartfelt apology. I am sorry, and I have never regretted anything more.

I pray you survived. I have spent a lifetime working with refugees in an effort to assuage some of the guilt I rightly feel, but it is a stain incapable of being expunged.

I am an old man now, and will die soon. I have bequeathed most of my assets, save what is due my son and daughter for their endless patience and love, to Yad Vashem. They may use it however they see fit.

Yours faithfully,

Edmund O'Doherty

'I don't understand. What is this?' Sol asked.

'Please, Mr Bermann, take a seat. I have a story to tell.'

The butler arrived with a tray, but nobody touched it as Charles began to speak.

'My father wrote that note in 1980. He was dead two weeks later. All of his life, he told us about his friends, the Behrmans, and how he wished he had done more to save them. Your family name was used in our house often, Sol, and though we never met your parents or your siblings, I felt like I knew you all. He often described the night, towards the end of the war, I think, that he and my mother had gone to the cinema and Pathé News showed images of the liberation of the Nazi death camps. He came home and locked himself in his study, and we didn't see him for days. The man I remember as my father before that night disappeared, and to my ten-year-old eyes, another man came out of that study a few days later. He was tormented – honestly, that is not too strong a word – he was absolutely tormented by what he had consigned your family to.'

The air was thick with expectation. Nobody spoke, so Charles went on.

'My father's family were in the precious metals and jewellery business for generations. That is, as you know, how they got to know your family. My father and mother often spoke of the friendship, so when your father asked for my father's help, immediately he went to the relevant authorities to set about providing a home in Ireland for you all. But Ireland was a deeply anti-Semitic country, and my father was the supplier to the Archdiocese of Dublin. We crafted all of the gold, chalices, crosses, thuribles and so on. The eucharistic Congress had been held in 1932 here, a world gathering of Catholics, and my family had the contract. We became very, very wealthy as a result.' He paused and swallowed, taking a sip of water from a beaker attached to his wheelchair.

'Once word got to the ears of the archbishop that my father was making enquiries to bring a Jewish family over here, he was summoned to the bishop's palace and told in no uncertain terms to desist in that course of action immediately. He was threatened with the removal of all Church contracts, and that would have meant not just a collapse of the family business but also of the family's social standing. He tried to reason with the archbishop, explain that Amos and his family were old friends, but the archbishop was having none of it. He did not want to see Jews coming into Ireland under any circumstances, and he was going to use whatever leverage he could to stop it. He gave my father this ultimatum and gave him no time to mull it over – he had to decide there and then. Fearing the worst for his business and his position, he agreed to do as the archbishop demanded. He told my mother and said that he regretted the decision the moment he had made it, but she sided with the bishop. She was a fiercely ardent Catholic, my mother, and so he had nowhere to vent his guilt at abandoning his friend. Eventually, weeks later, he defied both the archbishop and his wife and wrote to your father, suggesting that if he could get out of Germany by any means, then he would fund the family for as long as was necessary, but by then, well, it was too late. He never got a response to the letter. He was wracked with guilt. Each Friday night, he would light a candle and sit in his office alone, and my mother would tell us he was "In one of his moods". She would roll her eyes, I do remember that, as if he was being ridiculous. He worked all the time, and we grew in wealth and status as a family, but my father was hollow inside. He confided in his brother, my uncle, who told me years later. That night – when he went to the pictures, saw the images on the screen and thought about what he had condemned his friend's family to – was too much. He became obsessed, not just with finding your family but with helping refugees generally. He wrote to the papers, he used his position to highlight the plight of the European Jews, all the while desperately trying to find Amos and Sofia. Of course, my mother was mortified. Their marriage effectively ended at that stage. He was single-minded. I remember in May of 1945 when de Valera called to Dr Hempel, the German ambassador to Ireland, and offered condolences on the death of Hitler, my father stood outside the Dáil – that's our parliament – with a placard that said "No condolence from this Irishman. May Hitler rot in hell." He was arrested that time for being disorderly. He used his day in court to make an impassioned speech from the dock before being ordered to pay a fine. Eventually, his brother, my uncle, was running the business single-handedly while my father campaigned and searched for your family. I note from your message that the spelling of your name is different? Perhaps that made his quest even more difficult.'

Sol was unable to speak, so Donna interjected. 'Yes, a lot of Americans changed the spelling to make it easier, you know…'

'I understand. When I was an adult, my father asked me to help him, and I said I would but I had no idea where to even start, or if you'd survived at all. I did try. We went back once more in the early seventies to Brunhoff am Neckar, but there was no trace of the family there at all. In the end, we went to speak to the mayor. He told us that as far as he knew – and he was only a child during the war – the entire family had died in the death camps, and so we gave up.'

Charles wiped a tear from the side of his eye. 'I don't know why he said that when it wasn't true. Perhaps he thought it was, or it was kinder or something. He seemed like a decent man. My father went into a deep depression for months, and then one day decided that if he couldn't help the Behrmans anymore, there were many more displaced people, so he set up the Behrman Trust. He dedicated his life and most of his money to it, and the trust has been instrumental in improving the lives of refugees all over the world. You can look it up – TheBerhmanTrust.org. It's run by a board now, and I'm one of the trustees, but they are good people and do good work. At the moment, they are involved with the people attempting to cross the Mediterranean in boats. We have people on the ground in Greece and Italy, trying to help.'

Noah looked it up on his iPad and showed the website to Sol. Tears filled the old man's eyes. The Behrman Trust. He scrolled through pictures of children and adults, living in tents and on meagre rations. There was a lot of information on the website about the work they did, and it seemed to be a very active organisation.

The entire family crowded around the tablet, reading the text and looking at the photographs. In the 'About' section, there was a brief story about the Behrman family, and a photo of Sol's parents that he had never seen. It said his parents had perished in the Holocaust, and that the trust was dedicated to their memory.

Charles spoke again. 'My father was not a bad man, Mr Bermann, but he was not strong enough to stand up to the Church and his wife and the social circles they moved in. I know it was a failure that dogged him all of his life, and he deeply regretted his weakness. He told his brother, now long dead, how he wished he could have had the courage to defy the archbishop that day, especially as time wore on and the fate of the Jews became apparent in all its horrific detail. I know he would want me to tell you how very sorry he was.'

Conor watched as Sol stood. He was a tall man. He walked over to Charles and extended his hand, and the Irishman shook it. Both men held hands for the longest time, and Conor had that feeling once again that he was witnessing something momentous.

'Your father and mine were good friends. It hurt him so deeply that he got no help, and I'll tell you the truth, he remained sad about it to the day he died. My mother too. Their sadness was not all down to your father's reluctance though – it was survivor's guilt. They had lost so much, you see. All Jews of a certain generation feel that way, and it's hard to explain. But having said that, your father sounds like a good man. He didn't know what people like us were facing. And he was just trying to protect his own family, his livelihood. Who knows which of us would have acted differently? I'm so touched by what I've seen here today, and I wish they could have seen it too. Perhaps they are all together now, in heaven. Who knows? I hope they are.'

Another round of drinks arrived, this time with a bottle of sherry and a bottle of whiskey, and they drank a toast to the souls of the dead.

Sol said the mourning Kaddish for his family, the prayer for the dead, though he explained it should be with ten other Jews, and Billie looked up the words in English on her phone so Charles could join in.

Charles asked the butler to bring him a box of old photos. The old man looked through, flipping through one after the other. Eventually, he found the one he was looking for. It was a group shot, taken at the Phoenix Park in Dublin in 1929. In it were Sol's parents, looking young and carefree, and Charles's parents beside them, smiling for the camera; it had been taken on one of Sol's parents' visits. It was the photo used on the website for the Behrman Trust. Charles also found Christmas cards the Behrmans had sent, some of which contained family pictures of those relatives of Sol's who perished in the death camps. It was an emotional afternoon but a healing one. As they left, each giving Charles a hug, they swore to stay in touch, and Conor believed that they would.

CHAPTER 21

*S*unday morning dawned bright, and the boys were bouncing on Conor and Ana's bed to wake them up.

They were yelling. 'Granda is here, and he has a surprise for us, and he said we can't see it until everyone is there, so *get up!*'

Conor stretched and nudged the sleeping Ana. He knew what it was and that the boys were about to go crazy.

They shook her vigorously. 'Mammy, *wake up*! Didus and Babusya are here too, so it must be something cool.'

Ana groaned and tried to bat them away, but Conor got up and pulled on a t-shirt and jeans.

Jamsie had come down the previous night to see the boys win the under-tens county final, much to their delight, and afterwards, they'd all gone to Mario's for dinner. Artur and Jamsie, the proud grandads of the two lads, ended up playing penalties in the garden when they got home. Danika and Conor had watched out the window as they played in the almost dark.

'He is like boy with twins,' Danika said, pointing at her husband. Conor put his arm around his mother-in-law's shoulders. She and Artur had been such a support to him over the years, and he loved them dearly.

'*Vony lyublyat yoho*,' Conor replied, using some of his limited Ukrainian.

Danika beamed, delighted with his efforts. 'Yes, he loves them much.'

As Danika and Artur were leaving, Conor heard Jamsie explain how they would need to be back early in the morning to see the big surprise. They'd turned up in time like always.

'Joe, get off me!' Ana grumbled as Joe put his ice-cold hands on his mother's back.

They giggled, and Conor decided there would be no more sleep now anyway. 'Right, we're up,' he said, pulling the duvet back despite his wife's protests. 'Come on, Mammy. The boys want to see what Granda got them.'

Ana pulled on her dressing gown, and Conor thought she looked adorable, her hair standing on end, her face sleepy. He drew her in for a kiss as the boys groaned theatrically.

'Oh no, not kissing…ugh. Come on!'

Joe dragged Conor by the hand, and Artie pulled Ana, who was shoving her feet into her slippers. Her parents met them in the kitchen.

Jamsie called from the garden, 'Close your eyes, lads! No peeking!'

Conor covered Joe's eyes and Ana did the same to Artie as they ushered them out to the garden, releasing them both at the same time. There in front of them was Jamsie, a huge grin on his face, and in his arms was a ball of white fluff.

The twins were speechless.

Jamsie went down on his hunkers to be level with his grandsons. 'Now, lads, this is your puppy. He's a Samoyed, and he's got a special coat so that your mammy won't be allergic – we've checked. Your mammy even went to visit this little boy's mammy and daddy a few weeks ago to make sure. He is looking for a home, so do you think you could take care of him?'

'You knew?' Joe managed.

Artie's tears shocked everyone.

'Oh, Artie, are you OK?' Jamsie asked, worried now.

The boy nodded, unable to speak.

'When we say our prayers every night, we always pray we'll get a dog. It's our dream come true,' Joe said with such sincerity that Conor felt his eyes water too.

Jamsie put the little puppy on the grass, and it promptly did a wee on his shoe before running off to investigate a coloured ball. They watched, mesmerised, as the puppy played.

Joe and Artie laughed and immediately went to cuddle the little ball of fluff.

'What will we call him?' Artie asked Joe.

'Lionel?' Joe suggested.

'Perfect.'

'Lionel O'Shea, the latest addition to the family.'

'Lionel?' Danika asked, confused. 'What is this?'

'Lionel Messi – he's their favourite footballer,' Conor explained.

The boys ran to their granda and hugged him tightly as Ana and her mother cuddled the puppy. Lionel charmed everyone with his vigorous licks.

'Thank you so much, Granda. We never thought we'd ever get a dog, and Lionel is the best dog we could ever want. We love him already, and we'll take such good care of him. We promise.' The words came out in a tumble and it was hard to tell which boy was speaking, but Conor could see what it meant to his father.

Several minutes later, after everyone admired him and Lionel was put down on the grass once more, this time to play football with his adoring masters, Conor led everyone else inside for breakfast.

The adults, except for Artur, followed, leaving Joe and Artie to fawn over Lionel in the garden.

'You go in. I must replant this bay tree anyway, is not doing so good there.' He pointed to the beautiful herb garden he'd created for Ana. 'I'll watch them.'

'Thanks, Jamsie, they love him,' Conor said to his father as they crossed the lawn.

'I'm glad to do it,' Jamsie replied. 'Seeing their little faces light up is worth more than anything. I'm a lucky man, Conor, and I don't deserve it. I'm well aware of that. I left you and Gerry and missed all those special moments, and I feel like I'm getting a second chance with Joe and Artie.'

'Well, they love him, and I know those dogs don't come cheap. I looked. I hope you didn't break the bank. They would have been as happy with one from the pound, only that Ana is allergic.'

'Ah, sure it's no bother. I'm happy to do it. And this way we know for sure Ana won't have a reaction.'

Conor looked out the window at the puppy playing with the twins. 'Well, he's going nowhere now either way. They are well and truly hooked, so we might as well get used to being dog owners.'

He made coffee for Ana and his mother-in-law with strict instructions they were to sit and relax and have a chat in the lounge while he made breakfast, and he was soon frying sausages and rashers for the family.

'Can I help?' Jamsie asked.

'You can. Cut some soda bread there and make a bit of toast, would you?' Conor instructed as he fried rounds of black pudding and made scrambled eggs.

'Lionel picked this, so we're giving it to Mammy,' Joe explained as he came in from the garden with a little daffodil and placed it in a small vase for his mother before turning to go back out to Artie and the dog.

'Aren't you the best boys ever?' Jamsie said, ruffling his hair.

'And Daddy's not going to work today, so we're going on a picnic to Glenrua Woods 'cause there's amazing trees there for climbing. And now we can bring Lionel too and take him for a walk. Can you come, Granda?'

Jamsie hesitated, and Conor said, 'You're welcome if you've nothing else to do?'

'Well, in that case, I'd love to.' Jamsie smiled at his son, who was piling rashers and sausages on a large platter to keep them warm in the oven.

'I heard you rang Liz. She was over the moon.'

'Yeah, she seems lovely. We had a nice chat.'

Conor served up Ana and Danika's breakfast to them on trays. They were in the middle of watching some incredibly complicated-looking Ukrainian soap opera on TV that they were both addicted to. Sunday morning was their time to catch up on the carry-on of the huge cast, and Conor and the boys were generally confined to the kitchen. He then served his own and his father's breakfasts after putting the boys' and Artur's in the oven to stay warm.

'Thanks, this looks lovely,' Jamsie said, cutting a succulent sausage. 'What made you change your mind?' he asked, not looking at Conor.

'A family staying at the hotel at the moment. I'm kind of helping them. There are a lot of secrets and lies going back years with them, and I just kind of realised it was stupid not contacting her – she's my sister, you know? I felt a bit disloyal to Mam or something, I don't know, but she wouldn't want me not to speak to her. I invited her and her husband over. Now, I won't be having anything to do with her mother, mind you…' Conor said with conviction.

'You'd do right to give that one a wide berth, let me tell you. She's a piece of work. I don't know what I was thinking. Honest to God, she's a right wagon.'

Conor chuckled. There was some ironic justice in the fact that the woman Jamsie had left his mother for turned out to be the bane of his life.

'Well, hopefully Liz'll come over and we can all meet properly. I'm actually looking forward to it.' Conor bit into a slice of toast.

'And Ana tells me that you're going to get a big European conference into the hotel?'

Conor nodded. 'That's the plan, but to be honest, I don't know what's going to happen on that score. I haven't told Ana yet, but my partner, Corlene, wants me to buy her out – she's selling her share either way – but it's not an option. I don't think I could raise the cash, and even if I could, it's a huge debt to take on, even with her giving it to me for a fraction of its value. So it looks like I'll be getting a new sixty-percent partner, which I don't relish.'

'How much does she want?' Jamsie asked.

'Well, that's the sickener. The hotel is valued at around a hundred million, for insurance purposes now, mind you. I don't know what it would fetch on the open market, but possibly close to that. So she could technically raise at least fifty million by selling her share, but she's offered it to me for ten.'

'Ten million euro?' Jamsie asked.

'Yeah, which is an amazing deal if a fella had ten million euro, which I don't. I'm going to talk to Ana later, see what she thinks. We've no mortgage on this place, so we could mortgage this house, though it's worth nothing like that kind of money. But I'm fifty-five, so I don't know if they'll even lend it to me at my age, even in the circumstances, and then do I want to be saddled with a debt like that? I don't know.' Conor sighed and poured himself some coffee.

'But you would like to own it outright?'

'Well, I would, of course, but it wouldn't be me owning it – it would be the bank. I doubt I'd even pay it off in my lifetime, even if they agreed, and as I said, it's unlikely.'

'I'll give it to you,' Jamsie said quietly.

Conor laughed. 'If only it were that simple.'

'Actually, it is.'

Conor froze, a piece of rasher halfway to his mouth. 'What?'

'I'll give you the money. I have it, and once I die, it's being divided between you and Liz anyway, so you might as well have it now.' Jamsie explained.

'But how can you have that kind of money?' Conor asked, incredulous.

'I was in the business of buying retail units, shops as they used to be called, in places that were run down. I bought them for cheapish back in the early eighties. I knew they would be up and coming if I could just sit on them long enough. They were close to derelict in most cases, but I did them up, did most of the work myself and rented them out. The profit from one funded the next one. I sold a few along the way for cashflow reasons, but I tried to hold onto as many as I could. I had a few around north London, some in Islington, and you never really lose on London property. When I left England to come back here, I sold them all, and I made a lot of money. I bought a house in Dublin, and a nice car, but apart from that, the rest is just sitting there. You might as well have it.'

'Are you serious?' Conor asked, completely blindsided.

'Of course I am. Look, Conor, you and Liz are all I have. You let me back into your life despite everything I did, and you gave me these two little lads that I just am mad about, and Ana and Artur and Danika – I feel like I belong here with you all, and I certainly didn't deserve any of that. You did that, and it never occurred to you that I might have a few bob. But I do and I want you to have it.'

'But what about Liz?' Conor asked, still trying to process what was happening.

'Conor, there'll be more than enough left for Liz too, trust me.'

'And you're sure? You don't want to think about this? It's a massive amount of money, and maybe you should get advice?'

'I'm not much of a man for advice, I'm sad to say. A friend of mine advised me against leaving your mother, but I wouldn't listen. Over the years, I've been advised about all sorts of things that would be for my good, but as I said, I'm not much good at doing what people think I should. You're a good man, Conor, a better one than I could ever be. You're a great husband and father, and you're a good man to work for too – everyone says it. You deserve this chance, and I'm hoping I'm going to be the one to give it to you. I should have been there for you over your life, and I wasn't. I know this won't make up for that, but I want to try to make amends. I want to give you this, not lend it to you or invest in the hotel. I want to just give you the money, so if you'll accept it, then it's yours, with a heart and a half.'

Conor didn't know what to say. Was this really happening?

'What's a half a heart?' Artie asked as he burst into the kitchen, Lionel in his arms.

'Sounds gross,' Joe said, running after him.

'Can Lionel have a sausage, Daddy?' Artie asked.

'Definitely not. Granda got the proper stuff for Lionel, and that's what he's to eat, OK?' Conor warned, fearing for the dog's health if his diet was left to the boys.

'Can we get him a Barca dog shirt? Aaron Duggan has a Man U one for his chihuahua.'

Conor and Jamsie exchanged a look.

'We'll see. Maybe Santa can bring him one,' Jamsie said with a chuckle. 'Right, sit up at the table so, you two, and I'll get your breakfast.' He jumped up and grabbed a tea towel to take the warm plates out of the oven. He put on fresh toast and pressed the button on the complicated coffee machine Conor had installed.

'Juice or milk?' he asked his grandsons.

'Milk please, Granda,' they chorused together, Lionel sitting happily between them.

CHAPTER 22

*C*onor stopped off at the castle on their way back from the picnic in the woods later that day just to check on Olga and make sure all was running smoothly. Carlos was off, and she was managing on her own for the first time. To his surprise, Carlos's car was there, and Conor found him and Olga happily going over next week's menus in her office. He decided to leave them at it and passed no remark about it being Carlos's day off.

His family entered the castle, and Conor knew Ana and the boys – and now Jamsie – felt so at home there. Could this really be happening? That this would be his? All afternoon, his father's offer had swum round in his head. He'd had no opportunity to tell Ana, but he knew she would be thrilled. From lowly motor mechanic to owner of the most magnificent hotel in Ireland was some leap in a lifetime. Life had been kind to him, and he wondered what he had done to deserve it. Some people seemed dogged by misfortune, but everything in his life – his career and, most importantly, his personal life – was better than his wildest dreams.

Conor was not a religious man, but he believed in God and that the souls of the dead were around all the time, helping.

Well, Mam? he asked quietly in his mind. *What do you think?*

Conor could picture his quiet, gentle mother perfectly. She had adored him and Gerry and tried so hard to give them a good life after Jamsie left. That was all she wanted for them, a good life. She'd want him to have this.

The boys ran to reception to introduce Katherine to Lionel, and within minutes, they were mini-celebrities as staff converged to admire the puppy. Ana, Conor and Jamsie took the little dog for a walk in the garden after a while, fearing he was becoming overwhelmed, and the boys went to the kitchen. Ivan the pastry chef made them the most amazing ice cream sundaes whenever they visited.

'Will we have a drink while we're here?' Jamsie asked as they rounded the courtyard outside Grenville's Bar. 'We can sit outside here with Lionel.'

'Yes, let's do that. The boys were going to the playroom once they got ice cream, so we have some time.' Ana smiled.

They sat in a corner, waiting for the barman to serve them.

'Hi, folks. In checking up on us?' Harry joked.

'Exactly.' Ana grinned. 'I'll have an orange juice, please, Harry.'

'Have a glass of wine if you like. I'm driving anyway,' Conor said.

'No, it's fine. You have a pint with your dad. I'll drive us home.'

'Don't look a gift horse in the mouth, Son.' Jamsie winked. 'Not that you are a horse, darling Ana,' he added, and gave his daughter-in-law a squeeze as she slapped him playfully.

'Well, if you insist. I'll have a pint of Guinness please.'

'And the same for me,' Jamsie added.

As they chatted, Conor spotted Billie and Noah deep in conversation. They sat, their heads close together, and there was an intimacy between them that was palpable. They were joined shortly afterwards by Donna, Marko, Sol and Marilyn. They had mentioned that they were dining in the hotel that night as they had an early flight in the morning.

Ana waved, greeted Marko in Ukrainian and invited the group to join them. She texted her parents to come as well, as they would enjoy meeting someone from home. She knew they would be on the way back from mass, so they were only a few minutes from the hotel.

The two groups joined, and tables and chairs were pulled together. Lionel was much admired. Conor called Harry back and he took the extended order, and introductions to Jamsie were made.

'Oh, my word, you two are so alike,' Donna said, looking at Conor and his father.

'He gets his good looks from his mother though,' Jamsie said, and Conor heard the compliment there. Jamsie really did regret his life choices, and it was time to let it go.

The conversation went round easily, Sol telling Jamsie about his visit to Charles O'Doherty and showing him the photos he'd been given.

Conor saw Donna excuse herself to go order another round of drinks, so he joined her at the bar.

'Well?' he asked. 'Any news?'

'No, not a word. I'm trying to focus on all the good stuff. Billie is so happy with Noah. He's a great guy, and I'm so glad she found someone trustworthy. She's more vulnerable than she looks. And as you said, she and Marko are really getting along, and she and I are getting back to us, so apart from the actual purpose of the trip, it's been a huge success.' She smiled as the barman filled the order.

'Your dad was happy too, to meet Charles and all of that?'

'He really was. It kind of put it to rest for him. Knowing that, well, it makes it sad and uplifting at the same time. My grandparents were such melancholy people, and I never remember them smiling. If only they knew he was trying. If he'd succeeded, maybe they could have got more people out. Who knows? But how that man dedicated his life... And the Behrman Trust is incredible. I'm so happy for my dad – he is such a good father...' Tears choked her.

Conor drew her into a hug, not caring who saw him. 'I could see that,' he said, soothing her. He gave her a tissue, and she wiped her eyes.

'What must you think of us? Coming over here to your beautiful place with our tales of woe?' She looked embarrassed.

'We're all just human, Donna, and we all have a story.' He said sincerely and released her. 'Every single person you meet, no matter how together they look, is trying to manage their own problems, trying to be happy, and hopefully trying to not tear lumps out of anyone else as we do. Everyone has secrets, everyone has a past. You've got so much going for you now – a great husband, your dad who finally laid his ghosts to rest, and a daughter who loves you. I'd say you're doing great.'

She nodded. 'I just wish he'd call. I keep thinking maybe he didn't get the message, maybe his staff kept it from him, thinking it would damage him. I mean, it's hardly going to help. Not only does he have a child he doesn't know about, but he was deported from the US as an illegal immigrant. I'm sure if the press got hold of that story, his political career would be damaged, so I guess I can't blame him for not getting in touch. I don't care at all, but it's just Billie I worry about. She feels so lost...'

'Well, maybe, but I'm not so sure about that. Getting deported out of the US was fairly standard back in the eighties, so that wouldn't be seen as a big deal, and as for Billie, so what? He had a relationship years ago that resulted in a baby he never knew about? Why would anyone hold that against the man? Politics here are a bit different to the States – it's not all *House of Cards* stuff. We have a lot of faults in our system, don't get me wrong, but there is a tendency here to, as we say, play the ball and not the man. It means we have respect for people's private lives, and when they are criticised, often with very good reason, it's on their work, not their personal stuff. Usually anyway.'

Marko appeared then to help Donna with the drinks, and as they returned to the gathering, they never noticed who came into the bar.

A slight red-haired man, in jeans and a casual shirt, with an anxious woman by his side, glanced around. Conor was just about to sit when he spotted them.

He turned and walked towards them, a smile of welcome on his face. 'Liam, it's nice to see you again.' The two men shook hands.

The minister smiled, relieved to see a friendly face. 'Hi, Conor. I'm... Well, I'm not here on business actually. I'm looking for someone...' His wife took his hand.

'Billie and Donna?' Conor said quietly.

'Er... Yeah, I... Um...do you know?' He looked flustered, very far from the smooth politician Conor had met a few days earlier.

'Follow me,' Conor said, and led the couple back out into the lobby. 'Would you like to meet them somewhere privately?' Conor offered.

'Yes...if you could... That would be...better.' He swallowed.

Conor opened a small meeting room off the lobby. It had round tables and was set for a local heritage club committee meeting on Monday morning.

'Oh, I'm sorry. This is Laura, my wife. Laura, this is Conor O'Shea. This is his place.'

Conor shook the woman's hand. 'Lovely to meet you, Laura.' He said warmly.

'This is an incredibly beautiful place. Liam was raving about it when he got home.'

Her smiling enthusiasm was genuine, and Conor instantly warmed to her. She was in her late forties, dark haired and very ordinary. She didn't have that over-polished look some women, like Corlene, seemed to go for. He'd read somewhere she had a business setting up fruit and vegetable gardens in primary schools, and she looked like an outdoors kind of woman. Conor observed how she stood close to Liam as he confronted his past. He would go far in politics with someone like her by his side.

'Thanks. Yes, it is kind of special, all right.' He paused. 'Look, this isn't my business, but you have nothing to fear from Donna or Billie. They are really nice people, and I'm sure they don't want to make any trouble for you.'

'Thanks, Conor,' Liam said. 'I... Look, to be honest, I wasn't going to come. I nearly collapsed when I got the email. I hadn't even told Laura about that relationship. Well, she knew I was in the States for a summer and got deported, but I never mentioned about Donna. It was just a summer romance, you know? Another lifetime ago. But then I thought, this girl, this young woman actually, is my daughter, and I have to meet her, let the consequences be what they may. We'll weather it, won't we, love?' He turned to his wife for reassurance.

'Of course we will.' She smiled and rubbed his back.

'Right. Well, you two just hold on here, and I'll go and get them.' Conor said. 'Billie – she's named after you – will be delighted, but she can tell you herself.'

He went into the bar just as Artur and Danika arrived – there was much chatting in rapid Ukrainian. Conor approached and quietly asked Donna and then Billie to follow him out.

'What's going on, Conor?' Billie asked as they walked.

'There's someone here to see you,' Conor said, and saw the hope cross Billie's face.

'Is it my dad?' she asked, suddenly looking more like five than twenty-five.

Conor opened the door to the meeting room, and as they entered, Donna whispered urgently, 'Please stay.' He didn't want to intrude, but her eyes were pleading, so he agreed.

Donna and Liam stood, staring at each other.

'Hi, Donna, it's good to see you again,' he said at last, a genuine smile on his face.

'Hi, Billy. Or should I say "Liam" now?' Donna asked, the relief that it was going to be alright evident on her face.

Billie stood behind her mother, suddenly shy.

'I'm Liam for a long time now,' he said, 'this is Laura, my wife…'

The two women shook hands, and then Donna moved to the side so Billie was face-to-face with her father.

'And this is our daughter, Billie Romano.'

The two stood there, saying nothing, just drinking each other in. The resemblance was uncanny – the same red hair, the same eyes, they were both lithe and muscular. There was no denying the truth.

After what felt like minutes but probably was seconds, Liam Seoige opened his arms and Billie walked forward.

CHAPTER 23

*C*onor, Ana and Jamsie blinked as they emerged in the bright sunshine from the dark Georgian building that housed the Dublin solicitor's office. The deal was done, and Castle Dysert was now fully in the ownership of Mr Conor O'Shea. He couldn't believe it. Corlene, as she predicted, had to make a quick exit when Bláth MacEntire made a very thinly veiled attack on live TV, so the gloves were definitely off. Funnily enough, Conor saw a flash of the malice Corlene had mentioned; maybe the nation's darling wasn't as sweet as she made out. Either way, Colm left her, and he and Corlene were villa shopping on the Costa del Sol. Even Dylan didn't go too mad, as he really liked Colm.

The three of them walked down the street, feeling the warm sun on their faces. They passed a newsstand with a paper screaming the headline, 'Minister said to be "delighted" about love child.' Another one read, 'Seoige's bid for Taoiseach damaged?' And another, one of the trashy tabloids, 'Love-rat Liam lied.'

'Poor Billie. This is more than she imagined.' Ana sighed.

'They'll be fine. It's just a slow news day. He gave the big story to the *Sunday Telegraph*, and they got the scoop, so the rest of them are whining. I really don't think he cares either way. It's not going to hurt him. If anything, it makes him seem less perfect and more normal, so it might actually help his campaign. Either way, he's genuinely delighted to have Billie in his life. I spoke to him last week about the European summit – it's looking more likely with every day that passes – and he said Billie and Noah were coming over in the summer to spend some more time together, meet the rest of his family and all of that. So it looks like it's all worked out.'

'Now a celebration, I think?' Jamsie asked.

'Definitely,' Conor agreed.

They entered the dark interior of McDaid's off Grafton Street.

'Champagne?' Jamsie suggested.

'Well, you two go ahead, but I will just have an orange juice,' Ana said.

'Ah, what? We're staying in the big city tonight, no car, so you can have one drink to celebrate your husband becoming Ireland's fanciest hotelier surely?' Jamsie winked.

'Well, I could, but I won't.' She smiled and looked into Conor's eyes. 'Because not only is my husband the fancy hotel owner but next Christmas he is going to also be a daddy again.'

The End.

I really hope you enjoyed this book, if you did I would be delighted if you would consider writing a review on Amazon, I read every single one.
If you would like to hear more from me, and download a free novel, just go to my website www.jeangrainger.com to sign up for my newsletter. The free book offer has no catch I promise, it's free to join my readers group, and it always will be and of course you can unsubscribe any time.

ACKNOWLEDGMENTS

The idea for this book came out of a conversation with a friend about the ethical issues posed by this new DNA technology. I'm still not sure that our very essence, the thing that makes each of us unique should be available as a commercial thing to be exploited. Of course, there are tremendous advantages to these advances and regardless of what I or anyone else thinks they will march on anyway, but I do think it opens cans of worms that maybe people would rather stay shut.

This is the fifth book in the Conor O'Shea series and I had absolutely no idea when I wrote the first book, The Tour, that this man would find a place in so many hearts all around the globe. I am so glad he did though. I love him too.

Thank you as always, to my wonderful structural editor, Helen Falconer, my copy editor Abby Jaworski, my early readers, Jim Cooney and Vivienne Fitzgerald Smith, and of course my incredible advance team.

Thank you to you, my readers. My life has changed in so many ways because of you, and I am deeply grateful for your support and encouragement.

To Conor, Sórcha, Éadaoin and Siobhán, my darling children and to Diarmuid, without whom there would be no books, I love you all from the bottom of my heart.

J.G. July 2019

ABOUT THE AUTHOR

Jean Grainger is an Irish author, writing both contemporary and historical Irish fiction. She lives in Cork, Ireland with her husband and the two youngest of her four children.

Finding Billie is her fifteenth novel and is book 5 in The Tour Series.

f

ALSO BY JEAN GRAINGER

Made in the USA
Middletown, DE
09 May 2021